"These are stories full of menace and delight, drawing from that deep well of human complexity, perversity, sincerity, and hope. *Mystery Lights* is gorgeous."

—**KELLY LINK**,
author of *The Book of Love*

"Lena Valencia writes some of the best stories I've read in years, as sharp and finely honed as knives. Here are women who turn out to be powerful enough to meet the threats of their worlds in kind: their lives may cut them, yes, but they can cut back, and astonishing truths are laid bare in the process. Both bold and sly, in turns righteously angry and sinister, *Mystery Lights* offers a brilliant new vision of what it means to be a woman in this world."

—**CLARE BEAMS**,
author of *The Garden*

"I've loved Lena Valencia's brilliant, beguiling stories for years and read her debut collection in a single breathless evening. These are stories with teeth, both chilling and bold, about the strength and vulnerability of women and girls. Full of surprising turns, *Mystery Lights* reminded me of the incredible power of short fiction to speak the truth."

—**JULIE BUNTIN**,
author of *Marlena*

"B-movie aesthetics meet the cinematic splendor of the desert in these ten clever, neatly crafted, wryly stylized short stories. Against the backdrop of their desolate and often haunted landscapes, Lena Valencia's characters vividly come to life."

.YON,
he Dead

MYSTERY LIGHTS

MYSTERY LIGHTS

stories

LENA VALENCIA

TIN HOUSE / PORTLAND, OREGON

This is a work of fiction. All of the characters, organizations, and events portrayed in these stories are either products of the author's imagination or are used fictitiously.

The image of the meteors used on the cover is from the Rare Book Division of The New York Public Library. "The November meteors" The New York Public Library Digital Collections. 1881–1882. https://digitalcollections.nypl.org/items/510d47dd-e6cf-a3d9-e040-e00a18064a99

First US Edition 2024
Printed in the United States of America

Manufacturing by Sheridan
Interior design by Beth Steidle

Library of Congress Cataloging-in-Publication Data

Names: Valencia, Lena, 1986– author.
Title: Mystery lights : stories / Lena Valencia.
Other titles: Mystery lights (Compilation)
Description: Portland, Oregon : Tin House, 2024.
Identifiers: LCCN 2024014797 | ISBN 9781959030621 (paperback) | ISBN 9781959030683 (ebook)
Subjects: LCGFT: Short stories.
Classification: LCC PS3622.A4254 M97 2024 | DDC 813/.6—dc23/eng/20240402
LC record available at https://lccn.loc.gov/2024014797

Tin House
2617 NW Thurman Street, Portland, OR 97210
www.tinhouse.com

DISTRIBUTED BY W. W. NORTON & COMPANY

1 2 3 4 5 6 7 8 9 0

For my grandmother Robbie.

In the desert
I saw a creature, naked, bestial,
Who, squatting upon the ground,
Held his heart in his hands,
And ate of it.
I said, "Is it good, friend?"
"It is bitter—bitter," he answered;
"But I like it
Because it is bitter,
And because it is my heart."

—STEPHEN CRANE,
The Black Riders, and Other Lines

CONTENTS

MYSTERY LIGHTS

DOGS

Ruth had spent the morning thinking of ghastly things that could befall her protagonist. The script was a revenge flick about a supermarket checkout woman who—after years of dealing with callous customers, a lecherous boss, and a manipulative boyfriend—goes on a killing spree. One of the notes she'd received was that when the protagonist snapped, it just seemed to come out of nowhere, and that Ruth should make the bad things that happened to her worse. She should consider flashbacks to traumatic incidents in the protagonist's girlhood to create a more accurate psychological profile. "Dial it up," were the words the producer had used, which made Ruth imagine an old-fashioned cartoon villain turning a dial labeled *violence* from *moderate* to *extreme*, and cackling with glee as his captive writhed in pain.

Her ex-husband, Steve, had their daughter, Sabrina, for the long weekend, so she had booked herself three nights in one of the desert communities that used its proximity to uber-hip

Joshua Tree to jack up prices, which was all she could find last-minute. The area still looked like Joshua Tree but had fewer lithe desert witches and more drug addicts, or so she assumed. It felt decadent and almost too perfect to be paying hotel room rates for a trailer on a road called Trigger Drive. Decadent because she could just be writing in her office in her empty house, but she told herself she deserved it. She told herself it would be good to get away. That without the distractions of the city she'd really be able to nail down this beast of a script, which she'd promised to have revised three weeks ago.

But of course, yesterday, as she was on her way out the door to the too-perfect retreat, Steve had texted asking if it was true that Sabrina's teacher had extended the deadline on her English paper so that it was due next Tuesday instead of this coming Tuesday and could she spend the long weekend up at Big Bear with Hannah and her family? Ruth called him back and explained that their daughter was unequivocally lying. Ever since the incident with Jocelyn Mitchell and her mean-girl gang—either a nasty post about Sabrina, or some rude comments on one of Sabrina's posts (or was it both? Ruth couldn't keep track)—Sabrina had been "dialing it up": tears and melodrama, doors slamming, screaming. And now this, lying to her own parents.

Steve was on speaker as she drove. "Can you please just talk to her?" he pleaded. He loathed confrontation, the wimp.

"Trust me. I've tried. I doubt she wants to hear from me again. This one's on you."

"What did you say to her?" he asked.

She'd only been trying her best. Wasn't that all that could be expected of anyone? "It was really nothing. She's blowing it out of proportion. It's hormones!" She was yelling at Steve now, something she'd promised to stop doing. *I don't have the emotional capacity for an argument right now* was what the therapist would have wanted her to say. She prayed the turnoff that meant service would go out would appear so the conversation could end, but traffic instead slowed to a frustrating crawl.

"Okay, message received," said Steve, in that infuriatingly noncommittal way of his. "I'll get to the bottom of all this." They said their goodbyes and Ruth felt her shoulders relax.

This was, as far as she knew, the first time Sabrina had attempted to deceive her parents, and as she drove past the bland strip malls of San Bernardino and into the arid drama of the Mojave, Ruth's anger with her daughter melted away, leaving admiration for her boldness. Ruth had never been able to tell a fib with a straight face at Sabrina's age. Perhaps her life would have been easier if she had. And Sabrina's life *was* easy. That was what their fight had been about in the first place, that Sabrina wanted for nothing. So what if those girls had ganged up on her? Stop moping. Move on. She needed to toughen up if she was going to be anything in this world. Grow some thicker skin.

But this advice had only made Sabrina sob harder, screaming at Ruth about how she didn't *get* it and to get out of her room and leave her alone. Ruth, unmoved by the histrionics, had heeded her demands, comforted only slightly by the knowledge that Sabrina would be Steve's problem for the weekend.

It grew dark, and if it weren't for her GPS, Ruth would have missed the turn for Trigger, a dirt road off Highway 62. So far as she could remember, there had been no mention of a dirt road in the listing. Slowly, carefully, she steered the Subaru over rocks, wincing as brush scraped the sides, braking just in time for a coyote to trot through her high beams, out on its evening scavenge. Finally, the trailer appeared, gleaming in her brights.

* * *

NOW, AFTER A FITFUL NIGHT'S SLEEP on the thin foam mattress, she sat at the worn slab of Formica that passed as a kitchen table, where for the past three hours she had been staring into her laptop screen, cold coffee and blank yellow legal pad at her side.

Was the protagonist abused as a child? Was she involved in a sex-trafficking ring? Or maybe kiddie porn? Parents who took cash and looked the other way? Was she held captive, shackled in a basement somewhere on a quiet, tree-lined suburban street? She listed them all on her legal pad, each more ghoulish than the last, these ideas for how to "dial it up." This was how she used to work in the old days. Black coffee and a notepad she filled with grisly dismemberments and sadistic plot twists.

This script was, for Ruth, a return to form. It was supposed to be her comeback. She'd been something of an indie darling early on in her career. A woman filmmaker who wasn't afraid of blood and guts. Her first feature, *Blood Bouquet*, shot on a shoestring, was a cult favorite: a slasher flick featuring a killer bride. Then came *Cherry Split*, her most acclaimed work: a thriller about a stripper who picks off every man who's wronged her.

A-list actresses took notice. How refreshing it was, one said, to finally have a woman's take on the genre. A major studio had shown interest in her next project, slated to be her bloodiest yet, about a housewife who tortures her abusive husband to death.

But it never got made. In the early aughts, Sabrina was born, and Ruth couldn't finish the script. Her creative output slowed. She cobbled together an income to supplement Steve's admittedly heftier one by doctoring scripts and shooting commercials. She told her friends that she'd lost the bug, or that she was too busy parenting, but the truth was that something had shifted in her when her daughter came along: in Ruth's mind, every brutal rape, every strangulation, every artfully choreographed stabbing was happening to Sabrina. Her protagonist felt more alive than ever because, to Ruth, her protagonist was her daughter. She tried writing something else, changing course—a sweet coming-of-age tale—but producers scoffed. No one, they said, would want to see a Ruth Grayson movie without blood. Perhaps she'd gone soft after having a kid. It wasn't unusual for that kind of thing to happen to women.

Ruth and Steve fought, grew distant, and finally separated. Divorce papers were signed. It was mostly amicable. She threw herself into her freelance work. What was the point in trying to create something of her own in a system with the odds so stacked against her? Then, a couple of years ago, a programmer had discovered her old films and invited her to do a Q and A at a screening. The event was written up and made the rounds in cinephile circles. There was something so *feminine* about the rage of these working-class women protagonists, said the critics. A feral viciousness that couldn't be captured by a man. Interest in her films was reinvigorated. Maybe Hollywood was different now, she'd thought, more accepting of those it had left behind. Willing to atone by giving a forgotten woman filmmaker a second chance.

She frowned at her legal pad, ugliness now scrawled all over its first page. It made her a little sick.

A walk would clear her head. She filled her water bottle, slathered on sunscreen, and put on Steve's old, sweat-faded Trojans cap. The sky was a dazzling blue, the mountains dark and crisp against it. From her little trailer on the hill she could see the valley below, dotted with the browns and greens of desert flora. A fine layer of dust coated her running shoes as she walked. Her lower back ached from the cheap mattress and her morning spent slouching over the legal pad. She was mentally exhausted, too—all those images of violation and torture swirling around her like sick ghosts—but the desert's stark simplicity, the binaries of shadow and sun, of rock and sky, were a salve.

She put in her earbuds and played one of Sabrina's mixes. It had been a while since she'd listened—really listened—to the playlists her daughter had made her. This mix featured mostly sweet-voiced men singing about despair, true despair, not just the vapid tripe that Sabrina used to favor. She slowed her pace. How could Sabrina understand this sadness at fifteen? Part of Ruth wanted to throw her arms around her, shield her from whatever it was that was making her so upset, that was causing her to listen to these songs. The other part wanted to shake her for being so fragile. The desert spooled out ahead as she trudged heavily on, and a dulcet voice crooned in her ear about wandering streets at night, drunk on convenience store malt liquor.

She'd walked a little over a mile when, through the gentle guitar chords in her headphones, she heard a dog barking behind her. She turned, expecting to see a retriever straining a leash, a walker scolding him and apologizing. *He's harmless!* But no. Instead she saw—and she counted—five dogs. No leashes or humans. These were not the little terriers that warmed the laps of the wealthy in Beverly Hills. These were dogs you'd get to guard your shit. Two pit bulls, two German shepherds, and a gargantuan white mutt with quivering strings of slobber hanging from its jowls. She froze, facing the animals. They stood in formation, creeping closer and then bounding away, as if daring her to make a move. The leader, one of the shepherds, let out a low growl and flattened its ears against its skull. Its eyes turned to brown slits under a furrowed brow. It bared its teeth at her, revealing its black-spotted gums, and began to bark and snarl. Its jaw, Ruth realized, could probably crush her skull like eggshell. The rest of the dogs followed suit, emitting deep woofs. Ruth turned up the volume and continued walking. Maybe if she ignored them, they would go away. But when she cast a frantic glance behind her, she saw that they were following her, jaws snapping, hair on end, barks increasing in volume and aggression.

You can't reason with dogs. Ruth knew this. When she was fifteen, her parents had sent her and her younger brother away for the summer to live with their uncle Josh and his three pit bulls in rural New Hampshire, assuring the kids that they'd like the country, that they'd be good company for Uncle Josh. What they didn't say was that their marriage was falling apart, and they needed space to work it out.

The animals worshipped her uncle and treated Ruth and her brother like their own siblings, for better or worse. Priscilla, Annie, and Scotland: they were all well-behaved until her uncle left the room, at which point they became erratic whirlwinds of muscle and drool. They were embarrassingly sexual, too: Scotland's member, pink and shiny, appeared at random intervals; Priscilla and Annie licked themselves relentlessly. Needless to say, Ruth and her brother never had any friends over, not that they had any friends in that dreary town.

Ruth removed her earbuds. They were still following her, the dogs, their low growls suffusing the quiet desert morning with monstrous terror.

She'd been bitten once that summer, when she'd tried to take a bone from Priscilla. It was the first time she'd seen a wound like that. The blood gushed from the puncture, trickling down to her wrist as she stared at it, stunned. Its color was darker, richer than the ketchup-red ooze she was used to seeing in the R-rated horror movies the video store guy would let her rent if she asked nice enough. There was the sting of hydrogen peroxide, her uncle's rough hands tenderly wrapping her own in a bandage, a feeling of betrayal at the dog that she regularly played with, an ache for days after. But her uncle had scolded *her*, not Priscilla. "Never," he'd snarled, in that dark way of his, "take a bone from a dog." That taught Ruth. She still had the scar on her left hand, just below where her wedding ring used to be. It even throbbed from time to time. A reminder of her foolishness.

She was power walking now, emitting short puffs of breath with every step. She could run, she thought, but she knew that would only make things worse. Her uncle's dogs had gone into a sort of mania when she and her brother had run with them, becoming untrustworthy, reverting to wolfhood. It was after running with Ruth and her brother that the dogs had jumped on them, leaving muddy paw prints on their clothes. It was after running that they'd nipped at hands and ankles. Ruth was not going to run.

The desert dogs followed at a cautious distance. Their barks echoed through the hills. She wondered if their owners heard them, if they even had owners to call them off. A couple of them, she'd noticed, had collars. Her uncle's pit bulls would listen only to him. In front of her uncle, the three could have taken Best in Show at Westminster. In front of her uncle, they would sit, paw, and roll over. In front of her uncle they would fetch and actually drop the ball rather than make you pry it from their slimy maws. "It's because I'm the alpha," he'd said.

She breathed into her diaphragm. She closed up the bottom of her throat to deepen her voice. She imagined that she wasn't a petite forty-eight-year-old woman with nothing but an aluminum water bottle in the way of a weapon but a beefy six-foot-tall contractor, the kind of authority dogs happily bounded around, joyfully slobbering. She imagined she was her uncle Josh. "Down," she commanded in a baritone. "Get. Go away." A few of them tweaked their ears, but the leader barked louder, and the others followed along.

She pictured the headline: *Woman Killed by Dogs in Mojave Desert.* It would garner a few clicks, at least. Who didn't love a dead woman? *Dial it up.* Sure, she wouldn't exactly be a *young* dead woman, but her face was still pretty enough to play well. *Why on earth was she walking out there without a weapon?* inquiring minds would ask in the comments section. *It's sad, but it's her own fault,* they'd conclude. She'd gotten what was coming to her.

Then she could hear traffic zipping by on the 62, and she knew she was nearly to the end of Trigger Drive. Perhaps these dogs knew better than to cross the highway, with unhinged drivers racing by at seventy, eighty, ninety miles per hour and no cops to slow them down.

She dashed into the road. A car whizzed by her, honking. The animals scattered but regrouped. She heard another vehicle coming, stood at the center line, and waved her hands like a film noir ingenue. The mud-spattered blue Ford Explorer came to a stop.

"Can I get a ride?" she said breathlessly into the open window, not caring who the driver was. "Those dogs are chasing me." She pointed in the direction of the dogs, but the pack had dwindled to one. The leader was still eyeing her, sniffing the air, mangy and smaller seeming now, without its pack, more malnourished coyote than attack dog. The others had disappeared into the brush, as if they'd never existed.

The driver regarded Ruth as he took a sip of a comically large Slurpee and set it back down in his cup holder. He was a kid, Ruth saw, college-aged, probably just a few years older than Sabrina, with a narrow, pinkish face and aviators perched on a pointy nose. His wrinkled blue button-down shirt had a rust-colored food stain over the breast pocket. Unkempt brown hair peeked from under his beanie. He looked, thought Ruth, like the kid who gets bullied in the teen dramas Sabrina called "guilty pleasures." The one who gets the girl at the end. She softened and felt herself smiling.

He nodded at the passenger seat. "Just push that crap onto the floor," he said. His voice was deeper than she'd expected. The crap was several newspapers, a carton of Marlboro Reds, empty beer cans, and a box of Winchester .22 rimfire ammunition. She did as she was told, gingerly placing the box of bullets on top of the rubble. Ruth reminded herself that it was common to have firearms in rural areas—a gun was a necessary tool, like a screwdriver or a flashlight. Her uncle Josh had used his shotgun to cull the rabbit population of his backyard. It was perfectly normal.

Still, her heartbeat quickened as she thanked him profusely and latched the seat belt, cautiously avoiding trampling the pile with her dusty feet.

"Dogs, huh?" he asked, as he rolled his window up. On closer inspection, she saw his stubble, the sunken eyes behind his sunglasses. Not in his teens, she corrected herself. In his midtwenties, at least. Not a boy but a man.

She laughed nervously in response, realizing she would have to tell this man where she was staying. "I'm just at the top of the hill here." She gestured at the dirt road. He turned in that direction.

"Alone," he said. She couldn't tell if he meant it as a statement or a question, but there was something unsettling about it regardless. As if he'd had some sort of revelation.

For a moment she thought to tell him that her boyfriend was waiting for her in the trailer. Her giant, gun-wielding boyfriend, who lived in a trailer on Trigger Drive. But she was a horrible liar. He could probably sense the singleness on her—men could do that, she'd learned. "Uh-huh," she said.

With the windows up, the car smelled of cigarettes and dirty socks. Ruth pressed the button to roll down her window and get some air, but nothing happened.

"It's broken," he said. "Wiring's shot on the whole door. Costs a fortune to fix." She hadn't known he'd been watching her. The SUV bounced over a small hole, and she was briefly airborne.

"Here from LA?"

"Sherman Oaks." *Just give him your home address, why don't you*, Ruth scolded herself. He was going slow enough on the dirt road that she could jump out if she needed to.

"Lived in LA myself. Got into some trouble. Had to leave." He smiled, remembering. His teeth were stained red from the Slurpee. "What brings you to these parts?" He put the orange plastic straw to his lips and sucked noisily.

She clutched the door handle, contemplating what he meant by trouble. "Just wanted to get out of the city." This was as close to lying as she could get. She turned her face away from him. The desert crawled by outside, the spiny plants bleak and callous.

"Did you look them in the eye?" he said. "The dogs," he added. "They hate that. Makes them crazy."

Had she? She'd looked everywhere, taken it all in: spotted gums, spiking fur, strings of slobber, yellow teeth.

"Their bark's worse than their bite, you know," he said. "They wouldn't've hurt you."

"Well—" She fell silent as the driver slowed to a stop. "I'm a little farther up," she said. Her mouth went dry as he put the car in park, but she was afraid to take a sip of water, afraid to do anything this man might comment on. In moments like this, being visible was a liability. Her protagonist would have been completely calm, because her protagonist carried a hunting knife in an ankle holster and had no qualms about slitting the throats of men who creeped her out. Ruth was not Ruth's protagonist. Ruth wanted to disappear, to evaporate into the puffy white clouds in the sky. But she was here. And the driver was talking to her.

"You shouldn't be out here alone," he said, lifting his aviators and looking straight at her. She caught a glimpse of his eyes—dark blue, almost violet. "You got kids?"

"A daughter," said Ruth, silently willing him to start driving again. She didn't like stopping like this, with nothing around for miles but prickly foliage.

She thought of Sabrina's sad music, the true despair she'd know if her mother's body was found crumpled on the side of Trigger Drive. Her imagined headline shifted. *Body of Missing Female Filmmaker Found.* The postulations would be insane in that comments section, especially if this guy knew how to cover his tracks. They'd assume all kinds of things: an ayahuasca trip gone wrong, a serial killer, drug cartels. Research for a script that got too intense, which—hey—wouldn't be so far from the truth. It was fodder enough for a prestige podcast. The *CSI* episode practically wrote itself.

"I don't get it. Why women like you assume they can do the same shit that men can." He drank more Slurpee and slammed it down hard enough so that neon red liquid sloshed over his hand and into the cup holder. He cursed and wiped his fingers on his jeans, leaving dark smears.

Her hands grew hot. Her old dog bite scar, the divot below her knuckle, twinged. She half expected blood to begin spurting from it, stigmata-like.

"We're different," he shouted at the windshield. "It's just the way it is. I'm telling you this as a favor. I'd never let my mom come out here alone. You think the dogs were bad."

"I think I can walk from here." Ruth tried to keep her voice steady.

"How do you know I'm not some crazy serial killer?"

Ruth tried the door, but it wouldn't budge.

"I told you," said the driver. "Wiring's shot. I can only unlock it from the driver's side."

"Please," she said, "let me out."

"Like I was saying," he said, paying her no heed. "It's been proven. Women thrive in the home. Their job is to produce and protect their children. And a man's job is to protect a woman." He spoke in a singsong voice, as if repeating this fact by rote.

She realized what she needed to do now, if she ever wanted to see Sabrina again. She clutched her water bottle tighter, ready to strike if needed, and spoke low and slow, like she'd done to the dogs. "Let. Me. The. Fuck. Out."

He looked surprised, and then his face cracked into a laugh, revealing those pink teeth again. "You should see your face! Fucking city people." He slid his glasses back down his forehead, shifted into drive, and turned on the stereo, which blared a Dave Matthews Band song she remembered from her college years. He sang along off-key as they drove until, mercifully, they crested a hill and the Airstream appeared.

"This looks like your stop," he said.

She nodded woodenly.

"Hang on a sec." He lifted open the armrest behind the gearshift and rifled through the contents. She tensed, still gripping the water bottle. Though it was cold in the car, she could feel sweat droplets forming under her armpits. But all he produced was an unopened bag of beef jerky.

"The next time those dogs bother you, throw some of this at them. That's all they're after anyway."

She stood there, mute, holding the jerky, as he gave her a friendly wave from the driver's seat and puttered off down the hill, a dusty cloud trailing behind him.

It was quiet now, the kind of quiet that only comes in the desert, punctuated occasionally by the call of a lone bird out on a hunt. Her heart beat in her chest. A couple of ravens looped in the sky, their black feathers a shock against the blue. It had been a long time since she'd felt her own heart, since she'd felt that kind of fear. "What the fuck was that?" she said out loud to the hills and the birds. Nothing had happened, and for that she supposed she should be grateful.

Was the driver right? Had she been overreacting? Had she misread him, like she'd misread the dogs? Wasn't he just helping her? She thought again of Sabrina, how she was the same age that Ruth had been that summer at her uncle's, but how much younger Sabrina seemed now than Ruth was then, in her memories: Sabrina, who worshipped the raw voices of suffering men; who felt everything too deeply; who, like her mother, was an utter failure of a liar.

She tore open the jerky bag and put a plug in her mouth, sucking the smoky salt off until the meat turned dull and soggy and she swallowed it. She ate another and another that way, until her mouth burned from the chemical salt. She would not reward the dogs for barking at her, for scaring her into a stranger's car. She had not misread the driver; the driver was an asshole. She would not be taking any more walks down Trigger Drive. Sabrina did not need to toughen up; the world needed to be kinder.

In the trailer, she took special care to lock the door behind her. On the table was her notepad of terror. The scenarios scrawled on yellow paper seemed foreign now, quaint almost, written by a past self.

The script could wait.

She would go to her daughter. She would say, *I know it hurts, I'm sorry*. She would say, *It will get better, I promise*, the only lie she could bring herself to tell. Then she would take her daughter into her arms like she'd done when Sabrina was a little girl. Her soft, sweet little girl.

She gathered her things to leave. In the distance, something barked.

YOU CAN NEVER BE TOO SURE

It's the night before Thanksgiving and I'm at the Meals-2-Go section in the Gunnar College Café, stuffing Saran-wrapped turkey sandwiches into my backpack while the cashier stares obliviously at her phone. I was supposed to have driven back home to Colorado Springs this morning before the storm, but last night Chelsea stole a handle of Old Crow from the senior suite and we stayed up drinking and watching pirated episodes of *Survive! 1845*, the survival reality show that Chelsea's obsessed with, and next thing I knew it was noon today and Chelsea was shaking me awake to say that her car was here to take her to her flight home to LA. By the time I got my shit together, the roads were closed and the snow was beginning to really fall. I lied and told my mom I had a last-minute project that I had to work on for class because I figured it was a better excuse than sleeping in.

I pay for one sandwich and go back outside, where ice crystals attack my eyes. Squinting, I trudge on, thinking of the sandwich

I'm about to eat and the half handle waiting for me. I can just barely make out the path to the dorms. Chelsea's sleeping bag coat that she let me keep for the break feels like a freaking T-shirt in this weather, and immediately my nose begins to run and my snot to freeze. I take the long way to see if Clint Brewer's light is on. He's a transfer student from some East Coast liberal arts school who plays guitar and is super hot, and he told Chelsea he was staying on campus over Thanksgiving. Maybe, I think, this is the weekend to make my move, though I've hardly spoken two words to him and am an awkward mess whenever he comes into our room to talk to Chelsea. She says he visits to see me, but I know that he's definitely there for her. I see a light on and call his name, but the wind swallows it up. It's cold and I feel like a loser, so I keep on walking.

* * *

WITHOUT CHELSEA HOAGE AROUND this semester, I would have either dropped out or offed myself. It happened a couple of times last year, when I was a freshman—students offing themselves. The weather is what does it, they say. And the isolation. Chelsea thinks it runs a little deeper than that. She blames the lore. The cruel, jagged mountains that loom over us like they're plotting something. The same angry spirits that terrorized the settlers moving west and the prospectors hunting for gold. They grab on to you, she says, and they don't let you go. She's way superstitious and it's been getting more intense lately—I came home the other night and she had lit a bunch of sage leaves and was waving them around the room. "To cleanse it," she said. The room still smells like campfire.

One of her favorite bits of lore is the story about the Trapper. Every so often there are sightings of someone dressed like a nineteenth-century trapper slipping through the halls of the dorms. For whatever reason, maybe because it's balls cold, he's partial to the showers. There'll be muddy boot prints on the bathroom tile, mirrors steamed up at odd hours of the night. He always leaves something behind: a bloody rabbit's foot in the sink; a goose feather in the shower caddy.

He also takes someone with him: usually a girl. Chelsea says that a couple of decades ago, back in the nineties, this was happening a lot—the Trapper would be spotted slinking around and in the morning some girl would be missing from her bed. She'd come back a few nights later, dazed, with no memory of what had happened to her. Most would drop out soon after.

Then there was the Jasper abduction in '98. A group of senior boys didn't like the idea of this whatever-it-was sneaking onto campus and taking their girls. Protecting the school from creeps was their duty, after all. They stayed up nights, taking turns patrolling the halls of every dorm. No luck. No Trapper. They got frustrated, decided that maybe if they couldn't get ahold of him themselves, they'd trap the Trapper with a pretty sophomore: Kelly Jasper.

Of course, Kelly Jasper thought that she was just going to another party with her friends. The boys plied her with alcohol and invited her along for a beer run. She probably thought it was weird that they were taking the long way to the parking lot—the path by Jorgensen Creek—but was too wasted to say anything about it. She probably started screaming when they tied her to a tree, and screamed louder when the boys ran and hid to wait for the Trapper. She probably screamed a lot. She screamed until she wasn't screaming anymore, and the boys peeked out from behind their trees or bushes or whatever, and she was gone.

When she didn't show up to class the next couple of days, the administration began to worry, and the police started combing the campus and the town. The morbid whispered that she was another suicide. A few days later three cops found her in this tiny cabin in an aspen grove by the creek, maybe a ten-minute walk from campus. Some say she was skinning a deer by a roaring fire. Others say she was *eating* a deer, practically raw, blood trickling down her chin. Everyone remembers what it was she said to the cops when they found her, which was that the Trapper had taken her and made her his mistress. The cops said, "There is no Trapper, you are clearly here on your own." And she was like, "Well where did all these pelts come from?" And she gestured to the animal skins that hung from the ceiling, the bed, the wooden chair she sat on. "And don't talk like that or you'll piss him off." And the cops were like, "Okay, sure, but your parents are looking for you, just please come with us," and being cops, they forced her to.

"Listen," she told them from the back of the cop car, "he's not just going to go away. Those pelts are keeping him alive. You need to burn them, and the cabin."

The cops told her they weren't in the business of vandalizing private property and asked her why she hadn't just walked back to campus, didn't she know that she had been only ten minutes away?

But at that point she was done talking and just stared at the dark outside the window. At least that's how Chelsea tells it.

The newspaper took a picture of her that night that Chelsea and I found online. You can see the tear streaks through the dirt on her face. She has this dazed look in her eyes, like something snapped. "The stare of a doomed girl," Chelsea said as she enlarged the picture on my laptop screen until Kelly Jasper's eyes became gray clusters of pixels. Two weeks after the photo was taken, Kelly set fire to her room and died of smoke inhalation.

The kicker of this little bit of lore is that each one of those cops that took her, they all had these terrible things happen to them—one of them shot himself in the throat while cleaning his gun and bled to death in his garage. Another one lost his baby to this freak bacterial infection. And the third, well, he lost his job and just about everything else to his gambling addiction. Now he lives in a trailer in the Walmart parking lot.

The Trapper, though, he's been spotted a few times around these parts since then, stalking the halls, looking for a new Trapper wench. Chelsea says he's some sort of supernatural being; others think he's one of those back-to-nature Ted Kaczynski types who just wants his annual hot shower and coed lay, and that all that tragedy with the cops is coincidence.

She'll tell me these stories as we're going to sleep, bits of hearsay from other people on campus and things she's read online. We strategize escape plans in case the Trapper pays us a visit. I do this to humor her because the lore is just lore, I tell myself. She's given me a ring with a small amethyst affixed to it with copper wire. She got it at a meditation retreat in Northern California and it's supposed to ward off obstacles, according to her. I wear it on the middle finger of my right hand at all times—even to sleep, even in the shower, even though the metal stains my finger greenish gray. I wear it because you can never be too sure.

* * *

I GET BACK to my dorm just as George, the security guard, is zipping up his jacket.

"Still here?" he says.

"I couldn't get out before the roads closed," I say. "I'm stuck."

His pudgy face crinkles into a look of concern as I stand there, dumbly, half expecting him to invite me home with him and his family, where there will most likely be a turkey and green bean casserole and dressing and the whole deal. But he just throws his bag over his shoulder. "I think there are some seniors over in the Ponderosa who are celebrating," he says. "They do it every year. There's a pie-eating contest."

"Thanks," I say. I have absolutely no intention of going to the Ponderosa, the campus apartments where the rich assholes Chelsea used to hang out with live.

"You can call the main office if you need anything," he says.

"Have a good holiday," I say, giving him a salute. I'm not sure what the salute is for; it just seems like the proper thing to do.

"You too," he says, and he walks out the door and disappears into the curtains of falling snow.

* * *

CHELSEA'S ONE OF THE FEW here who, like me, don't ski. Skiing's all that's done at Gunnar College. Skiing when there's snow, which is practically year-round, and partying all the time. There's not much else to do in Gunnar, a tiny speck of a town in western Colorado, unless you're into studying. It makes the Springs look like Manhattan or something. If I weren't getting a free ride here, then I'd just forget college and move to Boulder and focus on my music. With the exception of Brewer, only assholes play music here. I thought I'd at least be able to join some wannabe Phish jam band, but all I've seen is these idiot ski jocks get stoned and try to pick out "Stairway."

Chelsea and I wouldn't be friends if we weren't roommates. She's from Los Angeles and is rich; I'm from Colorado Springs and not. She summers with her family in a villa on Lake Como, for example, and does coke with celebrities she's not allowed to name because they made her sign NDAs. She came to Gunnar because she was super into skiing and her parents have a chalet up here that she used to stay at with her old group of friends off-season, but they had a falling out and she started spending more time in the room, with me. Her old friends, she says, were assholes and made her hate anything to do with skiing. She says she'll never ski again. Whenever I ask her why, she changes the subject.

* * *

BACK IN OUR ROOM, I inhale a sandwich and wash it down with some Old Crow mixed with flat Diet Coke from the mini fridge while watching *Survive! 1845* on my laptop in bed. I'm supposed to finish my reading for my lit seminar, and I should have been slogging through *Jane Eyre*. I really *want* to finish it—the plot synopsis on Wikipedia made it sound pretty cool, with the crazy lady in the attic and stuff, but the language is so old-fashioned it just puts me to sleep. It's a holiday weekend and I deserve to relax. *Jane Eyre* can wait.

Instead, I watch as a middle-aged woman in a heavy fur jacket and hat is dropped off by helicopter in the Yukon in the middle of winter with nothing but a dead moose. If she survives for thirty days using only tools and materials from the year 1845, she wins $1 million. She's crying into the camera about how much she misses her two kids back in Omaha as she shakily slides a hunting knife through the moose carcass in an attempt to skin it when my phone buzzes with a text from Chelsea.

Are you losing it yet? Do you have enough food? Did you hook up with Brewer? Are you losing it?

No. Yes. No. No, I reply. *George tried to get me to go to a Ponderosa party.*

There's a pause, then a reply. *You should go if you want.*

She's testing me, I know it.

No way I would hang out with those ski-tards, I write back.

Miss you already, she says. *Gotta go out to dinner with the fam. Vom-fest.*

Miss you too, bb. Will call later.

I watch a few more episodes and drink some more till I get bored and decide that it's a good time to give Chelsea a call, but my phone is dead and I realize that I lent Chelsea my charger and it's in her purse, which is with her in Los Angeles.

"Noooo . . ." I say to no one. Maybe I *am* losing it. The Victorian-looking lady on the cover of *Jane Eyre* on the floor near my bed stares up at me, pleadingly. I'm not going to read it. I'm too drunk anyway, and too sleepy.

Then there's a gust of wind and the lights flicker out and there I am alone in the room, with the blue of my laptop screen saver pulsing like a breath.

The stories that Chelsea tells all start whirling through my mind and I get a little jumpy and take another sip of my drink, but it doesn't seem to help. If my phone had some juice at least I could text Chelsea, tell her what was going on, and it would be like someone was there with me. That's when I remember Brewer's window, how his light was on, and think maybe he has a backup battery or something, and how I'd rather be with someone, anyone, right now than by myself.

I get out of bed and feel around on the floor for a pair of jeans and slide them on. I run my hands through my hair. I briefly consider putting on some eyeliner but decide that it's better to show up makeup-less than with makeup applied in the dark. And then I'm off, following the dim glow of the tiny LED emergency light down the hall, imagining what will happen when I knock on Clint Brewer's door.

He'll let me in, I decide, and we'll sit in candlelight and play each other songs on his guitar. I've been working on a cover of "Where Is My Mind?" by the Pixies that Chelsea said would snag any boy who was remotely indie. I'm going over the chords in my head when I approach Brewer's door. I turn my hands to fists to keep them from shaking. I channel my inner Chelsea and knock.

"Who is it?" he says.

"Lily."

"Who?"

"Lily!" I say again, louder. "From down the hall."

He cracks open the door and light peeks out. I also smell weed.

"Oh," he says, "Chelsea's friend."

His eyes are red and he's wearing a Gunnar hoodie and basketball shorts and I have the sudden urge to throw myself at him, like literally fall into his chest and have him wrap his big arms around me. But that would be very weird, so I just stand there like an idiot.

"What's up?" he says.

I haven't rehearsed this part. What the hell am I supposed to say—that I was afraid of the dark?

"Can I come in?" I say.

"Do you guys mind?" he asks the concealed guests in his room.

"Whatever," says a girl.

"Is she hot?" a boy says. The girl giggles.

Brewer rolls his eyes at me. "You can come in if you don't mind hanging out with these idiots."

Inside, Rob Foley and Amanda Johnson are sitting on the floor. A camping lantern burns in front of them, casting dramatic shadows on their faces. My panic level is maxed out now. These are Chelsea's old friends. The ski-tards. The ones who snicker every time they see us like it's fucking eighth grade and call her the Hog behind her back (a variation on her last name, which I guess they think is real clever).

"Guys, this is Lily," Brewer says. He puts his hand on the small of my back and gently guides me into the room. I'm tingling.

"Lily, Rob and Amanda."

"Hey," says Amanda.

"Sup," says Rob. "Cool hoodie."

I'm wearing the Radiohead *Amnesiac* sweatshirt I found at a thrift store on one of my day trips to Boulder with Chelsea.

"Thanks," I say. Brewer sits down next to Amanda.

"Sit down," says Brewer. "Have a beer, while they're cold."

"We're trying to convince Brewer here to come out on the slopes with us," says Amanda.

"But he's being gay about it," says Rob. "Aren't you, Brewer?"

I sit down next to Rob, who is leaning against Brewer's bed frame. Amanda smiles as she hands me a beer from the fridge.

"I've got a screwed-up knee, I told you," Brewer says.

"Riiight," says Rob, then coughs out, "Pussy."

Brewer turns to me. "What are you doing all the way over on this side of the hall?" he says, his blue eyes dancing in the lantern light.

There's a draft coming in from the window above Brewer's desk, propped open with a crushed beer can. A candle near his laptop sputters out. I take a long sip of my beer as Rob packs a bowl.

"What kind of question is that?" says Rob. "The lady clearly wants to partake in the inhalation of the dankest weed this shitty campus has to offer." He passes me the bowl. "Greens?" he asks me. I shrug and take a hit. It's just okay.

"Thanks," I say, exhaling and passing it to Amanda.

"So," says Brewer, "did *you* see him, too?"

I have no idea what Brewer is talking about. "See who?" I say.

"The Trapper," he says.

My stomach turns a little and I wonder if they're playing some sort of trick on me.

"Oh my God," says Amanda, "stop." She hugs her knees.

"You know who the Trapper is, right?" asks Brewer. "Apparently it's a thing here. But it sounds like bullshit to me."

"Yeah," I say, playing it cool, "I've heard of him."

"Rob claims to have seen him in the bathroom down the hall," says Brewer.

"I swear," says Rob, slapping the floor to make his point. "He was taking a shower. I saw his boots. I saw his pelts. You know that's his MO before he steals a chick." I realize then, from the frown on his face, that this is no joke, that Rob actually thinks he's seen the Trapper.

"Why does it always have to be a chick?" says Amanda. "Maybe you're next."

"Don't be fucking stupid," snaps Rob. "The Trapper isn't into dudes. The whole reason he goes after chicks is because the guys he was with on his prospecting expedition ate his wife or whatever. He wants to replace her."

"Sounds like a romantic ghost," says Brewer.

Amanda scoffs. "He's not a ghost. He's a zombie or something."

"Zombies eat brains, babe, they don't steal women," says Brewer.

"Ghosts can't kidnap people," says Amanda.

"Ghosts aren't real, and neither are zombies, so it really doesn't matter," says Brewer.

"Whatever, you guys," says Rob. "I know what I saw." He turns to me. "You believe me, right?"

"I guess," I say, using the same noncommittal tone I use with Chelsea when she tells me about this stuff. I feel kind of bad for him, really. Was he the one who started Chelsea's Trapper obsession, or was it the other way around?

"See?" Rob says. "She's the only smart one here." He slides his hand onto my back, and I get a chill.

"How much of that dank weed did you have before you came over?" Brewer says to Rob. Then his eyelids lower and his face softens as he takes a hit.

"Lay off him, Clint," says Amanda, before nestling up against him.

So much for my chances with Brewer, I think, as I watch him pet Amanda's shoulder. I'll need to tell Chelsea that Amanda's basically called dibs.

"I was just thinking," he says to Rob, "that maybe Lily can go with you and confirm what it is you think you saw."

"If you're the one who doesn't believe him, why don't you go?" I say to Brewer. I'm surprised at the harshness in my voice.

Brewer looks at Rob, who is making cartoon ghost "oooo" noises with his mouth and wiggling his fingers. Am I actually riffing with the ski-tards? Is this happening?

"Nah," says Brewer.

"Too scared to ski, too scared to prove me wrong," says Rob. Brewer throws a balled-up sock at him.

It goes on like this for a while. I relax a little and realize that it's kind of nice to be around these people. Brewer pulls out his guitar and lets me play my Pixies cover, and Amanda and Rob are super sweet about it and ask me to play them some old Sublime songs. I'm actually having a good time. I start to think that I know nothing about the ski-tards, that maybe Chelsea has the wrong idea.

While Brewer and Amanda play blackjack, Rob puts his arm around me, which is a little weird, but it's been forever since I've been, well, touched like that, so I kind of like it. He's not Brewer but he's got a clean-cut, rich-kid look going for him, so why not? The Gunnar boys have never paid me that much attention. I don't rock a push-up bra and smoky eye like Amanda. She has clearly planned to look dressed up and dressed down at the same time, with her pink velour tracksuit and all that makeup. Rob, with his arm around me, makes me feel a little less jealous of Amanda, who is leaning closer and closer to Brewer with each hand he deals. Then Rob starts asking me about my music, which I have only talked to Chelsea about, and about the shows I like to go to. He tells me he has tickets to see his friend's band at a club in Boulder next weekend and that I should totally come, and I say maybe, because all I can think about is what Chelsea would think.

"I'm glad you stopped by," he says, hugging me tighter. His sweatshirt smells like weed and incense. He must feel me stiffen, because he asks me what's wrong.

"Nothing," I say.

"You can tell me," he says, playing with a strand of my hair.

"Why did Chelsea stop hanging out with you guys?" I blurt.

He puts his hands in his lap, shakes his head. "It's a long fucking story."

I'm silent, unsure if I even want to know. But he goes on anyway.

"It's chick drama," he says, "but basically Amanda and I used to date—we're just friends now. Anyway, Chelsea and I hooked up and Amanda got all pissy about it, and the two of them had a falling out, and I was just stuck in the middle. I sided with Amanda, because Chelsea was kind of a bitch about the whole thing, no offense."

"A bitch how?" I say.

"She started spreading all these rumors. Just immature gossip."

"Chelsea did that?" I say. But part of me isn't that surprised. She can be vengeful when she wants to be.

"I can't believe you didn't hear. It was like the biggest deal at the beginning of the semester."

He chugs the rest of his beer and crushes the can between his palms, letting it fall to the floor.

"She said I took advantage of her. Like I said, total BS, but we still had to have a fucking campus judicial hearing about it." I feel his body tense up, like he's annoyed just thinking about the memory.

I think back to a couple of months ago and remember how suddenly at the end of September, Chelsea started staying in at night, how she'd come back to the room looking tired, how she'd hole up and watch *Survive! 1845* and cry while I tried to focus on studying. That was when we started talking.

"I remember now," I say. He squeezes my shoulder again.

"You're a lot more down-to-earth than she is, I can tell."

"Thanks," I say, feeling uneasy. My leg has fallen asleep, and I stand up. On Brewer's bed, a phone-charging cable snakes out from his laptop. I remember why I came originally and plug in my dead phone, which comes to life with a glorious chime.

I have a string of texts from Chelsea, asking if I'm all right.

The power is out and I'm chilling with Rob and Brewer and Amanda, I write.

Rob Foley?????????

Yes.

I want you to be careful around him, seriously.

This is what I expected. She is so possessive. I decide to press her a little bit.

He's nice, I don't know what the big deal is.

Just trust me.

Drama queen. I'm about to text the words but know that it will just lead to her blowing up at me.

Why can't you just tell me?

"What's going on up there?" says Rob, swiveling his head to look at me.

"My mom's texting," I say. "She's worried about the storm."

"Tell her you're with friends," he says. Friends. I smile down at him.

There's a long pause, as I watch the dots that signal Chelsea typing blink on and off. Rob takes another hit from Brewer's pipe.

I'll tell you when I get back, she writes, finally.

I look at the back of Rob's head. My leg is in a position where if I pull my knee up and slide my foot forward fast enough, I can give him a good kick. Or I can slide down next to him and keep talking about bands. I drop my phone and fiddle with the ring Chelsea gave me. It feels like a million years since the first time we got drunk together, when she triumphantly burst into the room with a box of wine and told me that I needed to help her finish it if I didn't want her to get alcohol poisoning, but really it's been only a couple of months. Before those nights with the tears and that night with the wine she was a stranger, spending weekends and some weeknights at the chalet, leaving me alone in the dorm with my books and my computer and my guitar and my stupid, stupid thoughts. When she started talking to me, the weekends became something to look forward to, instead of to dread. But still, there were some major unanswered questions. Like why is she just now telling me about Rob? What happened with the ski-tards, really?

Rob pulls himself up on the bed next to me and leans into my shoulder. Just then a crash from outside the door makes us both jump. Brewer and Amanda, who have been making out by the closet with the camping lantern beside them, stop and look in the direction of the noise.

Brewer sees how freaked out we are and laughs. "It's the storm, you idiots," he says. Then he pulls Amanda closer and they start kissing again.

Reaching around my back, Rob takes the extinguished candle from the desk and relights it. "Now I can see you," he says. I stare at my sneakers as he leans in closer and whispers in my ear: "I want to show you the Trapper. They'll believe you."

His breath on my earlobe makes my whole body vibrate. He massages my knee, moving his hand up my jeans. I push it away, smiling to show that it's fine but to chill just a little bit, but he moves it back.

"I don't think so," is all I can muster.

"Come on," he says. He kisses my neck. I jerk away and he stops. "You like to watch?" he whispers, gesturing with his chin at Amanda and Brewer on the floor. It takes me a second to realize what he means and I'm glad that the light from the candle is dim because I can feel my cheeks turning bright red.

"It's cool," he says. "I'm just going to go take a leak. Then we can pick up where we left off." He gives my knee a pat as he stands up.

Once he leaves and shuts the door behind him, I stare at the writhing pile of limbs on the floor and decide that maybe I should make a run for it. Why didn't I simply ask Rob to walk me back to my room like a normal, sane human being? But then I remember what Chelsea said about Rob and wonder again whether I should believe her.

I step out into the hallway. In the gray light I can just make out the source of the crash: a branch has broken through the hall window, and snow and wind are blowing in through the hole in the glass. I realize I've left my phone on Brewer's bed and knock softly, but no one opens the door. I try the handle, but it's locked.

I sit down on the floor.

What kind of shithead fuckup doesn't go home for Thanksgiving? My mom and dad and little sister are probably sitting down together in front of the TV, watching *The Twilight Zone* like they do every year, which I used to think was so dorky, but right now I'd give anything to be there on our hideous tan sofa with the cat purring on my lap.

Within a minute or so I'm freezing. I don't want to let Rob or Amanda or Brewer see me have a breakdown in the hallway. I'm better than that. So I start back to my own room, one footstep at a time. I swivel the ring around my finger with my thumb, trace the jagged edges of the crystal, hope it does its job. The wind howls through the broken window and I can hear glass crunch under my feet. I stumble and fall into a wall. But it isn't a wall. It's leather, and smells like tobacco and mud and whiskey and rot, and it reaches out two arms and grips my shoulders.

They say there are two sides to every story. But sometimes, there are two stories. There's the lore, and there's the truth.

There's the Trapper, draped in furs, smelling like death.

And then there's Rob, sweatshirt hood draped over his head, smelling like incense and weed.

There's the Trapper's icy, callused hand on my wrist.

Then there's Rob's warm, smooth one, shoving me into the wall.

There's the Trapper's tassels flapping as he grabs me by the waist.

There's the clink of Rob's belt unbuckling.

I can't run, because moving would mean admitting to myself that this is happening. I ball my hands into fists and feel Chelsea's ring, heavy and hot, on my skin and I scream at myself in my head and miraculously I spin around and I feel my fist make contact with flesh, the crystal digging into his face, and there's that smell again and then the sound of fabric falling and what I see is the Trapper getting smaller and smaller, deflating almost, his clothes billowing around his shrinking body. Then my feet are freezing all of a sudden and when I look down I see it's because I'm standing knee-deep in a pile of snow in the middle of the hallway, and the Trapper is gone and then the snow disappears and Rob slaps his hand to his bloody cheek and shouts, "You crazy fucking bitch!"

But I've forced my feet to move and I am down the hall by then, my key finds the lock, the door opens, and I'm back in my room with the door shut and locked behind me.

My laptop's screen saver is still on, its dim blue light making the dorm room look like it's underwater. I pick up the Old Crow and take a swig. I drop my keys on my bed and walk to the window. My right hand throbs. It's wet with blood—not mine—gleaming black in the blue light of the screen.

I touch the windowpane. The wind is quieter now, and the snow has stopped falling. The power is still out but there's the moon, and the campus looks like a damn Christmas card, with globs of white all over the evergreens. Ice crystals are beginning to form at the lip of the sill on the inside of the room. Outside, a hooded shadow with his hand to his face trudges across the snow, toward the Ponderosa. I think of Kelly Jasper, wild-eyed in the firelight, as I lick the blood off my fingers.

MYSTERY LIGHTS

It takes forty-five minutes for your eyes to adjust to the dark.

Wendy squinted across the flat darkness of Marfa, Texas, as the instructions from an old stargazing book that belonged to her daughter, Emma, floated through her head.

The Marfa Lights viewing area was little more than a roadside rest stop with telescopes and a couple of covered benches that looked out over the desert. The tiny orbs of light that appeared floating above the horizon from time to time were an unexplained phenomenon. UFOs. Ghosts. Heat lightning. They appeared often enough for the viewing area to be landmarked with a plaque. There was a simple explanation for the lights that would appear tonight, however: drones, paid for by the network. She sat among the tourists and paranormal enthusiasts, with their cameras on tripods and phones in hand, whispering. The man next to her held a camera in his lap and took swigs from a hip flask. He offered some to Wendy, but she declined.

She was with her team. Katie, her meticulous assistant, whose doughy face made her look a decade younger than her twenty-five years, scrolled through emails on her phone. Perched next to Katie on the bench was Paul, Wendy's producer, sucking on a vape pen and taking his Dodgers cap off every so often to nervously run his hand through his thick blond hair. Paul and Katie had been here for days now, monitoring the marketing campaign. Wendy had only arrived late last night to supervise the conclusion, the campaign's finale, which was scheduled for tomorrow evening. She turned her wrist and looked at the glow-in-the-dark numbers on her watch. Ten thirty. Sixteen minutes late.

"Any word?" she whispered to Katie.

"No," said Katie, frantically scrolling, trying to refresh her mail. "They've never been late before. And service sucks out here."

When Wendy looked up, she saw the blue-green afterimage of Katie's illuminated phone screen in the sky. Damn. Her eyes would need to readjust if she wanted to see the night sky's full majesty. Then, off in the corner of the horizon, something else. A faint white circle of light, like a single headlight, but not anywhere near the road. It rose higher and higher up into the sky, glowing a bright white. More lights rose, twinkling from white to yellow to pale green, splitting apart in amoeba-like dances. The whispers of the people around them turned to excited chatter as they snapped pictures with their phones and cameras.

"Isn't it great?" murmured Katie.

"It would be, if they'd been on time," said Wendy. She pulled her phone from her purse to take a picture, but the man with the flask pushed past her, his camera beeping and whizzing as he attempted to capture the last visible orb, which rose higher and finally flickered out. Breathless whispers of "Did you see?" and "Did you get that?" bounced through the crowd. A couple of people even applauded.

"Thanks," said Paul, taking a bow.

Katie elbowed him in the ribs. "Dude, don't blow our cover."

"These idiots aren't paying attention."

"Kids," said Wendy, "let's get back to the hotel. We've got a big day tomorrow."

* * *

WHEN WENDY WAS ASSIGNED the marketing campaign for the *Marfa Lights* reboot, she was perplexed. The show hadn't been cool, or even all that good, in the nineties. It was contrived—basically *The X-Files* meets *Twin Peaks* with the Texas flair of corrupt oil-baron villains and a pair of improbably attractive Texas Rangers (a skeptic and a believer) solving the supernatural mysteries. So why bring it back? According to the notes she'd received from the network, it had a *fiercely devoted cult following.* Katie, who'd squealed when Wendy told her about the reboot, was one such devotee. Wendy had let her come up with some concepts, provided she did so on her own time.

Like Katie, Wendy had started out as an assistant. Her boss, the incongruously named Howard Meek, was a bloviating egomaniac who insisted that Wendy wear high heels "for your figure" and would go into detail about his dates with women, sharing stories about what he termed his "adventures in the bedroom" when she brought him his 11:00 AM coffee. All the men in the office looked up to him, said he was a genius. Last she'd heard, he'd retired after being honored with some sort of lifetime achievement award for his service to the industry.

Katie had it easy with Wendy, comparatively, who was more of a mentor than a boss. Which was why she'd submitted Katie's concepts alongside her own. As her own. The network had gone for one of Katie's. The wackiest, most expensive one.

The campaign pitch: they would create their own *Marfa Lights* episode, in real time. In the weeks leading up to the show, they'd partner with various social media influencers who would post cheeky doomsday videos claiming the world was going to end on October 14, the night the show premiered. That the end would be known by the lights in the sky. They'd send interns out late at night to stencil the show's tagline, *10/14 LOOK UP*, in the place of the usual teaser print campaigns in New York and Los Angeles. Then, for five nights before the premiere, they'd make their own Marfa Lights *in* Marfa—"With drones!" Katie had chirped—a convoluted magic trick to draw out the UFO hunters and generate buzz for the show. It had been Wendy's idea to have them show up at 10:14 PM. On the evening of the premiere itself, three hundred drones would take to the Marfa sky to spell out *LOOK UP*. Shuttles would be on hand to bring ticket holders to a drive-in movie theater down the road, where they would watch the *Marfa Lights* premiere.

There were all kinds of reasons the network should have said no. First off, it was happening not in New York or Los Angeles but in Texas, and seven hours outside Austin, at that. Secondly, it would take place at night, and with these kinds of experiential campaigns you depended on people to take pictures and post them. Smartphone pictures just didn't turn out that great at night. Thirdly, after all the permits and flights and hotels, it was expensive. But the network didn't seem to care about this. The network was obliging. The network had money to burn, apparently. Still, the whole campaign made Wendy a little uneasy. She was nearing her midfifties, aging out of her industry, which meant that any day she could be dropped for someone younger and cheaper.

She could not fuck this up.

Which was why, riding back to town in the black Texas night, she was grilling Paul about why the lights had been late. "I just want to know what happened, so that we can make sure it doesn't happen tomorrow," she said, trying to keep her tone as even-keeled as possible.

"I'll email them, okay?" he said, taking a turn a little too quickly.

Wendy knew she should be more careful about the way she talked to him. The truth was, Paul *could* afford to fuck this up. Paul's father was a big-shot executive at the agency. She could feel his aura of resentment filling the car with bitterness. Just when it was becoming unbearable, Katie alerted them both that she'd received yet another email from Teresa, one of the influencers they'd hired to help promote the show.

"What does she want?" Wendy snapped.

"A walk-on role."

"Don't respond to her," said Wendy. This was not the first time she'd asked, either. They'd explained that shooting had wrapped weeks ago and that they didn't even know if the show was getting a second season. Wendy had been opposed to the idea of working with the influencers all along. Too many variables, too little control. But Irv, her boss, had loved it. Paul pulled into the hotel parking lot.

"She's threatening to shut down our premiere."

Paul let out a sharp croak of a laugh. "This is your stop," he told Wendy.

"Aren't you getting out?" she said.

"Grabbing a drink."

"You too?" She turned to a frightened-looking Katie.

"Just one drink," said Katie, smiling apologetically. "Want to come?"

Wendy deliberated for a moment. "I've got work to do."

"We'll be at Lucky Star Saloon if you change your mind," said Katie.

"See you in the morning, *Mom*," said Paul, smirking. It was an inside joke they had, that they were her children. Sometimes it felt too real. Their taillights disappeared down the empty street.

* * *

WENDY, PAUL, AND KATIE were staying in what had once been a Bates-ish, all-American roadside motel that had been renovated into a sleek hotel with poured-cement floors, cowhide rugs, and record players in each room. This was, Wendy had come to learn in the short time she'd been in the tiny town, classic, self-aware Marfa: catering to the desert-minimalist-chic trend that was catnip to the Instagram waifs with their peasant dresses and Manson girl hair. Wendy sat on the bed and took off her boots, brushing dust off the soft leather. Her feet throbbed and blisters were developing on both ankles. She'd forgotten her hiking boots in Los Angeles and had spent the day trudging through the desert grassland of the drive-in theater in her city shoes, a pair of suede ankle boots that were totally inappropriate for the job.

She walked across the chilly floor in her tights, pulled a can of sparkling water out of the mini fridge, and called Chris.

"Howdy," he said. His voice was far-off, and she could hear the sound of a game in the background. Chris was a sports fan in the purest sense of the word. With no loyalty toward one team or another, he just loved to watch the games. Soccer was his favorite, and she'd sometimes wake up in the middle of the night to an ambient stadium roar and an announcer's cry of "Goaaaaaal" coming from the TV room.

"Hey," she said.

"How's the trip?"

"The drone pilot fucked up."

"Oh, no," he said, his attention elsewhere. "I'm sorry."

"Have you heard from Emma?"

The game sounds switched off then.

"Yeah," said Chris, "she's fine. Just figuring things out right now."

Their daughter, Emma, had, without telling either of her parents, dropped out of Smith and moved in with a friend in Brooklyn. After two weeks of successfully evading their calls, she'd admitted everything to them over the phone, saying she needed money to work on her music. Wendy had told her no, that if she was going to do what she was doing, she'd need to find a job. Chris had eventually talked Wendy into sending Emma a month's rent to tide her over, but Emma had refused to speak to her mother since that conversation.

Wendy sighed.

"Honey," said Chris.

"What? I just think that moving to the most expensive city in the world is unwise if one doesn't have a job, don't you?"

"You know what the job market is like for kids her age."

"Yes, which is why she needs to finish school and get that diploma so that we won't be paying her rent for the rest of our lives." It was an argument they'd had many times before. With Chris out of a job, they couldn't afford to do rich-parent things, like pay the rent on their daughter's ridiculously overpriced Bushwick loft. She took a furious sip of her sparkling water, wishing it were something stronger. It dribbled down her chin and she wiped it off. "Chris?" she said.

"It was one month. What did you want her to do? She's not going to make rent busking."

"She's *busking*?" This was new. She imagined her daughter on a subway platform, wearing her studded fire-engine-red motorcycle jacket—Emma's favorite, a relic from the eighties that had once belonged to Wendy—and strumming the Springsteen and Dylan songs Chris had taught her as tourists passed, throwing quarters at her.

"Can we talk about this when you're home?"

"Sure. Fine."

"I miss you. Bring me back a Stetson hat, can you do that for me?"

"Good night."

"Good night, Wen." He hung up.

Wendy stared at the phone, face hot with rage. She scrolled to her daughter's number. It was after midnight in New York. What kind of mother calls her child after midnight? She pressed the call button. The phone rang, then went to voicemail. "You've reached Emma. Just text me, okay?" her daughter's voice implored. She hung up.

The air conditioner switched off with a click. Muffled giggles and splashing came from the hotel pool. She typed the name of the bar into the mapping app on her phone. It was an eight-minute walk. Katie and Paul, Angelenos through and through, had driven there. Grabbing her bag, Wendy set off into the night.

* * *

LUCKY STAR SALOON was a tourist dive bar. Whoever had designed it had done so by focus group, ticking off all the boxes. Neon beer signs, check. A jukebox playing Hank Williams, check. Dark varnished wood everywhere, check. Dart board, check. Dilapidated pool table, check. There were craft beers, though, and a cocktail menu, and instead of a grizzled old barkeep there was a young guy with a coiffed beard who would have fit in at any coffee shop in Silver Lake. Paul and Katie sat at the bar in front of him, looking at their phones. The rest of the room was empty except for a booth of girls around Emma's age, all wearing brightly colored bobbed wigs and taking selfies with one another. When had this narcissistic ritual replaced conversation?

Paul looked up and caught her eye. "Shit. The boss is here."

Wendy waved.

"You came," said Katie. Her tone indicated that she wasn't so excited about it.

"I thought we may as well celebrate." She examined the cocktail menu and ordered a tequila drink called a Green Goblin. "What's up with those wigs?"

Katie inhaled sharply, as if about to say something, but instead looked down at her beer.

"They're high as fuck," Paul said.

Katie glared at Paul.

"What? They are! They told me—hang on, I wrote it down." He picked up his phone and read, "'We are here to bring purity through chaos. Serenity through disorder.'"

Wendy glanced over her shoulder. One of the girls was floating her palm over a lit candle, a euphoric expression on her face.

"Sounds like they've been watching our campaign," she said.

The bartender set her drink down in front of her. "Seven bucks," he said. She dug her Amex out of her wallet and set it on the bar.

"Open or closed?"

Wendy hesitated. "Open," she said.

"All *right*!" said Paul, giving the bar a slap.

The Green Goblin was too sweet, but she drank it anyway and ordered a second and a third as Paul prattled on to her about bad Tinder dates, television shows, and a new bar in Highland Park that served only Texas beers. She'd never really spent time with Paul outside work. *This is good*, she told herself. *Morale-building.* But Katie's morale looked like it could be better. She was ignoring them, mesmerized by something on her phone. After several minutes of staring intently at it, she left, muttering something about a call she needed to make. Once she was gone, Wendy took the opportunity to ask Paul what was wrong with her.

He shrugged. "She's probably just tired," he said. "Sick of me." He slouched on the bar and brought his bottle to his lips, smiling to himself. She thought of young Chris, driving her around the city in his gas-guzzling, baby-blue Ford Bronco, bottle of beer between his legs.

The girls behind them were playing the jukebox, singing along to a country song. One voice carried louder than the others, deep and breathy. Wendy gasped. It was Emma's voice.

She spun around on her stool and stood up, clenching her cocktail napkin, inspecting the faces of the girls in the wigs. The one whose voice she'd heard had her eyes closed and was belting out the chorus, her face contorted in a passionate snarl. Not Emma. But the voice was nearly identical. The song ended and her wigged friends clapped.

"You okay?" said Paul.

She stared at the cocktail napkin she was holding and unclenched her fingers, letting it fall. Her tongue was heavy, coated with the cloying syrup of her drink. She was drunk, she realized, as she clutched the edge of the bar to steady herself.

"I should get home," she said. "Big day tomorrow."

"Need a ride?" said Paul, eyeing the wigged girls.

"I'll walk," she said. "I could use some air, honestly." The bartender brought her the tab and she paid it, then stumbled through the door and walked the empty streets back toward the hotel.

In bed, she opened Instagram, typed her daughter's handle into the search bar, and clicked on the first result. A bunch of tiny square Emmas sprang to the screen. In the most recent photo, she sported an asymmetrical haircut, long chunks of platinum hair framing half of her face. Her heavily lined eyes were creased in a defiant squint, her dark lips curved in a pout. The caption had no words, just one of those emojis, a yellow girl smiling with scissors in her hair. Where was she? The photograph was taken outdoors—there was a street sign in the background. Wendy tried to zoom in but accidentally double-tapped the image, causing a white heart to bloom and disappear over her daughter's face. Crap. Her own account had no images—she used it only to monitor the various social media campaigns for work. It was her name, BendyWendy228, that Emma might recognize. Some doll that Chris had found once at Toys "R" Us and bought for Emma, and the two of them could not stop laughing. She was still Bendy Wendy whenever she went to yoga, whenever either of them wanted to disarm her in her bursts of temper. She looked at the likes underneath the picture: 476. There was no way her daughter would notice one more, was there? She put the phone down on the nightstand and stared at the shadows on the ceiling until sleep came.

* * *

THE TOUR OF THE CHINATI FOUNDATION, the shrine to minimalist sculpture that housed works by Donald Judd, among other artists, was supposed to be time off, a bit of culture before the big finale. Wendy had booked tickets for Katie and Paul, but Paul had texted moments ago declining, saying he had too much work. *Probably just had a hangover,* thought Wendy, sipping her third cup of coffee in the hotel café as she watched a group of girls pose for selfies in front of the mural across the street that said, simply, *See Mystery Lights* in bold white letters on a navy-blue background. It had rained overnight and was threatening to continue on and off today. Wendy prayed it would let up by the evening. Her head throbbed. She had hardly slept the night before. Katie walked into the café at a quarter past eight, fifteen minutes early. She looked tired, or tired as a girl her age can look, as she ordered a large coffee to go.

They walked out to the parking lot. "Rough night?" asked Wendy.

"Just some jitters about the premiere," Katie said, forcing a smile.

Katie's nervous silence throughout the short drive was interspersed with profanity at the wrong turns she took in spite of the GPS's directions. They still arrived at the foundation with enough time before the tour started to wander the grounds, a cluster of military buildings surrounded by a field dotted with Judd's rectangular concrete structures—picnic tables for giants. Their sharp lines stood out against the rippling yellow grass, alien and imposing.

"What do you think?" said Katie finally, inspecting the sculptures.

"I don't know yet," said Wendy. The blisters on her ankles burned. The truth was she didn't understand what the big deal was about minimalist art. Chris loved it. Used the word "sublime" to describe a painting that was nothing more than white paint on canvas. It felt out of reach to Wendy, who had spent her life in marketing, trying to make ideas accessible to the masses. Chris was the one who had insisted she book the tour.

"I think they're magnificent," Katie said.

They moved closer to one of the sculptures. It was taller than it had seemed from a distance—big enough for Katie and Wendy to stand inside, which they did, the concrete radiating a musty cool.

"Feel this," said Katie, running her hand along the sculpture's wall. "He poured the cement into plywood molds."

Wendy ran a hand over the concrete. It was textured with a swirling wood grain. A jackrabbit bounded by them, nose twitching. Thunder sounded in the distance.

"There's something you need to see," Katie said, and handed her phone to Wendy.

On it was a YouTube video titled *TURN OFF MARFA LIGHTS*.

"Is this one of ours?" asked Wendy.

"Just watch it."

"Greetings," said a young woman in a purple bobbed wig. She sighed heavily, her entire body deflating as she exhaled. Her blue-painted lips were turned down in a somber expression. "Sometimes, we are taken advantage of. Our youth, our beauty used to make others wealthy." She paused, nostrils flaring. "They've corrupted our language. Words like 'radical' are selling organic hand creams. 'Disrupt' is used by tech executives peddling apps. We're sedated by mediocre narratives that keep us in our beds and on our sofas, keep us from engaging with reality. You have the opportunity to stop one before it starts, friends. I'm asking *you* to disrupt, to spread your radical beautiful energy around the small desert city of Marfa, Texas, where yet another piece of bland nostalgia-bait is having its premiere. Hit them where it hurts, friends. Do what needs to be done. Purity through chaos. Serenity through disorder. Meet here on October 14 . . ." GPS coordinates flashed across the screen as she continued, encouraging people to come out to the viewing area on the *Marfa Lights* premiere date. "This is Teresa Montecito, signing off."

It had nearly six hundred thousand views. More than any of their own promos. She handed the phone back to Katie. "I don't understand."

"Those girls in wigs last night, those were some of her fans." Katie looked close to tears now, her face bright red.

"Katie," said Wendy, placing a hand on her back, tentatively. "What's wrong?"

"Her followers—her fans—they're kind of unstable."

"Unstable how?"

Katie winced and typed something into her phone. "See for yourself."

TERESA MONTECITO FANS WIG OUT, read the title of the video. In it, a group of wigged twentysomething girls were gathered outside an office building, chanting something inaudible. Two of them lit the contents of a trash can on fire. The shaky camera panned to a cluster of girls throwing bricks. Cheers erupted as the building's front window shattered.

"That was outside the office of a newspaper in Denver, after one of their columnists wrote an op-ed about Teresa's negative influence on young girls," Katie said. "Teresa sent a handwritten letter to each of those girls in the video, thanking them."

"Did you tell Irv?"

Katie stared at her boots and kicked a rock free from the dry dirt. "He's going to call you about it this morning."

"Christ," said Wendy. *It wasn't my idea*, she imagined herself saying to Irv. But that wasn't the way things worked. Katie was her employee; therefore the work she came up with belonged to Wendy. And Irv didn't care about details like that.

"We should go," said Katie glumly. "The tour's about to start."

* * *

DONALD JUDD HAD CREATED the structures at the Chinati Foundation to outlast him, the bespectacled tour guide told them; he was obsessed with permanence. She spoke with profound reverence for the work, a priest sermonizing, as she led them through arid repurposed artillery sheds full of waist-high aluminum boxes polished to a mirrored sheen, variations on the concrete ones outside. Wendy noticed several young women in wigs on the tour, surreptitiously snapping pictures of themselves with the art, despite the no-photo policy. Judd had installed floor-to-ceiling glass windows facing the structures in the field. Plastic buckets caught water that leaked from the roof. *So much for permanence*, thought Wendy.

The group filed out and walked toward the next building, which was nearly identical to the first. Inside were more rows of aluminum sculptures. The tour guide told them that this particular building had been a German POW camp during World War II. The peeling remnants of a German phrase were still visible on one of the brick walls. The guide translated it for the group: "It's better to use your head than to lose it."

Wendy's phone rang, then. It was Irv. She signaled to Katie to step outside with her.

He asked how things were. "Fantastic!" Wendy lied. She and Katie sat down on a bench, the phone between them, speaker on.

Satisfied with her update, Irv launched into an anecdote about his dog's groomer.

While he talked, Katie gnawed on her thumbnail. Instinctively, Wendy put a hand on her assistant's arm to stop her. Katie folded her hands in her lap.

Irv shifted topics. "I saw the Montecito gal's video." Wendy braced herself for a reprimand, a rebuke for getting Teresa involved in the first place. "The network *loves* it. What a concept! I don't know how you come up with these things."

Relief surged through her. He thought it was all part of the campaign. Wendy played along. "She's great, isn't she?"

Katie started to say something, but Wendy held up her hand.

"You're a true artist." Irv went on, telling them his twelve-year-old granddaughter was obsessed with Teresa and had a wig that she never took off. "You're gonna do great tonight," he said. "You always do." He had another call on the line and excused himself.

Wendy hung up. "That went better than expected," she said to Katie.

Katie sighed. "Does Irv know that this was *my* concept?"

"Does he need to know?" Wendy was annoyed now. Couldn't the girl see that Wendy had her best interests in mind?

Katie stood up.

"Sit down," said Wendy sternly. Katie did as she was told. She looked like she was about to cry. "Irv doesn't need to know who does what. You're on my team, that's all that matters."

There were tears now. Wendy hated tears. She pitched her voice up a register and spoke quietly, like she used to do to end fights with Emma. "I would have been the one to get in trouble if he didn't like it, you know. It goes both ways." She wasn't sure if this was the case. "The network wouldn't have gone for your idea if it wasn't a great one."

"Thanks," Katie sniffed.

Katie was mature. Katie knew her place. Katie would go far in this industry.

Wendy remembered Howard Meek again, how he had often taken credit for her work, and she had let him—the guys in the office had envied the fact that he'd found her ideas strong enough to put forward with his own, and Wendy, too, had basked in the glow of his approval, until she'd wised up and realized that he was taking advantage of her. But this was different. She was protecting Katie.

* * *

WENDY LAY IN THE HOTEL ROOM with the curtains drawn, phone in hand. Emma had posted a new picture to her Instagram account, or, rather, an old picture. In it, lanky fourteen-year-old Emma hunched over an acoustic guitar. Chris sat next to her, holding a ukulele, his mouth open in song. *Like father . . .*, read the caption. Wendy had taken that photograph on one of the rare Sunday afternoons when they weren't at each other's throats. Mother's Day, of all days. Chris and Emma had put on a show for her, performing the songs that Emma was learning in her guitar lessons, simple three-chord rock numbers. Some Nirvana. Some Police. Had Emma seen her like? Was this a message?

A knock. Katie, letting her know that it was time. Despite the serene expression on her face, the nails on the hand that clutched her clipboard were bitten to the quick. She flashed a tight-lipped smile and handed Wendy a lanyard with a *STAFF* badge clipped to it.

The three of them drove out to the now-congested viewing area. The glow of their headlights illuminated clumps of willowy girls in peasant dresses and wigs holding cardboard trays of tacos and glass bottles of soda from the nearby taco truck that had decided to capitalize on the crowd, which was now spilling onto the highway. Wendy grew nervous. The place was crawling with dozens of Montecito followers. She craned her neck, searching for anyone without a wig. No luck.

"They've totally lost it," said Paul, as they passed by a circle of wigged girls, eyes closed, holding hands and humming.

"A little confusion is fine," said Katie. "We just need them to be here, to document this."

"Katie's right," Wendy said, grateful that the girl had finally come to her senses. "It's already a story. We can spin it however we'd like after the fact."

"Whatever you guys say," said Paul, parking the car.

There was an electric anticipation in the air as they headed toward the viewing area. Wendy lost sight of Paul and Katie. She pressed into the crowd of shimmering wigs.

She was nearly to the viewing platform when she heard sirens. At first, she ignored them, momentarily forgetting that she was no longer in the city. It wasn't until bright white floodlights lit up the parking lot that she turned and pushed through the girls, moving toward the highway. There, the Presidio County Sheriff's Office had set up a quick perimeter with two cruisers shining their lights on the crowd. An officer with a megaphone commanded them to disperse.

Chants of "Fascist pig" rose in response. Wendy held her staff pass over her head, as if the ridiculous piece of laminated card stock on a lanyard would protect her from the impending riot.

"Officer!" she called to a cop who now stood on top of his car. He looked down at her, squinting in disgust. "Please," she said. "We have a permit."

Two more officers helped him down. She saw from his badge that this was the sheriff.

"Ma'am, your guests are blocking the road," he said, adjusting his cowboy hat.

Katie appeared at her side, with Paul. "We'll be busing them out of here shortly, sir," said Paul. "Just give us twenty minutes."

The sheriff seemed to be willing to comply, until something across the parking lot caught his attention.

Wendy followed his gaze. First, all she saw was a group of girls standing still, phones in hand, recording. Then the taco truck, swaying as girls hurled themselves into it. The cooks were out of the truck and trying to restrain them, but they were two against forty. It toppled with a crash. The crowd let out a cheer and jumped onto the truck's side, dancing and whooping. Wendy felt sick to her stomach. The deputies at the sheriff's side drew their guns and made their way toward the overturned truck. More sirens sounded in the distance.

The girls were throwing whatever they could get their hands on—tortillas, onions, raw meat. A soda bottle nicked the sheriff's head, knocking off his hat.

"Ow!" he shouted, clutching his forehead and putting his hand to his holster.

He dusted the hat off, put it back on his head, and drew his gun. It all happened so quickly after that. More cops showed up. The girls shouted, taunting them. One girl, whom Wendy recognized from the bar the previous evening, stood recording with her phone as a group of them jumped up and down on the sheriff's car, cracking the windshield. The deputies were overpowered, helpless. Two shots went off.

The sharp, dry smell of gunpowder brought her back to hunting trips with her father and brother in the Vermont woods. Wendy dropped to the ground, just like her father had taught her. She missed him violently then, choking up with emotion though he had died years ago. He'd never really understood why Wendy had left New England, thought there was something smutty and pagan about Los Angeles.

"The cops are shooting at us!" one girl shrieked, racing past Wendy's spot on the ground. A man's outstretched arm appeared in front of Wendy and she took it. It was Paul's, his face twisted into a look of panic.

"Get in the car," he hissed at Wendy. "Katie and I will deal with this."

Katie stood next to him, sobbing. Wendy felt her phone buzz in her jacket pocket.

"Hang on," said Wendy, brushing pebbles from her slacks, hands shaking. As she took out her phone, the screams amplified; the girls ran out into the desert and down the highway, yelling. There were multiple texts. One was from the shuttle bus driver, saying he couldn't get past the police barricade that had been set up. One was from Irv, saying that the *Marfa Lights* hashtag had gone viral, that the sponsors were all happy, and congratulating her. Another followed, asking what the hell was going on, and saying that she needed to report back to him ASAP. Then there were texts from Emma:

Mom, saw the vids from Marfa

u ok?

She felt a lightness, a joy.

"Check your phone in the *car*!" barked Paul. "It's not safe here."

Katie let out another heaving sob. "I told you guys," she said. "I told you guys."

But Wendy's attention was elsewhere. She knew this meant the end of her career, that no publicity was bad publicity until literal shots were fired, that she'd be blamed for everything that had gone wrong even though it had all been Katie's idea. But right now, what else was there to do but marvel at the canopy of desert stars above? At the fact that Emma had finally broken her silence?

She walked through the crowd to the edge of the viewing area, where the open desert began, and kept walking. *Purity through chaos. Serenity through disorder.* What had sounded like word salad last night was now resonant—prescient, even.

Gazing at the heavens, she was transported back to a trip she and Chris and Emma had taken to the Sonoran Desert a decade and a half ago. No porch lights. No flashlights. No screens. Just look up and the sky would unfold, each constellation becoming more visible as the three of them sat in camping chairs in the desert dust, necks craned skyward.

There was Cassiopeia and, below it, the galaxy Andromeda. Another fraught mother-daughter relationship, up in the sky forever. And there, rising from the horizon in perfect synchronicity, at 10:14 PM on the dot, was her very own constellation. Her triumph and her downfall. *LOOK UP.*

It was, truly, her best work.

THE WHITE PLACE

The best time to see the orb is at midnight on moonless nights, when it sets the white rocks of Plaza Blanca aglow with its pale, pulsing radiance. It hovers in the air, watermelon-sized, low enough not to be mistaken for the moon but high enough to be out of reach of the tallest man. Few people have seen it, because few people are near the rocks at that hour, when the desert gives itself over to the creatures that hunt their food under cover of night.

The painter is one of those few. When she can't sleep, she drives from her hilltop home through the surrounding desert. Probably not safe for a woman of her age with failing eyesight, but the painter is known for her stubborn nature. She drives and parks and walks through boulders and gravel, wrapped in a shawl of thick wool, like a witch in a folktale. This is how she found herself among the towering pale sandstone formations of Plaza Blanca, the White Place, staring up at the orb, bathing in its otherworldly glow. She gazes at it, memorizing its contours, the distinct emerald light it casts. Her vision seems to improve in its presence—the landscape around her is crisp and unblurred. There is no question. She must paint it.

* * *

IT IS CANNING WEEK. The kitchen is pure insanity. The painter prefers to stay in her studio when it's like this. She lives on a hill high above town, and her studio looks out on the cottonwoods of the Rio Chama valley, a green smudge. Soon they will be yellow, she thinks, slipping a piece of chocolate into her mouth and letting the muddy sweetness coat her tongue.

She has combed her long gray hair and pinned it up around her head. She wears a black ankle-length cotton dress. A silver belt embedded with turquoise stones hangs around her narrow waist, cold and heavy. She's reading a letter from the boarding school she attended as a girl, Miss Vesper's, requesting a contribution of artwork for their silent auction benefit. The nerve. After the ruler slaps and sore knuckles, the pinches from Mr. Foster in gym class.

A pair of arms wrap themselves around her waist.

"Hello, flower."

A kiss on the neck. Doublemint gum on the breath. The tickle of a mustache. The painter blushes and restrains a giggle; she is not to appear weak in front of him.

Mike has returned with Minkie and Angel, her two boisterous Samoyeds. Minkie pushes her face into the painter's leg, her nose cold and wet, collar jingling with post-walk excitement. She reaches a hand down and is greeted with a lick.

"Please don't call me names," she says.

"Sorry, ma'am," says Mike.

She thrills, the way he calls her ma'am.

She pulls away from him and carefully places herself on the armchair by the fireplace, wrapping a blanket around her shoulders. It's October, and the sun hasn't yet dissipated the morning chill. Angel trots over and curls at her feet.

"And where have you been?" she asks her lover, staring into the fireplace.

"Just out with the girls for a morning stroll," he says. "I like these."

He gestures to the charcoal studies on the easel. They are all of one thing, the only thing she's been able to draw, to dream, to think about: the orb.

"They're nothing," she says. "Just distracting myself." She likes it when he compliments her work, though she knows he is buttering her up because she's agreed to show his ceramics to her dealer, who's coming into town next week.

He pulls up a chair next to her and massages her hand. "Julio says the first frost is coming this weekend."

"You'll need to put the tarps over the garden tonight, I suppose," says the painter. "Are you staying for lunch?"

He moves the chair over to her other side and takes her other hand. "You know," he says, pressing his rough potter's fingers into her palm, "I can't do that."

Alice, her cook, has disliked Mike from the beginning. After it became clear that Mike was more than just a handyman, she told the painter that she refused to feed the help, that he could make his own meals. Which is why he can't stay for lunch, or dinner. If the painter wants to share a meal with him, she'll have to drive out to the little adobe house she gave to him, and they'll eat his cooking. Coarse, male cooking: steak and eggs, beef stew, hamburger.

He crouches next to her, watching the fire. "This isn't easy for me to say."

The painter braces herself. She has seen this day coming, the day he will tire of her. And though she knows she must not show her despair, though she tries her hardest to wish it away, it's still there at night, when she's alone with nothing but the fading warmth of the bedroom fire.

"Sandra's in trouble."

This is not what the painter was expecting. Sandra is Alice's daughter, seventeen and sullen. "What kind of trouble?" she asks, though she is fairly certain she knows.

"She needs a doctor. And she needs cash."

"This is none of my business."

Mike gets that helpless schoolboy look on his face. She realizes, then, that Mike is the reason Sandra needs the cash. She's not angry. She knows Mike can't help himself. He has a fervor for beauty, like her. He knows what it's like to be caught in the thrall. So many people live in that neutral zone, feeling fine about everything. But Mike feels everything deeply. It's there in the way his hands shape clay on the wheel, lovingly, as if it were a woman's body. Alice said he only wanted her money, that was the only reason a man in his late twenties would have anything to do with a woman three times his age. Maybe so. But the painter didn't care. He could have it. He could have whatever he wanted.

"Fine," she says. She stands, unlocks a drawer in her desk, and hands him an envelope of bills. "Take what you need from there."

"Thank you," he says. "You're a saint. Truly."

At lunch, the painter watches Sandra helping her mother in the kitchen. At first, she can't tell what Mike sees in her gangly limbs and perennial scowl, but slowly it dawns on her. It's the same thing her late husband saw in the painter herself all those years ago: her unblemished youth, so easy for him to control and manipulate. But she won, in the end, didn't she? Her grit and her energy and her love ultimately defeated him. She is here. He is not.

* * *

October 9, 1972
Dear Sirs,
I would like to report a sighting. There is a large, unexplained ball of light

Sandra chews on her eraser. She's sitting on the sticky vinyl sofa, binder splayed out on her thighs. If her mother comes home, it will look like she's doing homework. *A large, unexplained ball of light.* What does that even mean? It would be far easier if she'd seen a flying saucer, or a thin green man with big black eyes. But a glowing orb? Still, she keeps going. The editors of *UFO Country* get thousands of these kinds of letters a week. Maybe they'll actually believe hers. Maybe they'll even feature her in the magazine. She imagines passing it around to the kids at school, them taking her seriously for once. If it's in print, it has to be true.

She's nearly finished when she hears the crunch of tires outside and peeks through the shades to see the painter's Alfa Romeo in the weak yellow glow of the porch light. She knows it is Mike, who borrows the car frequently for joyrides. He honks once, twice. She shuts off the lamp and turns out the porch light. The sound of boots in the dirt. The doorbell rings. He bangs on the flimsy mobile home door, shouting, "Snake"—her nickname—over and over. She considers going out to meet him for fear he'll break it, sinking her in deep trouble.

Her mother is off tending to Alma, their ailing neighbor, and for once hasn't forced Sandra to come with her. Sandra was grateful not to have to clip Alma's gnarled toenails in that room smelling of death and bodily fluids. Much better to be home, where she can flip through *UFO Country* without her mother shaking her head and clucking her tongue in disappointment. But now she wishes she'd gone; she'd rather be changing a bedpan than sitting on the sofa, wondering whether Mike can break down their front door.

The plan was for her to take care of it, according to Mike. It. The child growing inside her. And Sandra, who usually went along with whatever Mike said, was on board with the plan, though she knew it was against the law. She even took his cash, assuring him that she could figure it out herself. She was seventeen, practically an adult. But then she told Leticia and Leticia told her what it meant to "take care of it," how her cousin's friend had bled for days and nearly died, how it was better to just have the child and be right with God. In all the years she'd known her friend, Leticia had never talked about God like that. So now Sandra isn't sure what to do. If she doesn't take care of it, she will have to tell her mother, who will throw her out, and then she'll have to move in with Mike, which would be bad news. But if she does take care of it . . . Sandra puts her hand to her belly. She prays, and this has become a frequent prayer, that the aliens will come take her away. She's sure that anything would be better than this.

Sandra thought Mike would be an adventure, something different, a distraction. She'd never really dated anyone—the kids at school treated her like an oddity, the white girl who wasn't rich, whose long brown curls fell over her shoulders in scraggly strands of greasy frizz, who wore torn jeans and the old flannel shirts that once belonged to her father, which her mother couldn't seem to part with though he'd passed away when Sandra was an infant. But the secret of Mike was a shield against all of that. For a while, Sandra had no longer dreaded going to school.

It was winter break last year when she first encountered him, and for once she wasn't slaving away at Mel's, the filling station where she worked after school. Her mother needed her in the kitchen—not their kitchen at home but the painter's. The painter's house creeped Sandra out with its empty walls, rocks and skulls on every ledge. It was freezing that day, and she was grateful for the heat of the stove. She plucked a chicken with her numb fingertips as her mother stirred a steaming pot of beans. Mike burst through the door with muddy boots.

"This a new girl?" he said. He had a rugged, dangerous look about him. A movie star jawline, like Paul Newman. Sandra tingled at the attention.

"That's my girl, Sandra," said her mother.

"Sandra," said Mike. In his mouth, it sounded dirty. He flashed her a smile. "Can she help me carry the groceries in?"

"Ask her yourself," her mother said.

"Yes, sir," said Sandra.

"You can just call him Mike," said her mother. "He thinks he runs things around here, but he's just the help, like us."

"Always good to see you too, Alice," he said.

Sandra stood, washed her hands, and eagerly followed him out the door.

"Mind the rattler," he said, pointing to the ground by his truck where two halves of a small snake lay curled in the dust. Sandra stuck her tongue out in disgust. Mike laughed, showing teeth.

"Got it with the shovel. A young one. Their bites are stronger. They don't know what to do with all that poison." He made snake fangs with two fingers, pressed them into her arm, and hissed. Sandra shrieked and giggled at his touch.

Mike didn't try anything that first time, obviously; he was smarter than that. She helped with the groceries, nothing more, though he did smile at her in that wolflike way of his. "You're stronger than you look, kiddo," he said, as she hefted boxes full of cans from the truck to the kitchen. "Kind of like our little dead friend out there."

* * *

SANDRA PADS BAREFOOT through the dark house into the kitchen. She stares out the back door. The Rio Chama valley glows in the moonlight. The air is thick with the sounds of night: the frogs and the insects, distant yelps of coyotes. And then, from the front of the house, Mike's blaring horn.

She slides her sneakers on and takes her father's sheepskin-lined denim jacket from the peg by the back door and begins to walk, then run. She knows this path well; she's been running it all her life, the path from the back door to Plaza Blanca. She knows it so well and she's sick of it, she's sick of the dust, she's sick of the rocks, she's sick of the cold mountains that surround the valley and make her feel trapped like a princess in a fairy tale. She sends out another signal to the aliens. *Please,* she telepathizes, *I need you.*

* * *

AFTER THAT FIRST ENCOUNTER, she'd see Mike at the filling station buying gas and cigarettes (Winstons), chewing gum (Doublemint), and pop (Tab), always paying with a twenty-dollar bill and telling her to "keep the change, Snake," with a wink.

Then came the spring morning when she and Leticia were walking back from the school bus stop because they'd decided to cut class and spend the day listening to records at Leticia's place. A familiar pickup slowed to a stop, and Mike leaned his head out and called to them.

"Crud," muttered Sandra.

"Is that—?" whispered Leticia.

"Yes."

Sandra had been selective about what she told Leticia about the hunk who worked with her mom, not wanting to trigger her friend's judgmental streak. Leticia wasn't completely innocent, but she was saving her virginity for college boys. Leticia could do this because she, unlike Sandra, had the grades for college.

Sheepishly, Sandra approached the truck. He was grinning again, he was always grinning, and this time she saw her own nervous reflection in his sunglasses. "Shouldn't you girls be at school?" he said.

Sandra was about to confess, to beg him not to tell her mother, but Leticia spoke first. "It's a day off," she said.

He sucked his teeth and shook his head. "Look, it's gonna get real awkward if I have to tell your mom about this. So why don't I just take you both home where you're safe? There are some crazies out here."

Sandra looked at Leticia. Leticia shrugged.

"Okay," said Sandra, and hoisted herself into the cab of the truck.

Leticia gave him directions to her house and then they were silent, Sandra in the middle, Leticia in the passenger seat. Mike seemed to be making himself larger, his frame pressing into her. The cigarette smoke on his leather jacket was so strong she was afraid her mother would smell it on her later. Leticia gripped Sandra's hand and squeezed it as they bounced over the dirt road that led to Leticia's house. When they arrived, Leticia opened the door and hopped out.

"You go along," said Mike. "I'll drop Snake here off." He placed a hand on the frayed denim of her jeans, his callused fingers scraping the skin on her knee.

Leticia's eyes burned into Sandra's. *Snake?* she mouthed, eyebrow raised. The girls had been friends since they were toddlers, taking the bus to and from school together, playing for hours on the land behind their homes, riding bikes, and pushing dirty Barbies with matted hair through the dust. There had never been a secret between them.

"May as well just take the ride," Sandra said to her friend, hoping she'd understand. She let Mike's hand rest on her knee for one, two, three seconds.

"Fine," said Leticia. "But call me, okay?"

Sandra nodded.

"It turns out I have the day off too," said Mike. Leticia was out of earshot now, walking toward her front door. "What do you say we spend it together? We can do whatever you want."

He glanced at her, desperate for her approval. It was intoxicating to have this grown man at her disposal, to do her bidding. She thought of the one place there was no chance of her mother catching her.

"Can we go to the movies?" she asked.

Mike eyed at his watch. It was half past eleven.

"Matinee doesn't start till 1:00 PM," he said. "We'll have to drive to the theater in Santa Fe. Cigarette?"

She nodded.

And that was that. Mike would meet up with her after her shift at the filling station and they'd spend an hour or two in his truck, sometimes fooling around, sometimes talking, sometimes just driving all over. He'd always get her home just before Julio dropped her mother off after work. She tried to be discreet about it, but some of the girls at Mel's started asking who the white guy with the mustache and feathered hair was and if she was willing to share. She would laugh and tell them to get their minds out of the gutter, that he was just a friend.

And he was a friend to her in many ways. He'd listen to her go on and on about aliens' attempts at communication through their lights in the sky, their crop circles in soybean fields. Her theory about how the closing of Project Blue Book, the air force's program for investigating UFO encounters, was yet another example of the ways the government hid the truth from its citizens. He didn't always agree with her, but his questions were challenges, not the straight-up dismissals she heard from Leticia and her mother. With Mike, she wasn't afraid to talk about the articles in *UFO Country*.

Mike had the same opinion about the government that Sandra did: it was not to be trusted. He told her about the draft lottery, tense evenings in front of the television, wondering if he was going to be called to his death. He wasn't, but his best friend was. From then on, Mike decided, he wasn't going to live the life dictated to him by a society that was actively trying to exterminate him. He wanted to be in control of his own destiny. So he packed everything up in a knapsack, hopped in his truck, and, in his words, "dropped off the face of the earth" for two years that he claimed not to be able to remember. When he finally came to, he was here in Abiquiu, lying in the flatbed of his truck, staring at a sunset so fiery he thought he'd died and gone to hell.

Curled up under the horse blanket in that very same flatbed, smoking cigarettes and staring up at the sun filtering through the leaves of a cottonwood after fooling around, Sandra knew what it felt like to be a woman. Mike let her drink beers and smoke joints, though he never partook in either. When she asked him why, his face darkened and he just brushed her off, telling her she asked too many questions. Sandra had a feeling it had to do with those two years he didn't remember. He had a similar reaction when she asked about the painter, if the two of them were, *you know.* "Anyone ever told you how pretty you are when you're quiet?" he'd say, squeezing her knee and changing the subject.

Then he got clingy. He wouldn't leave her alone. He didn't seem to care if her mother found out, which was a problem. She'd ask to go home, and instead of taking her there he'd make up excuses for her—she was working a late shift, she had drama club at school—excuses she wouldn't even bother sharing with her mother because they sounded so fake. He told her she should stand up to her mom, live her life, come clean about the two of them. "You'll be eighteen next year," he'd say, in that soft, persuasive way of his. "Old enough for anything." But every time she worked up the nerve to say something, she wimped out at the last minute.

* * *

AT THE ROCKS, she finds what she is looking for quickly. Tonight, the orb is not hidden in the folds of cliffs but is out in the open, like it wants to be found. She gazes upward. The light pulses gently, a full moon that breathes. She hasn't told anyone about the orb. Not Leticia. Not Mike, though she's come close. It seems like it wants her to keep it a secret. And she's gotten pretty good at keeping secrets.

All she wants to do is touch it, get its attention. In the dim light it casts, she searches for a stick. She finds one and hoists it upward, swinging it at the sky. The orb remains out of reach. She throws a rock at it and misses. This whole mess she's gotten herself into would be resolved if she just disappeared, if she erased herself. Everything would be simpler: for her mother, for Leticia, for Mike. She tries telepathizing *Take me* again, but the orb remains, indifferent. Finally, she shouts, her voice echoing through the valley: "Take me!"

At first, nothing happens. The orb continues to hover. Frustrated, Sandra plops down on the cold, flat rock. She feels a prickle, then an unearthly warmth comes over her. The shadows of the rocks become deeper. Above her, the orb is growing bigger. She stands as it grows and grows, big enough to engulf her. She knows that all she has to do is take one step. *If you walk in,* it seems to be telling her, *things will change for you.* It's giving her a choice, an option, and there's nothing Sandra hates more than having a choice, but there's nothing Sandra wants more than to have a choice. A choice means potentially making a mistake. But at least it's her mistake to make.

The orb begins to shrink, then, and she realizes with a sinking feeling that she's missed her chance. It fades, fainter and fainter, until it's just Sandra and the rocks and the faraway stars.

* * *

"IT IS CERTAINLY A DEPARTURE," says Greta of the painter's newest painting. It's an image of the orb in Plaza Blanca: a riot of blues and blacks and grays surround the sphere, a shock of white, with the rippling cliffs in the background. "Reminds me of that desert spiritualist stuff from the forties." The painter can see the dollar signs accumulating in her dealer's head. Greta, always one to dress for the occasion, wears scarlet cowboy boots over jeans and a black, Western-style shirt with a rose embroidered on the breast. She's purchased the outfit in Santa Fe, that great purveyor of cowboy uniforms for tourists. With her bright blue eyeshadow and red lipstick, hair teased up like she's been electrocuted, she'd make a perfect rodeo clown. The dogs follow her as she moves through the studio, wanting to play. She swerves out of their way, not a dog person. The painter could send them outside, but she likes seeing Greta uncomfortable.

"And the sculptures?" says the painter. She is referring to Mike's ceramics—palm-sized forms, glazed in vibrant white and turquoise, splattered with black dots. He's worked hard on this series, the painter knows. The shapes are familiar but alien, like shadows of rocks in the desert landscape. He's got something, she's sure of it. It's only a matter of convincing Greta and Fiona, the New York gallerist.

"You really like this guy, don't you?"

The painter doesn't appreciate Greta's tone. "I thought you said Fiona was looking for fresh blood, for something different next spring," says the painter.

"Fresh blood, huh?" says Greta, raising her eyebrows and smiling lasciviously. "For you, darling, I'll take some pictures and show them to Fiona. But only for you."

"Thank you," says the painter. The snap of the shutter echoes through the studio as the dealer photographs the sculptures with her Polaroid camera. The dogs, bored, take their places at the painter's feet.

Later, at lunch, Greta slides a copy of *Art Eye* across the table. "Hot off the press."

On the cover is a picture of the painter in her signature black dress and turquoise and silver belt, staring out at the view from her studio. *Alone in the Desert with Only a Paintbrush*, reads the headline. *The Life of the Solitary Feminist Pioneer.*

"I wish they wouldn't use that word," says the painter.

Greta slurps her stew loudly. "Solitary?" she says, as Alice and one of the maids whisk through the dining room with a crate of clattering glass mason jars.

"Feminist," she says, inspecting a chunk of beef on her spoon before dropping it back into her stew. "They're always trying to fit me into a neat little box."

"It gives you an edge," says Greta. "Makes the collectors' wives feel like they're doing something for the movement. You're lucky, you know," she says through chews of meat. "Not everyone has a cook like Alice. This stew is divine."

The painter is too nervous to eat. She promised Mike that Greta would love his forms, that she'd have them shipped back to New York immediately. She knows that Mike will not be satisfied with the Polaroids.

"Are you sure we can't ship the sculptures back for Fiona to look at? Not even just one?"

"Darling," says Greta, finishing her second glass of wine, "you don't want to do that. Just think—sending such a fragile piece across the country without any sort of insurance. What if it were to break? It's not worth it. Plus it's a series. You want her to see them all together, don't you?"

"Well," says the painter, folding her napkin and pushing her bowl away. "If you can't find any place to show Mike's work, I'm afraid you won't be able to show the painting either."

Greta blanches. The painter knows the painting is the big draw of the group show the gallery is planning. She also knows that there are other painters, that New York City is lousy with them, so she's gambling a bit. But she stands her ground. There is tense silence for a moment.

"I'll talk to Fiona," says Greta.

* * *

LATER, SHE VISITS MIKE. His house is filthier than usual. It pains her, this clutter. She loves clean surfaces, open spaces, planes of light. He pushes a pile of clothes off an armchair in the living room and gestures for her to sit.

"What did Greta say?"

"She took some Polaroids of the work. She's showing them to Fiona."

"I thought you said that Greta made the final call. That Fiona did whatever Greta decided."

"Yes, but maybe something's changed. I don't know. I'm not in that world anymore. I don't know the shifts—"

"Because you don't have to be," he snaps. "You've made it. You're rich. The least you can do is help out someone younger, someone struggling." He finishes up his Tab and cracks open another one from the ice chest by his feet.

"You just have to be patient. I'm sure Fiona will love them." A cockroach scuttles around a Mars bar wrapper by her boot. She doesn't mention the agreement she made with Greta.

Mike sips his Tab sullenly. "Fine," he says. He's drinking faster, like he's anxious.

"Is something else bothering you?"

He puts his head in his hands. "Sandra's going to keep it."

At these words the painter straightens. "*Keep* it?" she says. There's a buzzing in her ears, and she only faintly hears Mike's response. Something about what the Lord wants. Something about settling down. Something about destiny. Something about always wanting a child, and now's his chance. Something about family being the foundation of all good things.

She thinks back to the first summer at her now-late husband's family's lakeside estate, his sisters' and mother's strained smiles when she joined them to help in the kitchen, their insistence that she really shouldn't bother, wouldn't she be happier playing with the other children? She was nineteen at the time, not much older than Sandra, her husband well over twice her age. The two of them together had been a scandal, and his first wife had nearly bankrupted him in the divorce. The painter cried once on that trip, and only the once, in front of her husband. "There, there," he said, and explained that his family had a special relationship with his first wife, that it would take time for them to get used to the painter.

After that she told her husband that if she was to accompany him on the lake house trips, she'd need a studio with sleeping quarters made available, and to her surprise he obliged, letting her spend the days painting while he and his mother and sisters and their children splashed in the lake and loafed around the shore. It was there that she made some of the work that he showed at his gallery, that got the attention of some very important people.

But Sandra isn't like her. Sandra is from simple people, with simple dreams. Sandra will, at most, grow up to be a cook like her mother, or perhaps a secretary if she's lucky. That is, if she doesn't burn out on drugs like most kids her age are doing these days.

Mike has finished his rant and retreated to his studio in a huff. Part of her wants to tell Sandra that she can have him, for all she cares. She's too old for melodrama. But she knows she can't let herself be bested by a child.

She'd planned on spending the night, but instead she stands and leaves, starts the car and drives to where she knows she needs to be. There's a half-moon out, but still the rocks glow, ethereally pale. It is stupid, what she's doing, she thinks, as she gets out of her car. She crunches through the sand. This landscape! After so many years, it still excites her—its cold, dangerous beauty. So different from the soft flat fields she came from, the opposite of the quaint East Coast prettiness of her boarding school, and worlds apart from New York, where anything you desired could be obtained by simply hailing a cab. The desert is timeless, indifferent.

She trips over a rock and falls, pain flooding her body, reminding her why doing what she's doing is an awful idea. She lies there for a moment, inhaling the dirt, before finally pressing herself back up and wiping the gravel from her hands. She's winded and shaky from the fall, and this is when she notices the orb. Her pain disappears in the orb's light, and she sees clearly again. She reaches out to touch it and it lets her and the ice melts from her bones, the tiredness dissipates. She feels decades younger.

I need to keep him, she thinks. *I need to get rid of her.* And that is when it comes to her. Boarding school.

* * *

IT'S CHILLY OUT, but that doesn't matter to Leticia and Sandra, who are sprawled over the rusty lawn furniture outside Leticia's house reading the worn magazines Leticia has rescued from the school library wastebasket. They are missing covers, but otherwise their contents are intact. Sandra is absorbed in a banal article about what it's like to be a tall girl dating a short boy and how they make it work. *Our love is unconventional. That's what makes it special*, says the pull quote. The boy is a few inches shorter than the girl, but otherwise the two look like any other all-American teen couple, with straight teeth and blond hair. Big whoop.

"How do you read this crap?" asks Sandra.

"Don't be so stuck up," Leticia says.

Sandra leans back and puts the magazine over her face, inhaling the musty ink. It's been three weeks since she had Francesca at the filling station return the envelope of cash to Mike when he came in to buy his soda and cigarettes. She'd intended to write him a letter to go with it, but every time she tried it sounded corny, or mean, or phony. Since then, there have been no visits from Mike. She hopes that means he gets the picture.

"If you don't like them, you can go back to reading your alien rags."

"Maybe I will," Sandra says into the spine. The magazine slides off her face and onto the ground.

"Be careful with that one. I haven't read it yet."

She hears footsteps and labored breathing. Her mother is running down the hill toward them, waving a piece of paper in her hand. Her brown hair is down and trails behind her and for a moment, Sandra thinks, she looks beautiful.

"You didn't tell me you even applied!" she cries out, and hands Sandra the paper. It's an admissions letter from a school called Miss Vesper's College Preparatory School for Girls, which apparently Sandra has been accepted to. The letterhead says it's in Connecticut.

"I didn't," says Sandra. "This must be a mistake."

"But that's your name, there's no question." Her mother is ebullient, panting, her face blushing pink.

"Maybe it's a scam," says Leticia. "Be careful if they ask you for money."

Sandra scans the letter and finds the paragraph about expenses. The painter's name is there. She's a proud alumna. She'll be covering all tuition plus room and board, but Sandra must let them know if she'll be joining them as soon as possible, so that they can hold a bed for her.

She looks at her mother's grinning mouth. "Such an incredible opportunity," Alice says.

"I'm not going," says Sandra.

"What do you mean?" Her mother's face falls.

"You need me here to help out."

"Sweetie. Don't worry about me."

Leticia has taken the letter from her. "I'll bet there are some cute boys in Connecticut. Bet you'll find a husband quick out there."

Sandra shoots her friend a look that she hopes communicates, *Stay out of it.*

* * *

LATER, IN HER ROOM, she spreads out the letter and accompanying brochure on her bed and tries to picture herself walking through snowy New England. She can have the baby out there, give it up to a sweet childless couple. Come back in June with her mother none the wiser. She is unsure why the painter is being so kind to her, but her mother says not to ask those kinds of questions, that she's been cooking for the woman for nearly a decade and it's really the least she can do.

Two taps on her window. She pulls the curtain aside. In the waning afternoon light is Mike, with that look on his face. She knows she shouldn't, but she climbs through the window anyway. Her mother is in the kitchen making dinner and the last thing she wants is for her to hear him.

She lets him embrace her and kiss her on top of her head. He's come from his studio, and his hands leave smudges of clay on her sweatshirt. A soft feeling comes over her.

"It's over," he mutters, and explains how he's ended it with the painter so that the two of them can be together and start a family.

"Are you joking?" she says. This is not what she was expecting.

"When you gave the cash back, I did some thinking." He pleads with his eyes, skin perfectly golden, face a mask of silver screen perfection.

But then she hears pots clanging in the kitchen, smells the roast. This is the first time her mother has cooked something for them in what seems like months. Usually it's canned soup or Hamburger Helper or leftovers from the painter's house.

"I'm leaving," she says. "I'm going east. To school."

"I'll come with you. A fresh start." His eyes are wild as he leans toward her. She feels small right then, with his mass towering above her.

"Please go," she says, her voice a whisper.

Finally, with a dejected sigh, he turns and walks toward his truck.

* * *

THE TOMATO SOUP has developed a skin. The painter's appetite has disappeared after Mike's last visit, when Fiona called and said that Mike's forms were unsophisticated, that he'd be better off in a local gallery. Mike happened to be listening on the kitchen phone, thinking it would be good news. Instead, after the painter hung up, he walked to her studio and began to methodically smash each one of his forms on her floor. She watched him with bated breath. Then he told her that it was over. That this was her fault, that he couldn't be with someone so unsupportive of his work. She knows deep down that he'll get over it, that he'll come back because he needs her.

There is a slow, pulsing ache in her knee from where she fell. Though it's been over a month, the pain hasn't subsided, but now seems to have a heartbeat, as if it's become a sentient being. Miss Vesper's has heard nothing from Sandra, according to their secretary on the phone this morning. They'll need to hear back soon if she'd like to enroll in spring semester. The painter has tried to bring it up with Alice, who's promised again and again that she'll talk to her, she'll talk to her. She wonders if it's time to find a new cook, if her charity toward the woman and her daughter has run its course. Something crashes in the kitchen and the painter flinches. Alice curses. *What has happened in this house?* thinks the painter.

She finishes her tea, clears her throat, unfolds the day's paper and snaps it to get the attention of someone in the kitchen. Sandra comes in scowling, eyes cast downward, cheeks flushed.

"Can you get my pain pills?" the painter says, smiling sweetly.

"Yes ma'am," Sandra mutters, her mind clearly elsewhere.

* * *

HER MOTHER HAS PUT two and two together about Mike. Sandra is surprised it's taken her this long. At this point, she's sure everyone knows, including the painter. He's been staked outside her house in his truck every night for the past week. He's left Sandra three different notes, each detailing his love for her and his plans to follow her to boarding school, each more frenzied than the last. He doesn't know that Sandra hasn't replied to the admissions letter yet. Finally, her mother spotted him hanging around the house this morning in his truck while the two of them were waiting for Julio to give them a ride up to the painter's house.

"Why is that man here?" she asked Sandra. Sandra shrugged. She was exhausted, had been unable to sleep for fear that Mike would burst in and trash the place. She'd insisted on coming to work with her mother today instead of going to school, and her mother, in rare form, had complied. Sandra knew that the painter's house, with so many eyes on her, was the safest place to be.

The shrug was all her mother needed. As soon as she witnessed it, Alice understood what was happening and marched over to Mike, who started up the truck and drove away before she could get to his window. Then she returned to Sandra, her face reddening. She was silent during the ride up with Julio and while they prepared lunch. While Sandra was drying the dishes, a plate slid from her hand and shattered on the floor. A storm of curses burst from her mother's mouth. She wasn't to see Mike anymore, that man was no good, she was too young, didn't she know that she was endangering her mother's job, and on and on and on until she stopped just as suddenly as she'd started. Sandra heard the painter clear her throat like she did when she wanted something from the help and rushed out of the kitchen.

The painter is sweet to her, asking for her pain pills. As Sandra walks toward the bedroom, her eyes land on the easel. She recognizes Plaza Blanca, its cliffs and spires in shadow, the orb in the foreground. She forgets what she's doing and steps up to the canvas, though she knows that staff are strictly forbidden to look at work in the painter's studio.

She hears her name.

The painter stands in the doorway, a grave expression on her narrow face. She's grown thinner these past few months, gaunt and severe.

"What do you think?" she says.

Sandra realizes that though she's spent a good part of her life around the work of the painter, she's never thought about it, not really. The images have just existed, like the rocks and the bones the painter uses for her subject matter. But this, this one gives her the same jolt she gets those nights she goes out to Plaza Blanca.

"It's neat," she says.

The painter smirks. "I've been meaning to ask you about something. Please sit down." She gestures to a stool near the fireplace. Sandra obeys. The painter settles into the armchair, regal.

"I know Mike offered you cash to take care of your problem and you turned him down. Why?"

Sandra stares at her sneakers. "I'm afraid." She's alarmed at the ease with which the truth slips out of her.

"Honey, there's nothing to be afraid of."

There is silence. All Sandra can think of is blood.

The painter tries another approach. "Your mother tells me you don't want to go to that school, even after the strings I pulled to get you in. That's fine—I understand. Personally, I hated Miss Vesper's. So I'm giving you a way out. An option. End the pregnancy, while you still can. End the pregnancy and you can have whatever you want. This happens to girls like you all the time. But with money, the whole process is quite easy. I'll make up some excuse about the school that your mother will believe."

Sandra senses something in the painter's voice she's never sensed before, with all her grandeur and poise. She senses desperation, and realizes that she can ask for anything she wants. She wants to leave, doesn't she? To be rid of Mike, her mother, the whole thing? To start over? She can ask for money. She can ask for the Alfa. She stares at the orb painting and thinks of how it beckoned to her with a hundred different futures, how she just stood there. And now the painter is presenting her with a choice. But is it really a choice? Or is it just a disposal, the painter washing dirt off her soft, wrinkled hands?

"I'll go to the school," Sandra says. "I'll leave."

The painter smiles. "Good girl," she says. "Now fetch me my pills. You've made me and your mother very happy."

Numb, Sandra enters the painter's bedroom and takes the pills from the nightstand. She imagines swallowing them all, perishing with drama in front of the painter. But instead she walks out, hands her the bottle, and returns to the kitchen, where she spends the rest of her mother's shift in silent obedience.

Later that night, as she's about to fall asleep, Sandra hears the telltale crunch of wheels and knows that Mike is back. This time, her mind is made up. She won't cower. She stands, pulls on a pair of jeans, and slides into her sneakers. Again, she grabs her father's sheepskin-lined jacket from the peg. She slips out the back door, careful not to let her mother hear.

The cold outside is a shock. Sandra sprints across the valley by memory, her breath coming out in puffs of steam. Her feet barely touch the ground. The white rocks, spires majestic in the starlight, loom in front of her.

The orb glows above a pinyon pine. It pulses faster as she steps nearer, excited. Then it sinks until it is level with her face and expands, growing bigger and bigger until she is sure someone can see it from the road, but she doesn't care. She takes off the jacket, because the glow from the orb is warm and inviting. She steps into the light, granting her own wish.

BRIGHT LIGHTS, BIG DEAL

Rose helps you move into your first apartment on a sultry June afternoon. It's the day after Michael Jackson's death, and Brooklyn is in mourning for the King of Pop. "Thriller" and "Billie Jean" stream from the sound systems of passing cars. You and Rose moonwalk down the sidewalk in between sweaty slogs from the rented van up the stairs to your new room. Though you trip and skin your knee, she is scarily good at it, her dancer's legs gliding across the sidewalk in cutoff shorts and Converse. Hoots of approval at you both, the stupid dancing white girls, are shouted from car windows until you remind Rose that you've got to get the van back if you don't want to be charged extra.

The apartment is above a Mexican bakery in South Williamsburg. You settle in, get to know your roommates—a DJ and an actress—as much as they'll let you. They are both older than you by at least five years, hardened, used to the hustle. You are in awe of their bohemian lives. The actress works at

Beacon's Closet and is always bringing home bags of fabulous vintage clothes that she never invites you to try on. The DJ—you aren't sure what he does for his day job, though you're sure he has one. Most mornings, he's left the apartment by the time you wake and, if he doesn't have a gig, returned in the early evening wearing a dress shirt and ill-fitting slacks. Sometimes you go days without encountering each other.

Most of the apartment is carpeted with a grimy beige pile that never seems to get clean, no matter how much the actress vacuums. A faded print of Georgia O'Keeffe's *Brooklyn Bridge* hangs over the sagging vinyl sofa in the windowless living room. (You will forever associate that work with being young and stupid and dirty.) Your room off the kitchen is tiny, but at least it has a window, even if the window looks out over the auto body repair shop next door. On your short-but-long unemployed midmornings, the clanging racket of their tools reminds you that you are indeed in the big city, living the urban promise. You furnish the room with cheap Craigslist finds, trying to stretch out the cash allowance from your parents for as long as possible. A loft bed, a particleboard desk, the ubiquitous Billy bookcase. The floor in the room is uneven: someone has stapled linoleum over the carpet, and there's a slight squish when you walk on it. This doesn't matter though, since there's a layer of clothing, shoes, and objects on the floor at all times. You consider cleaning it up often but can't bring yourself to do it, and what's the point anyway? You're never there, or at least you try not to be. It's just a place to sleep.

At night, the refrigerator makes noise: a series of low rumbles followed by a keening whistle. Rumble, rumble, rumble, moan. Your landlord has told you to expect these sounds, that the refrigerator is old but still works fine. Sometimes, lying awake, you swear it's trying to tell you something.

Finding a job is harder than you expected. Your college friends seem to slide into them. Oscar works at a Chelsea gallery. Brendan is a junior banker at his father's firm. Kyle runs the ticket booth at a small off-Broadway theater. Jenna waitresses but is headed to school for her degree in library science this fall. And then there's Rose, your best friend: she's just been hired as an assistant at the literary agency Crawford & Shaw. You go shopping with her for business-casual clothes from Forever 21. Together you pick out a button-down oxford, a pencil skirt, a plaid blazer. She comes out of the dressing room and asks you what you think. You think she looks like someone who knows what she's doing with her life. "The blouse is gapping," you say. "I'll get you a size up."

"What do *you* want to do, Julia?" your parents ask you when you call and tell them about Rose's job. Rose was like a second daughter to them: she came home with you from school most holidays. She and her mother don't get along. From what you've gathered it has something to do with her mother's back pain, with the pills she takes for it, with the boyfriends she keeps around. You think her troubled homelife makes her irresistibly interesting, but Rose doesn't like to talk about it, changes the subject whenever you try.

But you: you need to know what you want! You don't tell your parents this, but you want to write for a media gossip blog. You want to be known in literati circles for your biting wit and your effortless fashion. You want to be featured in *New York* magazine's Look Book. You want to be part of the next Algonquin Round Table, the next February House, the next Brat Pack. You tell your parents there's nothing out there, you don't want to get sucked into working retail or waitressing, how will that look on your résumé? They tell you to keep trying, that something is sure to come up, and that you should feel free to use your emergency credit card in the meantime, that you can always, whenever you want, come home. You want to tell them that you are home, but right now that feels like a lie.

You spend your days riding the subway, headphones on, listening to mixes made for you by your high school boyfriend, basting yourself in nostalgia. You read the *New Yorker* cover to cover. You make yourself as compact as possible: those are the rules in a city with this many people. So you put your tote bag on your lap, clamp your knees together. Never make eye contact. Hours pass this way in your cocoon, the rumble of the train taking the edge off everything, interrupted only by the bass-heavy acrobatics of showtime performers and pleas from the homeless people stumbling through the cars.

At night the playing field is leveled between you and your employed friends. You are all back to your college selves, except amplified, because now you are adults in the city. You happen to live in an ideal location: a street lined with bars of all kinds. Overpriced speakeasies, swanky cocktail lounges, unironic dives where the regulars give you and your friends dirty looks. The names of the bars become shorthand for the pattern of the night: pregame at Fastball, then the Pines for boozy slushies, Roxanne's for dancing, O'Malley's for a night-cap. You and your friends take to the streets like you are the first twentysomethings to ever go out in Brooklyn.

Nights like these, the city opens up for you. Photo booths, beer-and-shot deals, late-night chicken cemitas from the Mexican bakery with chipotle peppers that burn the roof of your mouth. And there are men, too. You've never thought of yourself as remotely attractive but apparently that assessment is false. The moment you enter the heady fog of a bar packed with the weekend crowd, something shifts in you and your night becomes about two things: getting as drunk as possible, and getting fucked. You skip dinner so that you can get your buzz on quicker, and soon you disappear into the evening's sweaty gauze. You make out with basically anyone, go home with many. You seek the thrill of a new tongue in your mouth, bitter with beer and cigarettes.

One night Oscar invites the gang out for celebratory karaoke: he's just had one of his photographs selected for a juried gallery exhibition. Three whiskey sours later you're up on stage doing your rendition of "Rehab" and you have the whole bar singing along and Oscar snapping pictures and this, *this* is why you're here, for nights like these with friends who know you, really know you, who've held your hair back as you drunkenly vomited out a dorm window, who've stayed up all night with you on Adderall-fueled binge-study sessions, who've put up with your bullshit and know all your secrets. The crowd cheers as you walk off stage, and you're so happy you want to float away. It's a feeling you wish you could hold on to, bottle and keep, because you know it won't last. And you're right, in a way. Six months from now you won't be speaking to these people.

When you get home one morning after (Union Pool, a finance bro with blow) and check your email, there's a message from your mother's friend from college, who lives in the city and knows you are looking for work. She's passed your name along to a friend of a friend who manages executive assistants at a credit rating agency in the Financial District and is hiring. You reply quickly, possibly too quickly. A job interview is scheduled for the following week. You have no idea what a credit rating agency is, but you fantasize about a desk overlooking the skyline, the click-click-click-click of high heels on marble. Maybe this is your path.

Rose invites you to a private book launch party for the novelist Phoebe Forsyth at a Dumbo loft. While you're getting ready together at Rose's Greenpoint railroad apartment, you confess that you've never read anything by Phoebe Forsyth. Rose, running a straightening iron through her strawberry-blond hair, tells you it doesn't matter, most people are just there for the scene. She looks like a different person in her black miniskirt and the Louboutins she got, she says vaguely, as a gift from work. Next to her in your floral polyester shift from H&M and ballet flats, you feel like a child. Rose assures you that you look amazing, incredible, so hot.

In Dumbo, she steadies herself on your arm as she toddles over the cobblestones in her heels. As you laugh together, you see yourselves as an outsider might see you: two girls in the big city, having a blast. In the elevator, Rose swats your hand. You've been absentmindedly scratching the bug bites on your arm. "That only makes it worse," she hisses. Once inside the loft, she sees someone she knows and you are left standing in a throng of well-dressed strangers, Manhattan glittering at you from across the river. You weave through the crowd, toward the bar, and order a beer. You watch Rose laughing with a pert young clump of who you can only assume are assistants, from their ages and how they carry themselves, like they're in on some secret. You catch her eye, but she turns back to the group and continues laughing until a serious-looking man in a suit puts a hand on her. He's older and has a slight paunch but is handsome in a DILF-y George Clooney kind of way, and when Rose smiles at him he breaks into a grin, crow's-feet crinkling.

Your phone buzzes. It's your roommates. Earlier, you poured yourself a bowl of Lucky Charms and noticed the cereal was squirming. For a moment you blamed your hangover, so bad you were hallucinating. But no—these were wriggling grains of rice, tiny white maggots drowning in the milk. Pantry moth larvae, you discovered after a rudimentary Google search. They'd gotten in everything: the rice, the crackers, the pasta. You were midway through cleaning out the cabinets when you realized it was time to go, and now your roommates are texting you, asking where all their food went. You try to explain about the moths, but it doesn't quell the barrage of messages. You turn off your phone and slide it into your purse.

You get closer to the window to take in the view but keep catching glimpses of your own reflection: a silhouette with the downtown skyline inside it. You hear "Julia" and turn around. It's Freddie, who graduated two years ahead of you. He looks exactly the same: stocky build, black leather jacket, black jeans, black Chuck Taylors, the muted post horn tattoo, impeccably coiffed black hair. At school he was a bit of a joke, the weird dude who was into B movies and krautrock, but here, in Brooklyn, his look feels unforced and natural, as if he has always existed this way, birthed from the pavement, slick with cool. He hugs you and you inhale leather and cigarettes.

He invites you downstairs for a smoke, and the two of you catch up outside, your banter interrupted every four minutes by the rumble of trains over the Manhattan Bridge. You wonder if this counts as networking, which is something you've promised Rose you'll do. He's a freelance writer, he's covering this event for the *Literalist*, a book industry gossip blog that you've heard Rose mention often since she started her new job. You ask him how to break into the industry, and he tells you to start your own blog if you want to get noticed. "You need to have a voice, or a story, but preferably both," he says matter-of-factly. "Remember Jon Slauson, the conservative news anchor?" You have no idea what he's talking about, but you nod. "The intern he was sexting with? That was my friend Grant. He let me publish the messages on my blog after they broke up. It opened a lot of doors for me, that post." You mull his words over as he asks you what you're doing here and you tell him you came with Rose. "I thought that was her up there with Crawford," he says. "She looks different. You kids grow up so fast."

Back inside, the party has grown louder. Freddie says he's grabbing a drink and then evaporates into thin air. Though you have nowhere to go, you circumambulate through the publishing professionals like you have somewhere important to get to, smiling and apologizing as you brush against bodies. You make these rounds several times—the window, the bar, the exit, the signing table. The only person who seems to notice your rotations is the pouting Phoebe Forsyth, leaning against the signing table, very clearly not listening to whatever yarn a graying lug of a man is loudly spinning in her face. She narrows her eyes at you and cocks her head. You flash a weak smile and continue on your mission to nowhere. What are you hoping for? To stumble into a meet cute by accidentally spilling your drink on someone? To be offered a job? Rose has abandoned you; she's nowhere in the crowd. You finish your fourth and final beer and float out into the evening.

* * *

THE JOB INTERVIEW: you have dressed carefully. Your black tights. The maroon A-line dress you found on sale at Macy's, not too tight but not too loose. On your way there, it starts to rain. You buy an umbrella from a subway vendor that snaps the second you open it upon emerging from the stop and you get drenched. You spend a frantic eight minutes in a Starbucks bathroom fixing your makeup and attempting to dry yourself as best you can by contorting around a weak stream of hot air emitted by the hand dryer. Infuriated patrons slap the door and curse you. You emerge damp but presentable and dash across the street to the credit agency's building with a minute to spare before your appointment.

The lobby of the building is puke-pink marble, but your heels do make that click-click-click-click when you walk on it. Connor, an anemic-looking HR associate in loose-fitting khakis, not much older than you, conducts the interview in his cubicle. He runs you through the basics. Duties, hours, perks, casual Fridays. Then a bald man with bushy eyebrows wearing an expensive-looking suit appears and introduces himself as the managing director of business development: your potential boss. "So nice to meet you," he says. His teeth are bleached a blinding white. You follow him to his office. *You've got this*, you think. Out the window is a rainy downtown. He gestures to a modernist leather sofa and tells you to sit down and relax, and that this is a chance for the two of you to get to know each other. You plant your gaze on the bowl of fruit on the coffee table as he sits down next to you, close enough so that you can feel his warmth, smell the sharpness of his cologne.

Soon he's looking over your résumé and nodding. "You worked for your father in high school?" he asks, and you mutter in assent, because you did work in your father's real estate firm briefly in high school, filing paperwork, your only office experience. He tells you about his kids, how they would never work with him, they think he's the devil because he makes money at his job. He sets your résumé down on the table and looks at you. "My daughter's about your age. Hardly talks to me, but certainly doesn't mind spending my money." He lets out a guffaw at his comment, and you make yourself laugh with him. Why is he telling you this? Why isn't he asking you what skills you can bring to the position? What your five-year plan is? You start to say something, an apology of sorts, but before you can get the words out he leans back on the sofa and delivers a monologue about the importance of executive assistants, how the agency couldn't run the way it does without them. He takes a banana from the bowl on the table and peels it. "You want some of this, dear?" He brings it to your face so that its damp sweetness grazes your lips. You aren't sure what to say, but he's staring at you, breathing his old man breath in your face: cigar and mouthwash. You quickly weigh the pros and cons and say no thank you. He shrugs, takes a bite, and continues to talk, eyebrows wriggling, mouth full of mush, about how they aren't training college kids for real jobs, just the glorified frat houses of Silicon Valley. No one has any ambition anymore. You smile politely.

"Not you though, Julia," he says. You startle at the sound of your name. "You're a very put-together young lady." He winks at you and grins with those white teeth of his, a look that makes your skin crawl.

The office grows stuffy. You can hear him breathing as he waits for a response, but you're mute. Everything slows. Your bites itch. You resist the urge to scratch in front of this man. "You okay, kiddo?" he says softly. A tiny voice in your head screams at you to stand up and you heed it and stand. "Sorry," you croak. The boss glares, vexed. He starts to say something, but you book it out of there, sobbing through the columns of cubicles, getting lost once or twice until finally you find the elevator bank. You imagine heads turning to stare at the spectacle of the blubbering girl, but when you sneak a glance, no one is paying any attention.

Your parents are furious that you bombed the interview. You've made up some weak lie about what happened, that you had a panic attack and left. You couldn't bring yourself to tell them the truth because you knew they would immediately ask you if you were sure, was he really coming on to you, or was he just being friendly, and was it a generational thing, perhaps? You'd rather be scolded, honestly, which you are: "We can't support you forever," your father says. "You're too old to let your emotions rule your decisions," says your mother. Then she tells you, in that syrupy, apologetic way of hers, that you have until Christmas before they cut you off. You tell them it's October, that you just need more time, that it's their duty as parents to support you. "Try again," says your father. "Maybe they'll give you a second chance."

You manage to hang up without screaming at them. From your loft bed, you stare at the floor below. The clothing is a writhing sea, the loft bed your boat, your safe space. Then a pair of jeans starts to move. There's more rustling. You gingerly climb down the ladder to investigate and see a gray blur dart over a blouse. You pick up the blouse, shake it off. Small black pellets fall to the floor.

A bath will solve your problems. A bath will soothe. A bath will clarify. The Plath quote echoes in your head: *There must be quite a few things a hot bath won't cure, but I don't know many of them.* Maybe the protagonist of *The Bell Jar* isn't someone you want to be identifying with. Nevertheless, you turn on the tap. The water comes out slightly orange, but you let it run anyway. It will be like a mineral soak, you tell yourself, people pay top dollar for those. You squirt some of the DJ's Dr. Bronner's in the water and the room fills with the scent of eucalyptus. You undress and sink into the tub, steam curling around you. Your bites sting, but the memory of the managing director and his teeth fades away. Your mother is right. You are too emotional. A cockroach waddles across the ceiling, and though your instinct is to leap onto the ledge of the bathtub and smash it with a shampoo bottle, you stay put and watch it go on its way, marveling at the grace and coordination of its tiny legs. There are worse things than moths and cockroaches. You emerge from the tub a new woman.

It is decided: you will take the day off life. This is something you and Rose used to do in college when things got rough. It involved a bottle of wine, a joint, junk food, and Rose's complete *Sex and the City* DVD collection. There is nothing in your pantry, thanks to the moths, so you leave your apartment and go to the Mexican bakery and purchase a cemita, Flamin' Hot Cheetos, Bugles, peanut M&M's, and a six-pack of Miller High Life. You climb up the stairs to the apartment, up the ladder to your loft bed. Safe in your tower, you pack a bowl and gorge yourself, a millennial Homer Simpson, slurping and burping until the food is mostly gone and two beers have been consumed. It's in this state of drunken, gassy euphoria that you conceive of a name for your blog: *Bright Lights, Big Deal.*

* * *

ROSE TEXTS YOU WANTING to grab a drink at Relish, a trendy speakeasy on the Lower East Side. You think this will mean waiting in line to get a table, but when you get there, you see that she has somehow enchanted her way into a seat by the window. She's birdlike, frail almost, in her crimson silk blouse with poet sleeves. You hug.

"You've lost weight," you say.

She grins. "I feel like it's been forever," she replies.

It has been a month since the party where she abandoned you, the last time you saw her. She texted you a few days later, apologizing, saying she'd needed to do something for her boss. Since then, she's been busy with work, so you've been hanging out with Oscar and Kyle, with an occasional Jenna cameo when she's not working. Brendan has abandoned the group entirely by doing the unthinkable: quitting drinking. Outwardly you've been supportive, but with your friends, you question how long it will stick. Oscar says he's doing it for attention. Kyle agrees, saying that Brendan never had much of a personality anyway, and maybe now his sobriety will give him one. You all clinked glasses to that proclamation.

But you can't deny that all the shit-talking and rehashing of college lore feels empty. Out with them, you find yourself missing Rose, wondering what she's up to. You don't tell her any of this as she orders a glass of grüner veltliner and you order a seventeen-dollar whiskey cocktail inexplicably called the Bret Easton Ellis.

Conversation is stiff at first. She asks about your job search and you tell her the truth, or part of it: that you've been devoting time to your blog. The part you don't tell her is that you've written only three posts in the past three weeks, rambling narratives about the minutiae of daily life in Williamsburg. Since then, seven people—if the analytics are correct—have visited the site. Then, and this is probably the Bret Easton Ellis loosening your tongue, you tell her about your job interview. Her face falls.

"Men are such fucking pigs," she says, and stares out the window. She sniffs a little and in the dim light you make out tears fuzzing her mascara. And then she tells you about Dale Crawford, her boss. It was kind of hot at first, she confesses, the attention, the dalliances in his office when she worked late nights. It was intellectually stimulating too: the man was the genius behind so many of the great authors of the past two decades. According to him, she was his protégé, she had a golden future in this industry. He would introduce her to the right people, show her the path. She was on track to becoming an associate agent. And then there was the hotel room where things got a little rougher than she wanted. ("Did he—" Your throat catches and you can't bring yourself to say it. "Was it—" "No," she says, definitively, "but it wasn't fun.") Something shifted after that. Either he lost interest or his wife found out, Rose wasn't sure. But Kim, the other assistant, who'd always been jealous of Rose and Crawford, ended up getting the promotion, and is now being a total bitch to her and giving her the most mundane busywork. Rose isn't sure how much longer she can take it. She gulps her wine, hands trembling. "I'm sorry," she says, but for what, you don't know.

From there, the night devolves into its usual debauchery. Rose flirts with the bartender and your drinks are on the house. The bartender finishes his shift and the two of you follow him to another louder, sweatier bar where you meet his friends. Normally you'd home in on one of the friends, always slightly less hot than the bartender, but tonight you're unmoored, off your game. You feel horrible for Rose, but even in this instance she seems to have bested you: not only does she get the salaried literary agency assistant job while you get your unemployed subway rides, but she gets a steamy affair with her boss while you get the creepy managing director.

Then it's last call and Rose is leaning against the bartender and whispers that she's fine and you should go, so you wait for the J train with several other facsimiles of you: smudged makeup, swaying slightly, trying to act sober though you've been filling yourselves with poison for hours.

That night, you dream there is a tall, thin figure standing in your room, staring up at you. The floor is clean. The figure is made of the clothes that were on the ground. Its head is your purse, its torso made of balled-up underwear and bras, its legs crumpled blue jeans. When it sees you looking down at it, it opens its mouth and lets out a rumble, rumble, moan like the fridge. You wake up in the morning and look down, expecting, momentarily, to see a clean floor, but the clothes are scattered where you left them.

You spend the week scouring job boards, avoiding your roommates, riding the trains. You read a post online about Jon Slauson, the ousted news anchor, how his wife and kids have left him and he was spotted at Duane Reade in sweatpants, buying out their HARIBO selection. Rose's story nags at you. Crawford touching her shoulder at the launch, the way he smiled at her. Freddie said you need a voice or a story, but preferably both. Here's your story. Well, not your story exactly, but it's not like Rose ever told you *not* to share it. You deserve a break—you've been diligently plugging away at this blog for weeks. She'll be proud of you, grateful, even. Crawford's a predator, and predators deserve to be punished. You open the *New Post* tab and start typing. As you type, you can see her perched atop the rumpled sheets of the hotel bed, shivering a little in the AC. She's alone—Crawford's gone home. Maybe she's pulling on that Forever 21 blouse you two bought together, wondering if she'll have bruises on her arms from where he held her down. The way the story tumbles out of you, it's like you're possessed; the feeling is electric. When you finish, you read it aloud to yourself and get a little chill. You can't post this. But then you think of Rose and the bartender the other night, the way doors seem to spring open for her. The way doors opened for Freddie when he published those sexts. This is your door. You haven't even named Rose, just referred to her as *the assistant*. You hit *Post*. You even email Freddie a link to the published piece, hoping maybe he'll pitch the story to his editor at the *Literalist* and link to your blog. He writes you back almost immediately.

No offense, but this kind of shit happens everywhere all the time. Everyone knows Crawford is a creep. I'll try, but I doubt my editor will care about this.

Fine, you think, *fuck you*. You keep refreshing the analytics page, hoping for the views to tick up. You need some air. You ride the trains.

You emerge on the Brighton Beach boardwalk. It's cold but sunny, and there are shirtless Russian men out on the benches, their bellies glowing white in the late fall sunlight. You lean against the railing and watch the surf. Some preteen boys are playing tag in the sand, coats flapping. It's getting rough—they are not just tapping one another but shoving and collapsing into the sand, laughing maniacally. When you were that age, you and your friends played a game you called gladiator—a variation of king of the hill—on a steep hillside by the baseball diamond. The rules of gladiator were, simply, to get to the top of the hill by any means necessary, which usually meant hurling your opponent down the slope. There were torn tights, bloody knees, ruined uniforms. You loved that game, even though the other girls were bigger than you and often you ended up at the bottom, giggling on your back with grass-stained khakis. Maybe your problem is that you *like* being a loser.

You get a cryptic text from Freddie. *Thanks for the tip.* You text back a series of question marks and he tells you that his editor green-lighted the Crawford story and to check the *Literalist*. Your cell phone is a useless magenta Motorola Razr so checking the internet means you need to go home. You bolt back to the train, which has never been so slow, and the term "crusader for justice" begins to flit around your brain, along with all the valiant anger that comes with it. You're basically a hero, a savior. Inside your apartment you rush to your laptop and open the *Literalist*. There it is, at the top of the page, with that trademark *Literalist* snark:

Shocker: Top Literary Agent Has Affair with, Is Creep to, Female Underling. Freddie has even included an excerpt from your blog post in a block quote. You click *Read More* and scroll down to the comments. You skim them, frantically, and take a moment to process what it is you're seeing.

I call bullshit.

A petty takedown by a disgruntled millennial.

Since when can't consenting adults have sex?? This is relevant . . . why?

They are all defending Dale Crawford. You close your laptop, stomach rioting with nerves. The fridge is getting louder and louder, rumble, rumble, moan, until it's pitched to a roar. You know what you need to do: you call Rose. To your surprise, she answers.

"I just wanted to check in," you tell her, voice shaking.

"Well, I got fired." She emits a croaking laugh.

"That's so fucked up," you say. "You could probably sue them, you know."

"I don't need legal advice from *you*," she says.

"I wasn't—"

But Rose isn't done. "This is what you wanted, isn't it? You had to fuck it up for me. You're jealous."

"No," you say. She needs to understand that you were only trying to help.

"I don't have a cushion," Rose goes on. "I don't have an *emergency credit card*. If I don't find a way to make money, I have to go home to live with my insane mother."

The way she lobs that information at you, you just know she was saving up that little fact and brooding over it, letting it ferment until it flowered with blue-green mold like the leftovers in the takeout containers the DJ is always leaving on display in the fridge. Rose knows you better than anyone, knows where to push when she wants it to hurt. Well, good for her, she's succeeded. And even in your frazzled state on the edge of tears, you hear that quiet voice that you so often ignore, telling you that this knowledge she has, the fact that she knows you better than anyone, this is a *liability.* The way you trusted her and let her into your life, the way you trust everyone as if you were a child, this is what gets you into trouble. It's the reason you're in this situation now, the reason you got into that situation with the managing director. You want to crawl into your clothes pile and disappear forever. You take a breath, about to unleash this storm onto Rose, but realize you don't have the words for it. And Rose cuts you off before you can begin, anyway: "That wasn't your story to tell. Don't speak to me again."

You drop the phone and the fridge noise returns, deafening. You cover your ears but can still hear it. On the floor, your clothes roil and squeak; you see a flash of pink tail. The clothes are rising now, taking shape, looming above you. Tiny pink rat noses peek out of the eyeholes, rats fall from the mouth as the garment creature lets out a scream and opens its arms. You fall into its soft, cool embrace, smell soiled laundry and the rancid-sweet odor of rotting animal. When you come to, you are on the cold linoleum, covered in your dirty clothes. Someone is knocking on your door, calling your name. It's the DJ.

"Come in," you muster.

He jolts almost imperceptibly at the sight of you, then resumes his deadpan expression. This is New York, after all, you will be just another anecdote on his list of Crazy New York Stories. "We have bedbugs," he says.

The exterminator leaves you with a checklist of what needs to be done before he comes in to treat the apartment. You gather the clothes from your floor, from your closet, and bring them to the laundromat. It takes three trips back and forth and countless loads, but eventually you clean every single piece of clothing you own. Your coats you bring to the dry cleaner. Everything else goes in bins in the middle of the living room, where it will stay for weeks until the exterminator completes his various treatment cycles. As you deal with it all, the folding and the washing and the dragging of the bins from the 99 Cents store back to your apartment and the packing and the stacking, hot rage bubbles inside of you. After all you've done for Rose. The audacity, to treat you like this.

You say as much to Oscar and Kyle one Fastball happy hour in the booth beneath the inflatable stag's head, the same one Rose knocked off the wall while dancing on the tabletop so many months ago. Jenna isn't returning your calls for some reason. She's probably studying, but a paranoid part of you wonders if it might be because of Rose. Kyle makes his little nervous laugh, and Oscar just gives a noncommittal "Yeah" while staring at something in the distance. He's preoccupied with his upcoming show and the fact that a gallery has reached out, wanting to represent him.

"I mean, you did get her fired," says Kyle.

"Just give her some time," says Oscar. But something has shifted.

* * *

IT'S A LOT, Rose and the bedbugs and what's going on in your inbox: reporters wanting to speak with you; horrific, typo-riddled threats from trolls; and a cease-and-desist letter from lawyers representing the Crawford & Shaw Literary Agency, demanding that you take down the post. They rankle you in a different way than the bedbugs do, they itch and nag at your soul. Despite their letter, you do nothing.

Rose leaves a message, wanting to talk, offering a weak apology, she overreacted, blah, blah, blah, more twig than olive branch. You ignore it. A day later she texts, and you ignore that, too. You don't have time in your life for people like her, ungrateful people. How many Thanksgivings did your family feed her? How many Christmases did she crash?

With the floor devoid of clothing, your room feels different—bigger, though it's still very small. You are brooding in your nest of a loft bed when Freddie texts, inviting you to the *De Trop Magazine* launch party, which happens to be at the exact same time as Oscar's opening. Freddie says it will be a great chance to network, that practically all of NYC media will be there. The choice is simple. You tell him yes, please add your name to the list.

The *De Trop Magazine* launch party, sponsored by Bangable Vodka, is at a warehouse in Bushwick. There's a line to get in, and you diligently stand in it, hugging your pleather silver jacket tight around you to stave off the frigid autumn wind. At the door, a heavyset man with scraggly red facial hair and a sickly-looking woman in racoon eye makeup are writing the numbers 1 to 10 on name tag stickers and handing them out to the party guests. The bearded man looks you over and Sharpies a 6 on a sticker. You ask him what it means. He tells you with a straight face it's how bangable you are on a scale of 1 to 10. He draws a little line under the 6, lest you be tempted to flip it over. You notice he wears a 2. His colleague, a 9. "Lighten up," he says, clocking your fallen expression. "It's a party."

You get a free Bangable Vodka tonic from the gamine in white lipstick at the bar and scan the crowd for Freddie. Everyone there is cool, so much cooler than you. A nightlife photographer in a leather fedora roams through the crowd, snapping pictures of the scene. A DJ spins a clubby Katy Perry remix. There's gritty powdered soap in the grimy bathroom soap dispensers and graffiti everywhere and you can't tell what's affectation and what's authentic.

A craggy-faced man in horn-rimmed glasses (7) is talking to a group of 10s in gold lamé leggings about the good old days in the city in the eighties, pre-Giuliani, when you could smoke anything anywhere in the East Village and blood ran through the cobblestones of the Meatpacking District when the clubs let out at dawn. What must it be like to live in a place for that long, to watch it change?

"That one loves to hear himself talk, doesn't he?"

You register the icy blond bob, the pink lipstick, the air of elegance. It's Phoebe Forsyth. There's no number on her black turtleneck.

"Where's your Bangable ranking?" you say, trying to be funny, but it comes out in earnest.

Phoebe smirks and smooths her sweater. "This is cashmere." She takes a delicate sip from her plastic cup. "What do you do?" she asks, not bothering to introduce herself.

"I'm a blogger," you say, and it just rolls out of you like it's the truth.

"Ah," says Phoebe. "Tell me, how does one make it as a blogger?"

Is she making fun of you? Is she asking for advice? You hear a shrill laugh and see that the crag-faced man and the lamé leggings 10s are doing bumps of cocaine together.

You feed her Freddie's line: "You need a voice or a story, but preferably both." She seems impressed by this, and soon you and she get to talking, despite the pounding bass line. The nightlife photographer takes a picture of the two of you mid-conversation, and your heart sings. Phoebe tells you she's here because she worked with the founder of *De Trop* in the eighties. You tell her about your job search, about your bedbugs, about your roommates. She keeps asking questions, and eventually you find yourself talking about the managing director.

"Oh, honey," she says, shaking her head. And for a moment you think she's going to hug you and tell you it's all going to be okay. "If I ran away every time a boss flirted, I'd still be flipping burgers at Wendy's in Wichita."

You don't know how to respond to this. You're dizzy all of a sudden, the room around you hot and loud and oppressive. You take another sip of your drink, which has turned to melted ice. To your relief, you catch a glimpse of Freddie across the room. "I have to go say hi to my friend," you say, and walk in his direction.

Freddie's with his friends, all clones of Freddie with their black clothes and expensive-looking hair, all wearing name tags sporting 8s and 9s. Freddie introduces them as his coworkers and you as the one who broke the Crawford story, and they make small "oh yeah" noises like they remember but you can tell they are just pretending. Freddie wants to introduce you to Ted McDowell, the editor in chief of *De Trop.* He knows everyone, apparently, got his start in the eighties working for a big-name magazine. And he's looking for writers, young ones. "There he is," says Freddie, and you see he's pointing to the crag-faced man in horn-rimmed glasses, who is now talking to Phoebe Forsyth. The song switches to a track with a bass so heavy it feels as if it's coming from somewhere within you, a plodding heartbeat. At that moment you realize you can't be in that warehouse anymore, that whatever scene this is, it's not yours. You tell Freddie vaguely that you'll be right back and weave through the crowd of hipsters wearing their Sharpied numbers until you reach the sidewalk.

You feel very alone out there, more alone than you've ever been, probably. Your ridiculous silver pleather jacket is no match for the icy wind barreling down the street. You light a cigarette just to look occupied, since this city seems to have something against people who don't look occupied, people who don't have an occupation, and you aren't even allowed to complain because you have an emergency credit card. The sidewalks are alive with groups of friends laughing, couples leaning into each other in the wind, cars blasting hip-hop and reggaeton and—still—Michael Jackson. Your mother's words echo: *You can always come home.* You realize with a little thrill that you are walking distance from the gallery where Oscar's opening is. It's ten thirty, so surely the gallery is closed, but there's an afterparty at the bar down the street. You would give anything to be with people who know you right now, with their warm familiarity.

* * *

"THERE SHE IS!" Oscar shouts from the booth where he's holding court. There's a bitter edge to his voice. Rose is there too, seated next to Jenna. Even Brendan has turned up. No one will meet your eyes except Oscar. "Where the fuck *were* you, Julia? Why are you wearing a 6?"

"I'm so sorry," you say, self-consciously peeling the name tag off and shoving it into your jacket pocket. "I had a work thing."

"Bullshit," Oscar snorts. "Since when do you have a job?"

"I was networking," you say.

This sets Oscar off. He lays it all out for you: How everyone's had enough of your crap. How you won't shut up about how you can't find work, then you got your best friend fired from her job, and you can't even make the time to show up for your other friend—him—after he spent all those nights listening to you bitch about your privileged problems.

The bar has gone silent. People are listening, waiting for you to say something. Your friends—the people you thought were your friends—stare into their drinks, except Oscar, who glares at you with shining eyes.

You realize what you must look like to them: an opportunistic monster. You at the very least owe Rose an apology. You could save your friendship now by saying that Rose was right—it wasn't your story to tell. But when you try to find the words to say you're sorry, they aren't there. You have nothing to say to Rose, or to Oscar, or to any of them. It's time to go home.

The body shop has put up its Christmas decorations, though it's not even Thanksgiving. The glowing, eight-foot-tall animatronic Santa Claus who rotates his head to the tunes of Christmas classics reminds you of your impending financial doom. You fall asleep to a tinny rendition of "O Come, All Ye Faithful." The fridge groans in response.

The next day, your parents ask if Rose will be joining you for Thanksgiving this year, and you tell them that you actually won't be coming home for any of the holidays because you want more time to job-search. When did it get so easy to lie to them? The truth is that the idea of facing your mother and father is too much to bear. You know that once you are home with the tidy kitchen and Joanna the maid who does your laundry and tidies your things and the giant TV and the pantry that is mothless and always full of food, you'll want to sink into that coma of bourgeois comfort and never leave. You do your best to ignore their dismay, to push aside their disappointment in you, their only child, the failure.

Both roommates leave for Thanksgiving, and you have the apartment to yourself for four blissful days. A staycation, you tell yourself. You eat pizza in the bathtub. You drink wine in bed. You get high and watch reality television into the night and let your dishes pile up in the sink. You sleep until the afternoon. You ride the subway and keep thinking you see Rose everywhere, but they are just look-alikes, uncanny doppelgängers that exist only to make your stomach flip-flop and your hands tremble. You won't see Rose for another several years, when you are both completely different people. You will look back on this as the nadir, as a Very Sad Time, but in the moment it's not so bad. In the moment this is what's to be expected, this is what you deserve, this is you getting your thick skin.

You find your photograph with Phoebe Forsyth from the *De Trop* launch on a party blog and stare at your face, blown out in the flash, mouth open, drink raised in mid-gesticulation. Thankfully the 6 is concealed by your arm. What are you saying? It's a Julia you don't recognize, a carefree Julia, a desperate Julia, with her silly silver jacket and smudged eye makeup.

You keep interviewing for jobs. An eco-friendly lighting manufacturer in Industry City says you are overqualified for the receptionist position. A marketing firm in Midtown says they are looking for someone with copywriting experience. Through your alumni office, you arrange an informational lunch interview with a VP of a major magazine publisher. Over enormous salads in the company cafeteria, she tells you that New York is very competitive, and that if you want to find a job you should consider moving to another city, like Boston.

By the time the coffee shop on Bedford Ave. calls about your job application, you've forgotten you even applied. You schedule the interview, thinking nothing of it. They offer you the job on the spot. The pay and benefits are nothing compared to the credit agency, but it's something to do, it's your own money, barely enough to cover rent. You spend your days lugging bags of beans, steaming various milks, and knocking grounds out of the portafilter. The morning shifts go by fast; the afternoon shifts are slow enough for you to notice the way the light moves across the tile floor. You can hear the relief in your parents' voices when you tell them the news.

The actress is moving out at the end of the month, and to your surprise she offers you her bike. You accept, bewildered at the kindness, thinking that you'll sell it once she leaves. But you decide to take it out one morning, just to see what it's like. You're nearly sideswiped by a bus. It gets easier as you spend more time on the streets, though, and soon it's replaced your subway rides. And though the wind turns your cheeks and fingers to ice, though your legs cramp and strain up the inclines of bridges, you feel as high as you did on those sweaty nights with your college friends. You forget about the managing director and Rose and Oscar and the rage roiling your insides. When it's just you propelling yourself through space, things come into focus in a way they never did before.

You weave through traffic in Downtown Brooklyn and bounce over the wooden planks of the Brooklyn Bridge, dinging your bell to scatter pedestrians. Every ride, the city reveals another secret. A block made entirely of red brick, sidewalks included, in Ridgewood. A flock of green parrots roosting on a spire at the entrance to Green-Wood Cemetery. A house with elaborate mosaics of glass and stone cascading down its side in Jamaica, Queens. There are the smells: the toilet bowl breeze of the East River, the fish market on Chrystie, the hot dogs and Nuts4Nuts and car exhaust. And, of course, there are the people. Sometimes, even though it's cold, you park your bike and sit with a steaming slice of pizza, watching the glorious vignettes of other people's lives unfold. Being around strangers all day is a kind of balm for the loneliness that finds you when you're on your computer in your room. The affection you feel for this place is so strong that you wish you could fit it in your arms for an embrace. Even if it doesn't feel like your home, *because* it doesn't feel like your home, you can never leave.

On Christmas Eve, you and some of the other baristas go out for drinks after closing. Together, you wind through the forests of sidewalk Christmas trees in the direction of some bar you've never heard of, talking shit and goofing around. Giant illuminated snowflakes are suspended over Bedford Ave. The whole place is lit and jolly and you want to sing a fucking carol, even though you've been listening to Christmas music all day at work. One of your coworkers hands you a flask and you drink from it, bourbon glowing in your throat. It's the first time you've been out with people who didn't know you when you were an eighteen-year-old college freshman. They know nothing about your study sessions, or your secrets, or *Bright Lights, Big Deal*, which you've let go fallow and will delete before winter's end. With these people, you can be yourself. You can be anyone.

TROGLOXENE

Max was home.

It had been ten days of sleepless nights punctuated by nightmares, ten days of television news crews in the front yard, ten days of headlines like *11-Year-Old Girl Still Missing in Cave* and *How Long Can She Survive? No Luck on First Expedition to Find Lost Girl*, ten days of fast food for dinner (if there was dinner) after her parents' long hours at Forrester's Caverns, overseeing the rescue team. But now, after an additional three days of staring at her sister through plexiglass in quarantine at that dismal Phoenix hospital, Max was home—not home exactly, but back at their vacation rental in Quicksilver Springs—and Holly was looking forward to things going back to normal.

The first dinner after she was back they had spaghetti with meatballs and a kale salad. Holly watched, nibbling a piece of kale, as Max spooled one generous helping of noodles after another around her fork, shoving each into her mouth. When she was done with the pasta, she grabbed a handful of meatballs from the serving dish and took a bite before laying the obliterated mound on her plate and slurping the sauce off her fingers. Marinara bloodied her chin. It was all Holly could do not to gag.

"So hungry!" exclaimed their mother. "That's good!"

"Well, there wasn't much to eat down in the cave, was there, Maxie?" said their dad.

Max shook her head. Before the rescue team had found her and been able to lower food down, Max had survived—for eight days—on the four KIND bars in her fanny pack.

There was something weird about Max's face, thought Holly. Something off. Max had always been the pretty one, while adults used words like "unconventional" to describe Holly. But now Max's eyes, once a crystal green, were dulled and bloodshot. Her shimmering golden hair had lost its sheen and hung limply around her face, which was sharper now, more angular. She twitched at every fork clank, sniffling and shifting in her chair.

"Can you turn off the lights?" Max asked.

"Of course, sweetie!" crooned their mother. They spent the rest of the meal in darkness.

After dinner, Holly FaceTimed with her best friend, Justine, back home in LA, as she did every night. In the middle of their conversation, Max walked into Holly's room without even knocking.

"Get out of here!" Holly screamed. Their parents might have been letting Max do whatever the heck she wanted, but Holly sure wasn't. Max started to say something but stopped when Holly glared at her. She retreated and left the room, thank God.

"Did she drink her own pee?" Justine asked. "That's what you have to do, you know."

Justine was always asking the grossest questions.

"No, disgusting," said Holly. "There was an underground stream."

"You know you are going to be the coolest eighth grader. Marie Jackson was asking me all these questions about you." Marie Jackson was the daughter of a famous actor, and one of the most popular girls at La Brea Middle School. Justine and Holly hated Marie.

The conversation shifted, as it often did, to Justine's crush on Sean, who was in her summer performing arts day camp. Sean was late for rehearsal today. Sean had skateboarded by Justine at the park and nodded at her. Sean had liked one of Justine's posts. *Who cares?* Holly wanted to scream at her friend. But she never did. Through her earbuds, Holly heard a clatter coming from outside her room. Still holding her phone, she tiptoed down the hallway to the dark kitchen. In the dim glow of the digital clock on the microwave she could just make out Max's slight silhouette at the counter.

"I've got to go," she whispered to Justine. "Talk tomorrow."

She flipped on the light. Max jerked her head up and bared her teeth. She was grasping a metal serving spoon, poised to eat cereal and milk from a large mixing bowl. It looked like she'd dumped the entire box in there. "Turn it off!" Max hissed.

Holly did as she was told. "What the heck are you doing?" she whispered.

"I was hungry," said Max, between slurps of cereal.

Holly lingered for a moment. Something was up with Max, she could tell.

"What are you looking at?"

"Nothing, freak," said Holly.

Back in her room, she listened to the spoon clinking against the metal and wondered what had happened to her little sister.

* * *

THOSE TEN DAYS that Max was gone had been scary and boring at the same time. That was what Holly had felt in the Forrester's Caverns State Park ranger station: fear and boredom. Boredom while waiting for her parents to finish meeting with the park manager so that she could go in and talk to him. Fear while staring at the puffy, watery look on her mother's face in the manager's office. Holly sat down in the folding chair next to her dazed father, the metal cold on the backs of her thighs. Two police officers stood behind the park manager, a heavyset man who introduced himself as Ranger Garcia.

"I'd like you to tell the officers here *exactly* what happened." He spoke to her in an artificially high, soft voice, enunciating each word, like someone talking to a small child.

One officer held a pen and notepad, expectantly.

She looked to her mother, who avoided eye contact. Her mother had said very little to Holly since the incident.

"Go ahead and tell them what you told us, Hols," said her father.

So she did: that they'd been hanging back behind the tour group. Holly had been minding her own business, and when she turned to check on her sister, Max was gone. She'd called out to her, even shined her headlamp into the shadows beyond the dim green in-ground lighting that illuminated the stalagmites surrounding the walkway. When Max didn't answer, Holly immediately ran to tell her mother. While she talked, the officer scribbled furiously.

Garcia looked as if he believed her, but it was hard to know for certain. He slid a laminated map of Forrester's Caverns across the desk. "Can you show me where you were when you *last* saw your sister?"

The map reminded her of a diagram of the digestive system. She traced her finger through the cave entrance and into the caverns, all with dumb names. The Candelabra Room was where she'd last seen Max, but if she told them that, then her parents would know that she'd waited until the Hall of Echoes to say anything. She pointed to the Forrester Passage, which came right before the Hall of Echoes, and handed the map back to Ranger Garcia.

"Thank you," he said. "I'm sure this isn't easy for any of you, but I want you all to know that my guys have made Max their priority. They *will* find her."

Her mother began to cry again. Then it was time to go.

In the car, after they'd picked up Burger King for dinner—a rarity for the family—her mother turned around to face Holly for what felt like the first time since Max's disappearance.

"This is your fault, you know," she said. "You should have been watching your sister."

"Lisa," her father said, weakly. "Don't."

Her mother sighed and turned back around in her seat. The greasy fug of the fast food made Holly queasy as the saguaros whipped by on either side of them. Was Max beneath them at that moment, in some far-flung underground passage? She hoped the jacket her mother had forced Max into was keeping her warm in the cave's chill.

Back at the vacation rental, Holly lay flat on her bed and stared at the ceiling. She could hear her mother in Max's room, sobbing. It wasn't until the next day that she realized her parents had left dinner in the car.

* * *

THE MORNING AFTER Max came home, their mom made pancakes for the girls, but only Holly was awake to eat them. She sat at the table, gloomily sopping up syrup as her parents traded glances in a coded language that Holly was sick of trying to read. When Holly asked what was going on, her dad said that the two of them should go on a hike before it got too hot and give her mom and sister some space. Holly tried to protest, but it was futile.

They drove to an "easy" trail along a wash. Holly huffed along, sweating beneath the stupid hat her father forced her to wear. They were each carrying a gallon of water in addition to their water bottles, "just in case." Her backpack straps dug into her shoulders.

She was so sick of the desert. "You'll like the Southwest," their father had told her and Max, when he'd informed them that their family vacation this year would be to Quicksilver Springs, Arizona, two hours outside Phoenix in the middle of nowhere. "It looks a lot like that computer game you're obsessed with." He meant *Colony*, which was set on a desert planet. As it turned out, it was better on the screen than in person. Sure, she was into the giant rocks, and Max had found a tarantula in the yard one night. But the extreme heat was dizzying, and after a few days, she missed walking around the Third Street Promenade with Justine, eating churros and checking out boys. And then, of course, the cave incident had happened.

"Dad," she said, "when are we going home?"

"Soon," said her father. "The doctors want to make sure your sister is okay to travel."

"Can *I* go home?"

He stared at her. There was a stripe of white on his nose where he hadn't rubbed in sunscreen all the way. "Out of the question," he said.

"I can stay with Justine," Holly said.

"No," said her father. "Believe it or not, your sister needs you right now."

Holly doubted that. She'd felt something unexpected after Max had disappeared: the relief that came with being sisterless. People felt sorry for her, and she liked it. She liked not having Max there to steal her clothes; she liked not having her interrupt her FaceTime calls with Justine; she liked not having to call shotgun when one of her parents drove her somewhere. Max had it so freaking easy. People cooed over her all the time about how pretty she was, how "darling." It was nice for Holly, with her lanky limbs and oily skin, to be the center of attention for once. But whenever this notion crept into her head, she pushed it away. It was evil, she knew, and she felt awful for even thinking it in the first place.

The terrain became rocky, the trail narrowed, and soon they were scrambling single file over boulders. Holly stormed ahead of her father, determined to get this death march over with. She was about to climb over a particularly large rock when her father yanked her wrist away. "Look out!" he cried.

Nestled in the handhold that Holly was about to grab on to was a scorpion, its shiny black tail curled to attack.

"I could have gotten stung and *died*," shrieked Holly. "Can we please go back to the house?"

The dazed expression that he'd had the whole time Max was gone flashed across her father's face. "All right," he said robotically.

* * *

LATER, HOLLY CAME DOWNSTAIRS to find Max on the couch, watching TV, which was against the rules. The shades in the living room were pulled down. "How come Max gets to watch TV before dinner?" she asked their father.

"Why don't you go help your mother?"

Holly groaned and walked into the kitchen.

"Oh good," her mother said, hand in a chicken, "you're here. I'm making a roast chicken for your sister, and the rest of us are going to have grilled cheese and broccoli. How does that sound?"

Holly despised broccoli, which her mother knew, but she wasn't about to get into it with her. "You're making an entire roast chicken for Max?"

Her mother washed her hands and dried them on a dish towel. "It's what she specifically requested, and the man at the grocery store gave it to me for free. How cool is that?"

Holly didn't say anything. She massaged her shoulder, sore from walking with the water bottles that morning.

"She's not going to eat the whole thing. Stop giving me that look." She picked up a bag of onions from the counter and handed it to Holly. "I need two of those, sliced. Then you can get started on the herbs."

Holly sighed and began her work. The dull knife slipped each time she tried to cut through a bulb. Her eyes teared up.

"There's a news crew coming tomorrow to interview us as a family," her mother said, churning a pepper mill over the chicken. "I bought you a new dress. It's on your bed."

Normally Holly would have been thrilled at the prospect of being on TV. But the idea of spending another day in this miserable house made her want to retch. Plus she was sure that whatever her mom had gotten her was butt-ugly. "Can't I just wear normal clothes?"

"Where did I put those giblets?" her mom said to no one, and wandered out of the kitchen. *Typical. Leave me to do the work while you go off and dote on Max,* thought Holly, wiping her nose on her sleeve. A scream came from the dining room. She dropped the knife and ran toward the sound. At the dining room table, their mother was trying to wrestle the bowl of chicken innards away from Max. Their father watched, helpless.

"Sweetheart," shrieked their mother, "you *cannot* eat those raw!" Max didn't loosen her grip on the bowl. "Charles," she said, "*do* something."

Their father crouched beside Max. "Give that back to your mother, please," he said.

"But I want to eat it."

"Maxine, that will give you a very bad tummy ache." He reached his arm down to pull the bowl away. Max let out a snarl and gnashed her teeth at his wrist. Their father jerked his arm away just in time.

In a flash she'd shoved the glistening mess into her mouth and swallowed.

"Max!" their mother cried out.

"Oh my God, that's so gross!" said Holly. Max flashed her a bloody-toothed grimace.

Their parents looked at each other, mouths agape. "Come on, Max," said their mother. "We're going back to the hospital."

"Lisa," said their dad, "let's not catastrophize."

"I don't want to hear it," their mother spat. "After everything—"

Holly tensed, anticipating a fight. Thankfully, their father held up his hands in surrender. "Fine," he said. "Go ahead."

She slung her purse over her shoulder and grabbed Max by the wrist. "I'll call you," she said, slamming the door.

Holly and her father stared at the bowl that had held the glossy innards. Then her father picked it up with a frustrated sigh and dropped it into the kitchen sink. Holly found a paper towel and wiped the droplets of chicken liquid from the tabletop.

* * *

WHEN HOLLY HAD FIRST PULLED her mother aside to tell her that Max was missing, her mother had told her the cave was no place for goofing off. They'd paid good money for this tour. She demanded that Holly go get her sister and tell her that since the girls had been so horrible all day, fighting over Holly's silly sweatshirt, and now this, there would be no ice cream, no souvenirs from the gift shop on the way out.

"Mom," Holly said in a trembling whisper, "I'm serious."

Something wild lit her mother's eyes. She called out Max's name, running deeper into the cave. The tour guide stopped her lecture on cave geology and followed her mother, lips pressed to her walkie-talkie, shouting code. Her father went next, chasing after their bouncing head lamp beams. Holly stayed put, the confused voices of the tour group around her echoing off the walls.

No one knew how Max had gotten so far away from the group. She was found all those days later a dozen miles from where she'd run off, in a part of the cave that was closed even to park staff. The hypothesis was that she'd floated down the underground stream. It was a miracle she had survived.

How was what Holly wanted to know. But her parents had warned her not to ask Max questions about the cave, that she'd tell them in her own time. Holly had read up on Forrester's Caverns during those days alone in the vacation rental. She knew about how the cave had been discovered by uranium miners, that the bats that lived there were called trogloxenes because they left the cave to feed, that cave fish had no eyes and were called troglobites since they lived *only* in the cave and never left. There were weirder things about the cave, too—conspiracy theories. UFO sightings near Mount Vista. A two-headed rabbit skeleton found at the entrance. Rumors of a thirty-foot-long snake seen slithering through the Hall of Echoes.

The websites that made these claims looked like they'd been built in the nineties, filled with capital letters and long-winded screeds. Most of them focused on creatures called mudmen: humans who'd gotten lost in the underground maze and become mutants who lived on raw flesh. It was the uranium-tinged water that was responsible for the mutation, apparently.

It was nonsense, Holly knew, but what if it wasn't? Then what?

* * *

THOUGH IT WAS WELL after 9:00 PM by the time their mom shuttled Max back from the hospital, they gathered around the table to eat as a family because their dad had gone ahead and prepared dinner. Their mother recounted what the doctor had said. It turned out that raw chicken was only dangerous if it had salmonella, which would have manifested symptoms by the time they arrived at the ER. "You gave us quite a scare," she said to Max. The shadows on her face were intensified in the candlelight—a compromise, since Max had thrown a tantrum when Holly switched on the overhead light in the dining room. Across the table, Max was slowly breaking down the chicken with her hands, shoving the flesh into her mouth.

"Why are you letting her do that?" Holly said. It was truly disgusting, and Holly couldn't believe that her parents weren't saying anything.

"Holly," said her dad, "just eat your dinner, okay?"

She pushed a mushy broccoli tree around on her plate. Her father should never be in charge of cooking. "I'm done," she said before bringing her half-empty plate into the kitchen and letting it clatter loudly on the tile countertop.

Her father called from the dining room, demanding that she come back and help clean up.

"Make Max do it," she yelled. She slammed the door to her room. She was astounded by the BS she had to put up with from her parents.

Holly eyed the Walmart bag on the bed that held her new dress. She took one look inside: pink. Why did her mother do this to her? She knew pink was Holly's absolute least favorite color; Holly had told her a thousand times. She threw the dress to the side of the room and flung herself onto her bed, where she started up *Colony* on her laptop and wandered around the planet killing everyone she saw and picking up their supplies until her mother knocked on the door and told her lights out.

A yowl from the front yard woke her. She pulled aside the curtains and peeked out the window. The house didn't have a yard, really—it was just a fenced-in patch of desert. The moon made the sand glow a dull gray. A rabbit darted by, followed by a dark blur. A coyote? The blur stopped. It was Max. She had the struggling rabbit in her hands. She lifted it to her face and tore into its skin with her teeth. Max looked up for a moment, seeming to sense Holly, but then returned to whatever it was she was doing to the animal. Holly lay back down in bed. There was no way she could have seen what she saw. She was dreaming, or something. She drifted into uneasy sleep.

* * *

IN THOSE DAYS THAT fogged together after Max went missing, Holly's parents would leave at dawn to meet with the rescue workers at the caverns. Holly cobbled together meals from pantry items left behind by previous renters: mushy beef stew out of a can, Triscuits and salsa, Cup Noodles, its Styrofoam container faded and yellowing. She spent hours on *Colony*, chatting with strangers, slaying demons. It felt good to be anonymous, to have nothing to worry about except where to find ammo. When her parents came home for the night, her mother would retreat to her room for the evening, leaving Holly and her dad to eat their burgers and fries alone, the crinkle of wrappers and the gentle pop of peeled-back condiment plastic the only conversation they could manage.

Ranger Garcia told them that keeping attention on the rescue meant resources for the rescuers, and resources for the rescuers meant they would find Max sooner. Her parents agreed to let the press photograph them as a family. They stood in front of the vacation rental in the scalding late-afternoon sunlight as reporters took their picture, her parents' expressions stoic. A gold cross pendant glinted on her mother's neck. She had let Holly put on lipstick and mascara, and Holly had even snuck on some foundation, which sat hot and waxy on her face. Her mother's hand clutched Holly's shoulder, the first contact she'd had with her in days. Holly tried to focus on Mount Vista in the distance to keep from breaking down as the cameras clicked and flashed around her. Finally, her father wordlessly led the three of them inside, where they all disappeared into their rooms.

The photos had run in several major newspapers. Max's plight had now turned viral, and Holly soon began to get messages from friends back home, from people at school who she hadn't even realized knew who she was, asking how she was doing and sending prayer hands and heart emojis. They used hashtags on social: #SaveMax. #ForrestersCaverns. #CaveRescue.

Strangers were using those hashtags, too. There were theories. Holly pored over these. People had exhaustively analyzed the maps, posting their findings on YouTube, speculating where Max could be. Some said she'd run away from abusive parents. Some said the whole thing was a hoax, that her family had created a stunt for attention. Others assumed Max was dead, citing statistics for missing children. Holly clicked through videos and message boards. None seemed to offer anything resembling an answer.

* * *

BY THE TIME the news crew came, the house had lost the musty scent of dust mixed with putrefying garbage. Now it smelled like the coffee her mother had brewed. She'd woken Holly at dawn and tasked her with a sizable list of chores: getting rid of the containers of rotting flowers; taking out trash from the overflowing wastebaskets; washing dried tea bags and hardened black coffee silt out of mugs; disposing of the fast-food wrappers that littered the living room.

Sadie Jones, the reporter, was younger than Holly had expected her to be. She had straight black hair and flawless makeup. She'd be asking them questions, she said, and they could stop if things got too intense. There was a warmth in her voice that made Holly want to tell Sadie everything. A crew member turned on a light. Max hissed at him, but if he noticed, he pretended not to.

Holly wriggled in the stiff new pink dress between her mother and sister on the sofa. Because rousing Max had been an ordeal, Holly had not had the chance to tell her about her strange dream. Their mother had managed to wrestle Max into an equally itchy-looking purple dress and braid her hair just in time for the news crew. Still, the gray circles under her eyes made her look like one of the dwarf ghouls in *Colony*.

"Can you talk about the moment you realized Maxine was gone?" Sadie asked their mom, who had done a less-than-perfect job with her own makeup. There were streaks of poorly applied concealer under her eyes, and a dusting of mascara on her lower eyelids. Holly felt a pang of embarrassment on her mother's behalf as she began to tell the story—the same one Holly had told to Ranger Garcia.

The dress became stifling, then. She imagined herself interrupting their mom, telling everything to Sadie: the fight, what she'd said to Max to make her run off. How she'd waited nearly twenty minutes before telling their parents about Max's disappearance, because she hadn't actually believed that Max was gone. Instead, she tugged on a loose piece of fuchsia thread in the hem of her skirt until their mother nudged her to stop.

Sadie's eyes were glistening now. "How in the world did you get through the agony of not knowing where your daughter was?"

"Prayer," their mother answered, to Holly's surprise. Holly hadn't seen their mother pray once and couldn't remember the last time they'd gone to church. The reporter nodded, smiling warmly, and turned to Max. "And Maxine, that must have been very scary down there in that cave. What did you do to keep your spirits up?"

Holly could feel Max fidgeting. She smelled like sweat and moldy towels.

Holly doubted their mother had been able to coax Max into the shower this morning.

Then Max let out a long, whistling shriek—something between a cat in heat and a bird of prey. The same noise, Holly realized, that had woken her the night before.

For the briefest moment, Sadie dropped her reportorial professionalism, her mouth frozen in a shocked O, hand to her chest. Max stood and sauntered out of the room.

"Did you get that?" Sadie asked the cameraman.

"Maxie, honey?" called their mother, and followed after Max.

"I'm sorry," their father said to Sadie. "She's probably tired. Maybe we can reschedule?"

* * *

AT LUNCH, HOLLY'S PARENTS ANNOUNCED that the family was finally—finally!—going home. They would fly out of Phoenix Friday afternoon—the day after tomorrow!—and be in Los Angeles by dinner. Holly ran around the house singing goodbyes to random objects. "Goodbye, ugly painting," she said to the portrait of the neon-green cactus above the television. "Goodbye, stupid sombrero," she said to the hat hanging on the wall by the front door. "Goodbye, tacky house!" Her parents looked on with mild amusement. She was being a ham, as her mother would say. So what. For the first time in her life, Holly couldn't wait to go back to school.

"Chill," said her mother. "Your sister's taking a nap."

"I. Don't. Care," she sang.

She FaceTimed Justine, but Justine wasn't picking up. She scrolled through Justine's social media: video after video of her on the beach in the red-and-white polka-dotted two-piece she'd bought with her allowance money, the one with the push-up bra that her mother had forbidden her to wear until she was in high school. Marie Jackson was in some of the videos, as was an older boy with patches of stubble dotting his chin and upper lip. This, Holly gathered, was Marie's older brother. At least now Holly wouldn't have to hear about Sean Levinson all the time.

Holly played *Colony* until her eyes grew itchy. Her parents hadn't even bothered to check to make sure she was in bed. It was well past midnight when she shut her laptop and gazed out the window, half expecting to see Max outside. There was nothing but the desert, of course. But she thought she saw—no. It was probably just a plant, a man-sized cactus, far too big to be Max, in the moonlight. She walked down the hall and poked her head into Max's room.

The mildewed odor that she'd smelled on Max earlier was tinged with a metallic stench. In the thin strip of light coming through the curtains, Max's bed looked empty. Holly stepped inside and switched on the bedside lamp, flinching as her toe grazed something wet. On the floor was a bloody animal carcass—a rabbit, from what she could make out. She clamped her palm over her mouth to keep from screaming and turned to run out of the room. Standing in the doorway was Max. In her hand was another dead rabbit. She dropped it and ran to Holly, wrapping her arms around her waist, crying.

"Dude," said Holly. "*What* is going on?"

Her sister spoke. "They want me to come with them. Tomorrow night. They've been sending watchers to make sure I do it. Or they'll take me. Or I'll—" At this, Max broke down, sobbing. Holly held her quivering body.

"Or you'll what?"

"The sun kills us," Max managed to choke out.

The cave must have been so scary for Max, who was, as their mother said, fragile. Now she was imagining things and acting out. Had she read the conspiracy theories online?

"No, no," said Holly, stroking her sister's greasy hair.

Then Max told Holly about what had happened to her down in the cave. How she'd tripped and slid down some shale, and when she realized she couldn't climb back to the walkway had searched the tunnel for another way up. It was there that a group of creatures had found her shivering and wrapped her in furs, fed her dried fish and rabbit. At first, she was frightened, but as the days went on, she'd grown to love it down there in the dark with the mutants. She had a knack for hunting. She'd also been drinking contaminated water from the stream, which meant that her evolution had begun, they told her; she was becoming one of them. Once it was complete, she wouldn't be able to survive in the human world. But then one of the rescue workers had found her and she'd been forced to come home.

Holly was truly impressed with her sister's imagination. "This BS might work with Mom and Dad, but it's not working with me," she said, but as she looked around the room, littered with tufts of fur, she didn't know what to believe.

Max pushed her away. "I liked it down there, with them," she said. "I liked it better in the cave than in this stupid, boring house with you and Mom and Dad."

"You ungrateful brat," spat Holly, feeling unusually defensive of their parents. "You have no idea what we went through while you were down there."

"You told me you wanted me to disappear," said Max. "So that's what I'm doing. And now I have to eat." She pushed past Holly out the door.

Max's words stung. She'd kept that from the park manager, from her parents: the fight. The sisters had been bickering all day because Max had stolen Holly's yellow hoodie and spilled ketchup on it and Holly had snapped in the cave, calling Max a weirdo loser freak. "Get lost," she'd commanded, her words echoing off the cave's cold walls. "Just go away. Disappear!" Then Max had run.

Now, Holly swept up the tufts of rabbit hair and wiped the puddles of blood from the hardwood floor with a paper towel. She changed the red-spattered sheets, stuffing them into the closet. Doing everything she could not to throw up, she shoved the rabbit carcasses into a trash bag and took it out to the bins by the garage.

When she finally slept, she dreamed she was playing *Colony*, shooting grimacing elves that, on closer inspection, were Maxes. She woke with a wet face. She'd been crying in her sleep. She just wanted to be home where things were normal, but she was starting to think that normal wasn't an option anymore.

The next day, Holly spent most of the time on her phone, scrolling mindlessly, lingering on Justine and Marie's beach adventures. The rest of the time she spent checking on Max, making sure she was still there. Her sister, as usual, was asleep. Her parents kept asking Holly what was wrong, wasn't she excited about leaving? She wasn't, not anymore, not after the incident with her sister last night, not after she'd lost her best friend to vapid, rich Marie, but she said yes anyway.

Again, her parents let Max choose what she wanted for their candlelit dinner. She asked for In-N-Out and devoured three Double-Double burgers, Animal Style, and two orders of fries. This time, her parents didn't praise her appetite.

Max's skin was pale and shiny, almost translucent, like the grilled onions she'd picked out of her burgers and placed in a greasy pile on her plate. Holly could see the veins in her temples pulse as she chewed her food. A shadow of fine black hair had appeared on the backs of her hands. Her yellowed nails seemed to have grown talon-like overnight.

Holly's mother was making the pouty face she made when one of the girls was sick.

"When we get home, we're taking you to Dr. Singh. This could be a thyroid condition."

Max only grunted.

Holly couldn't bring herself to eat.

"What's going on, Hols?" said her father. "Is it a boy?" It was weird to have her parents notice her for once.

Holly shook her head.

Max glared at her.

"This time tomorrow night, we'll all be sitting around our dining room table at home," said her father. The joyful glow on his face made Holly furious. She wanted to scream at both of her parents, tell them that it was too late, that Max was lost already.

"No we won't," she said instead, doing her best to keep her voice from trembling. She felt a sharp kick under the table from Max's sneaker.

"I don't know where all this is coming from." Her mother stabbed at her salad with her fork.

Holly tore a fry into smaller and smaller pieces. "Never mind," she said.

After dinner, her father insisted that all four of them drive up to Mount Vista for one last desert sunset. It was a short walk to the peak. They watched in silence as the sky turned blazing orange over the valley. While her parents took pictures, Holly felt her sister's hand grab her own, her long nails lightly scratching Holly's palm. It was ice-cold. "I don't have a choice," whispered Max. "It's not your fault."

Holly said nothing. What was there to say? She pulled her hand away.

* * *

SHE TRIED TO STAY AWAKE that night to listen for Max, but eventually she sank into sleep until the clank of the gate woke her up. Holly pulled her curtains aside. The sky was cloudless and the stars were dazzling. If she missed anything about the desert, she would miss them.

Max was at the yard's edge. Next to her was a man, or something man-shaped. It wore no clothes. Its face was ghostly pale in the moonlight, its body caked in dirt. Where its eyes should have been there were black slits, narrow and gill-like. It put a hand on Max's shoulder.

Now, *now* was the moment when there was still time to do something, screamed a voice inside her. She pulled on her hiking boots and stumbled down the stairs. If her parents heard her, so what. Once out the front door, she called to Max, who turned around long enough for Holly to see that there was something different about her eyes. Her bloodless skin shone silver. Then she and the mudman took off toward the mountains at an inhuman speed.

Holly ran after them, lungs straining, faster than she'd ever run in gym class, summoning every last bit of strength in her body. Coarse brush whipped her legs, but she surged ahead, Max's stringy hair always just out of reach. She ran like she should have run back in the caverns, the first time Max had disappeared.

Her foot hit a rock or a branch or something, and Holly went flying. For the briefest moment she thought her speed had launched her airborne, and she was headed straight for the stars. But then she felt the sting of the gravelly sand as she landed hard on her palms and knee, the sticky warm blood leaking from her wounds. She tried to stand, but the pain was too much.

"Max!" she called again, as the two forms bounded away like graceful nocturnal animals, becoming smaller and smaller in the moonlight.

All around her was the cacophony of the desert at night: a din of whistles and chirps and cries of distant creatures. She gazed off toward the mountains, trying to catch a final glimpse of her little sister. There was nothing but miles of sand and boulders and shrubs. She'd lost her. Max was gone.

THE RECLAMATION

DAY ONE

THE AC IN THE van was broken, and Pat was sure she stank. It was eighty degrees and climbing, hot for a November morning in the Coachella Valley, and even with the windows cracked it felt airless.

There were twenty of them. Twenty women business leaders in two passenger vans eastbound to an undisclosed destination in the middle of the Mojave for the Glow Time Retreat, an entrepreneurial wellness and self-actualization boot camp led by Brooke Soleil, host of the Stop & Glow podcast and lifestyle brand.

Stepping into the conference hall in the Palm Desert hotel where her husband, Roman, had dropped her off for the welcome breakfast, the first thing Pat had noticed was how much older she was than most of the women, by at least two decades. She'd half expected it. She supposed it was a good thing, networking with younger women. Perhaps she'd find some potential customers. Or perhaps she could call Roman and tell him to turn around and pick her up immediately, like an anxious child on her first day of summer camp.

Pat had never considered herself to be someone who gave credence to self-help gurus. Brooke's podcast had started as a guilty pleasure and turned into a habit. Then Roman surprised her with a pass to the retreat, and here she was. She should've spoken up, told Roman that sure, she listened to Brooke's podcast, but this was just too much. Eight days in the desert was not Pat's idea of a good time. Her and Roman's admittedly rare vacations were to cities: Chicago, New Orleans, New York, one glorious week in Paris. A childhood spent on miserable, ill-conceived camping trips all over California with hippie parents had soured her on the outdoors. Not to mention the price tag. It wasn't like they *couldn't* afford it, though it also wasn't like Roman—the obsessive budgeter who'd wooed her in their late twenties with the fact that he had a savings account with money in it—to make that kind of purchase without spending weeks agonizing over it. And perhaps he had, silently, sparing her his grief. Oh God. This was all her fault. She'd hardly slept the night before, her mind spinning in anxiety spirals, refusing to let her get a minute's rest. She slid on her vintage Prada shades, closed her eyes, and leaned her head back on the seat as the women behind her gushed to one another about Reiki.

"You okay?" It was her seatmate speaking, a tattoo-sleeved millennial in silly knockoff Nina Ricci sunglasses that covered half her face. "I have some Dramamine in my bag if you need it."

She began digging through an ancient canvas messenger bag festooned with enamel pins and buttons. She moved in shifts and twitches, a manic energy that set Pat on edge.

"No, thank you," said Pat. "Just tired is all."

"I'm Celeste," she said, holding out a hand glinting with silver rings.

"Pat," said Pat, taking Celeste's clammy hand in her own.

"You sell vintage clothes," said Celeste, and, noticing Pat's look of surprise at her knowledge, added: "The meet and greet." She tapped her head and grinned at Pat. Earlier that morning, the group had been herded into a circle in the hotel conference room and forced to share who they were and the entrepreneurial pathway they envisioned for themselves. Pat had been so nervous about speaking that she hardly remembered what anyone else had said. "I run an independent fragrance start-up. Hierophant," Celeste continued. "Here." Reaching into the pocket of her cutoffs, she produced a tiny glass vial filled with amber liquid.

"I don't really wear perfume," said Pat.

"Just give it a try," Celeste said.

Pat uncapped the bottle and put it up to her nose. It smelled astringent, with a hint of cedar. She frowned.

"No," said Celeste. "That won't tell you anything."

"Excuse me?"

"You need to put it on your skin. That's how you know what the profile is. Fragrance reacts differently to each of us, depending on our unique bodily oils. It's kind of magic that way. Dab some on your wrists and then rub them together."

Pat did as she was told, then sniffed her wrist. Aromas of campfire, pine, and salt water emanated from her skin. She closed her eyes. For a moment she was far from the desert—on a beach, her feet in cold, wet sand, aged twelve and back in Big Sur with Judith and Frankie. When she opened them, Celeste was staring straight at her through her ridiculous glasses, an idiotic smile on her face.

"What do you think?"

"It's not really for me," said Pat, rubbing her wrist on the van upholstery. The beach with the cold, wet sand was not a place she wanted to return to.

"Well," said Celeste, "it takes a while to find the right profile. I'm trying to set up a fragrance concierge that matches people to their scents on my website but am having trouble locking down funding. These finance bros don't like giving that kind of money to girly stuff, even though the gendered idea of fragrance is so antiquated and exclusionary . . ."

She went on like this. Pat tuned out. She didn't know if it was the heat or the perfume or the dust coming through the cracked window, but she felt unmoored, woozy, like she'd been drugged. Outside, Joshua trees blurred past, their branches tipped with small, spiny orbs, their bark black from a recent fire. She leaned back and closed her eyes as the van bounced over rocks and potholes. Soon Celeste's chirping was drowned out by a roar, the roar of the ocean, the chill of the Pacific water washing over her toes.

She woke as the van rumbled over a cattle grate. In the distance she could just make out what seemed to be a large campsite.

The vans parked and the passengers disembarked silently, taking in their surroundings. Small shrubs dotted the land as far as the eye could see. Dark mountains spread across the horizon. It all looked prehistoric, devoid of human life, and if it weren't for the power lines in the distance, a herd of brontosauruses wandering through wouldn't have seemed out of place.

A wiry, grim woman in a teal pashmina greeted them, clutching a clipboard. "I'm Tanya," she said in a quivering voice. "Welcome to Touchstone Retreat Center, home of the Glow Time Retreat." She attempted a brief smile. "Ms. Soleil intends this retreat to be a device-free space. Please power off and hand over your devices." She held open a black Stop & Glow tote and went from person to person, collecting phones. Pat reluctantly dropped hers in the bag. Before she left, she'd told Roman she most likely wouldn't have service where they were going, but she hadn't expected her phone to be confiscated. She hoped he wouldn't worry.

Celeste followed suit, dropping a phone and an iPad into the tote with a flourish of her wrist. "Such a relief, isn't it?" she said. "I shipped my teenagers off to my sister's and told her I was off-grid. They're her problem for the week!"

Underneath her glasses, Pat noticed, Celeste was much closer to Pat's age than she'd originally thought.

One of the women was making a scene. Her husband was alone with the baby for the first time. She needed to be reachable.

"Please," Tanya repeated, panicked, shaking the bag in the woman's face.

"Hon, it will be *fine.* I promise!" Celeste called out to the frazzled woman. "You've gotta let go sometimes."

"Ma'am, I'm going to have to ask you to get back in the van if you won't surrender your device," said Tanya.

Defeated, the woman slumped her shoulders and walked back to the van. Tanya whispered something to the driver, and both vans took off down the road.

"Jesus," said Pat. "It's nonrefundable."

"Some people are just so tied to their lives," said Celeste, shaking her head.

The vans disappeared into a cloud of dust.

* * *

TANYA ANNOUNCED THAT SHE would give them a tour of the center, and the group dragged their suitcases and duffel bags through a smattering of picnic tables, protected from the elements by a canopy of tan weatherproof fabric. This was the dining tent. Radiating out from the tables was a circle of glamping yurts: their homes for the duration of the retreat. Beyond those, a firepit and a shared shower building that had the faint whiff of a truck stop bathroom.

Finally, they were assigned yurt numbers and dispersed. Pat entered hers, grateful to be out of the sun, and surveyed the spartan interior. Besides the two cots, the only furniture was a small shelf containing Brooke Soleil's four bestsellers. On each cot was a beige backpack branded with the Stop & Glow logo, the letter *S* inside a line drawing of a sun. Pat set her bags down and unzipped the pack, turning it over and emptying its jewel-toned contents on the bed. There was a magenta aluminum water bottle (branded), a mustard-yellow plastic ballpoint pen (branded), a navy-blue compass (branded), an emerald-green spiral-bound notebook (branded), a collapsible metal straw (not branded), and a turquoise folder (branded). In the backpack's front pocket was a travel-sized bottle of Soleil Detoxifying Facial Spray and a small glass pot of Soleil Desert Sage Set Your Intention Facial Serum. The suns stared up at her like eyes, expectant. Pat opened the folder, which contained photocopies of talks Brooke had given: one on "Fast-Tracking Your Inner Truth" and a second entitled "Perception, Projection, and Perseverance," which had gone viral last year after Brooke delivered it as the keynote at a mindfulness conference.

Pat had moved on to inspecting the shelf when Celeste walked in, trailing a cloud of a church-like odor that Pat recognized as frankincense.

"Hey there, roomie," Celeste said, with a hysterical laugh, as if the fact that they'd been placed in a yurt together after randomly sitting next to each other on the van was some hilarious joke.

"Hello again," said Pat, trying to sound friendly.

Celeste took off her sunglasses, and Pat couldn't help staring at her face as she let her bags fall from her hands and sprawled on the cot. How did someone her own age carry herself with such youthful abandon? Celeste sat up and grabbed hold of the backpack. "Is this our swag bag?" she said. "Far out!"

Pat grunted in assent.

"First retreat?" asked Celeste from the cot, inspecting each object she pulled from the bag and laying it carefully on the bedspread.

"A gift from my husband," Pat said. Roman was concerned about her well-being; she knew by the way he'd been treading so softly lately, constantly asking her how she was feeling and surprising her with candy, trinkets, and finally a pass to the retreat. She wasn't okay, not really, not since she'd lost her lease on the consignment shop that had been her life for the past thirteen years. She missed the scraping of the hangers on the racks, the feel of the furs and satins, brocades and velvets, the way the garments hung expectantly, waiting for someone to take them home again. And though she did sell an evening gown or some costume jewelry from time to time on her Etsy storefront, it wasn't the same. "I'm not like a Brooke superfan or anything. Just listen to the podcast on occasion."

"That's sweet of your hubby," said Celeste. "And I'm sure you will be by the time you leave. Brooke's got a rare wisdom about her. She changes people. She changed me, at least."

"So you've done this before?"

"No," said Celeste, dreamily. "This was a fiftieth birthday gift to myself. I'm die-hard. One of the original Brookies." Pat had seen the term on various Facebook groups to describe fans of Brooke Soleil but had never heard it used in conversation. "You're going to love it," said Celeste. "You and I are going to have the best time."

* * *

THE WOMEN HAD BEEN WAITING nearly an hour for the Inspo Session with Brooke that was supposed to begin at two thirty, fanning themselves with their branded notebooks and spritzing themselves with facial spray, casting eager glances at the empty stool that had been set out for Brooke to give her first talk. The canopy over the dining tent provided little respite from the afternoon heat. Tanya hovered, reassuring the group that Ms. Soleil would be here any second now. Pat was about to beg Tanya to call a van and take her back to the hotel, nonrefundable retreat fees be damned, when the one they'd all traveled so far to see glided into the tent. Brooke's face was smaller, softer than it appeared on her Instagram posts. She brought her hands together at her heart center and smiled. She was ageless. At times she looked no older than seventeen, and then the light would hit differently and she'd look seventy, some sort of desert crone-goddess.

"Thank you for giving yourself this time," she said. "I'm so excited to guide you on your journey to entrepreneurial wellness and success. Let's all give ourselves a round of applause for being present. It's Glow Time!"

The crowd clapped, and Pat along with them. It was strange to see Brooke in the flesh, this being who had lived in her ears and on her phone for the past year.

"I want us to start with an affirmation," Brooke began. "You've probably all heard this one before, but say it along with me anyway." She closed her eyes and brought her fingertips to her temples. "My mind knows," she said. She crossed her arms over her chest, giving herself a hug. "My heart shows." Her palms fluttered down to prayer position at her sternum. "My self glows." The group repeated the affirmation until Tanya signaled that it was time to stop.

"Our work begins today," said Brooke. "And it is work, I assure you. It will not always be easy. In fact, it may never be easy. We'll travel to some dark places together. But we'll come out stronger. We'll emerge actualized, like the phoenix from flames." She paused, emitting a wind-chime tinkle of a laugh. "What am I saying?" she said, shaking her head. "Our work doesn't begin today, of course. We've been at it for our entire lives, for the lives before this one. Today, we *continue* that work."

She took a seat on the stool. "Every so often, I bring potential Stop & Glow investors out here. It gives me a chance to test their mettle. The weak, I've learned, tend to be problematic shareholders. I try to avoid them." She took a sip from her own magenta water bottle. "The one I'm going to tell you about was a young man from old East Coast money. Private jet. Driver. Boarding school. He was used to *luxury*." The way she accentuated the word conjured images of palm-shaded cabanas and silk robes. "As you know, I've been living out of a backpack in my camper van for the past two years. That's why you all got the same backpack, a reminder that this place is not about luxury but rather about finding space within yourself to *feel luxurious*."

She went on, describing the walk she'd taken him on, how he kept commenting on how barren, how desolate the landscape was, how he'd never understood the appeal of the desert. He didn't get why she made it so hard on herself, running a successful career wellness start-up like Stop & Glow from a rusty old camper van in the middle of nowhere.

"These investors," she continued, "they think because they have money you want, you'll agree with them. But I didn't agree with this man. Instead, I told him to lie down on his stomach. Just right there, on the dirt. He was uncertain at first, but he did it, and I did the same. And as we lay there—very slowly—things came alive. First we saw a little spider scuttling along. Then a stinkbug or two, leaving tiny footprints in the sand. When a rattlesnake approached, he almost jumped up, but I told him to just be still. And you know what? That rattlesnake slithered right by us. And soon the place was positively teeming with life!"

She was pacing with excitement now, and Pat found herself getting excited with her. "After about twenty minutes or so, I stood up. And slowly, he joined me. 'I get it now,' he said. That night, he wrote me a check for about four times as much as I'd anticipated." She clutched her hands to her chest in gratitude as the crowd applauded.

"But this isn't a story about winning over the investors. Materialism will get you nowhere. No—I shared my *perspective* with him. I taught him to use his mind to alter his perception of the situation. And that's what I'd like to teach you all to do in this next exercise which I call, simply, the Quieting. I want you to follow me outside."

Brooke led them out of the dining tent, past the yurts, and into the raw desert beyond.

"As you may have guessed, I'd like for all of you to get down on your stomachs. Your task is to lie still and observe. And when I say 'still,' I mean absolutely no movement. With mindfulness this is possible. Each time you move, Tanya will make a mark on your body. At the end of ninety minutes, the person with the fewest marks wins."

Celeste was the first one down on the ground. The rest of the women joined her, their faces solemn masks. Pat followed, envisioning herself rising an hour and a half later covered in marks.

Tanya marched through the rows, a drill sergeant with a paint pen, the kind wielded by used-car salesmen to write prices on the windshields of their vehicles. The women around her squealed as Tanya dabbed them, but Pat stared straight ahead, a sphinx, trying to focus on the mountains in the distance. She wondered what the climate was like up there, if it was as hot, if there were houses, if there was someone inside one of them, gazing out a window toward her.

Her father was always waxing on about the beauty of the desert, trying to get her interested in the plants and constellations, the rocks and bones, but for Pat all it meant was sunburn and fatigue, snakes and angry cacti, or screaming in terror as her father dangled her—age three—over the edge of a canyon while her mother laughed. Her parents insisted this had never happened and she was misremembering, but it came back to her each time she stood at any sort of precipice, that tingling in her feet.

She needed to use the bathroom. She should just get up, she thought. Just forget it all, head back home to Burbank and the familiar comforts it held: Roman, her garden, her cat.

"If you get distracted, focus on what's in front of you," Brooke called out. So Pat did. There was a small rock about arm's distance from her face. She trained her focus on the rock. A fly landed on it, cleaned its little hands, and flew off. A lizard darted by. There was a serenity that came from focusing on these simple objects, so calming, in fact, that Pat became drowsy.

She was startled awake by Brooke announcing that the challenge was over and asking everyone to stand. Shakily, Pat rose and dusted herself. She looked around at the other women. Some had one or two red dots on their skin, others had more. Celeste, standing next to her, had maybe a dozen speckling her tattooed arms and back like a rash. There were even a couple on her forehead. "I guess I was just wiggly today," Celeste said with a shrug and a laugh, though Pat could sense her aura of disappointment. Pat scanned her own body, checking for dots in case she'd moved while sleeping, but found none. "You, queen," said Brooke. Pat realized she was talking to her. "Tell me your name?"

"Pat."

"Pat," Brooke repeated. How strange to hear her name in Brooke Soleil's mouth. "Pat is our winner of this challenge. Congratulations, Pat. Your focus and fortitude will serve as an inspiration for us all this week. You glow, girl!" Brooke clapped, and the rest of the women followed, their applause interjected with yelps of "You glow, girl!" The back of Pat's neck stung with sunburn, her lumbar region ached, but despite the pain, she smiled.

DAY TWO

AFTER THEIR MORNING MEDITATION and Flow Intention Yoga, both led by stone-faced Tanya, the second day was spent performing Mindful Silent Service, which was essentially just chores around the property done in complete silence. Pat was assigned bathroom duty and spent a good part of the day scrubbing and bleaching, attacking the mildewed tiles of the bathhouse with a thick-bristled brush. She'd never been bothered by this kind of work and was grateful to have an excuse not to socialize with Celeste, who was far away in the dining tent.

Later, at the evening Inspo Session, they sat around the fire as the sun set, the sky rioting in pink and orange. Pat's stomach gurgled. Breakfast, lunch, and dinner were glass bottles of

GlowShakes, Brooke's meal-substitution smoothie, sky blue from a type of algae called spirulina. This was not enough to keep her satisfied, and she wondered how any of the other women could be sated by the strange drink. Celeste had tried to sneak in trail mix, but Tanya had confiscated it, causing a stir in the dining tent. The GlowShakes, Tanya explained, were part of Brooke's Depletion for Creation philosophy, or D4C, something she talked about at length in season 2 of her podcast. If you took away the creature comforts you were used to, something new and beautiful would grow in their void. Celeste had snapped back that she was quite familiar with Brooke's teachings and demanded to speak to Brooke herself about the meal plan. Tanya told her that she was welcome to speak to Brooke at the fire circle that evening. In the end, Celeste surrendered her reusable plastic pouch of nuts to Tanya, who tucked it away in her omnipresent Stop & Glow tote. "Sorry about that," Celeste said to Pat after it was over. "I get a little crazy with low blood sugar."

Now they sat in silence, staring at the flames, conversations buzzing around them. "Fires are *so* dangerous this time of year," Celeste said, loud enough for the women in front of them to turn their heads. She went on to inform Pat that a friend of hers had lost her home in Palm Springs as a result of carelessness with a backyard firepit. "Burnt to bits," she said. "Everything incinerated. Can you imagine?" Thankfully, Brooke emerged before Pat had a chance to respond. Pat was embarrassed. Embarrassed for Celeste, who, since she'd failed at the Quieting, seemed unable to refrain from criticizing all aspects of the retreat, but also embarrassed for herself. Surely the other women thought she was aligned with Celeste because of their proximity in age. Then the group hushed.

Brooke stood in front of the fire in a loose-fitting linen smock and pants, her blond hair rippling down her shoulders.

"As you may have discovered by now, this is not a space for the weak. Look at the landscape around you. The great painter Georgia O'Keeffe once said of the desert that it was a place which knows no kindness with all its beauty. Take that in. This is not a spa retreat. I repeat. This is not a spa retreat. Remember, you are phoenixes."

She went on, reviewing her expectations for the next several days. Pat was oddly soothed by Brooke's absolutes, which normally she'd question. But there was something about the landscape, about the fire, about Brooke's purr of a voice that she found refreshing. The land around them that had once felt so empty, so hostile, came alive in the dusk light; the creosote bushes and Joshua trees danced across the hills; the jagged rocks flashed pink in the sunset. For the first time in a long time, it felt like everything was going to be okay. Pat envisioned a new consignment boutique, the rows of garments carefully steamed and hung from racks to be browsed by fashionable types of all ages, the types of people who knew that things just aren't made the way they used to be.

"This next mission is called the Letting Go. I want you to take a moment and reflect on a hurt that lives inside of you. This shouldn't be a physical ailment. This is an emotional wound. I know what mine is—it's the gaslighting, the cheating, and the general unkindness I dealt with for years from my ex-husband." The crowd murmured. Brooke's marriage, and her overcoming the emotional scars she suffered as a result of it, was a popular Stop & Glow topic of discussion. Pat winced at the mention of the ex, who'd been such a bastard to Brooke. Celeste nodded along, entranced. Pat was relieved. The last thing she wanted was for the woman to embarrass her by bringing up the trail mix incident.

As Brooke went on, Pat located her emotional wound with ease. The day the landlord emailed to let her know that her lease would not be renewed because he was selling the building, resulting in her loss of the store. That failure. And the loss of direction that came with it.

"Bring that pain to the surface," Brooke said. "To the skin. Then show Tanya where it is."

Tanya approached, carrying a small, zippered pouch (branded). From it, she pulled a contraption that Pat didn't recognize.

"She can't be for real," Celeste whispered to Pat. "I don't see what getting a tattoo from Tanya has to do with anything we're supposed to be getting out of the boot camp."

So the contraption was a tattoo gun. In the twisted expression on Celeste's face, Pat saw that she was looking to her for some sort of answer. She had never been looked at in that way before. She'd always been the bewildered one, stumbling into whatever minor successes she'd found in life.

"Scars are reminders of our resilience," she whispered, with a newfound authority. Had she heard that on Brooke's podcast, or had it just come to her, through the magic of the firepit?

"You will be the first," Brooke said, and Pat realized with a jolt that Brooke was pointing at her. She stood and walked to the fire.

DAY THREE

THE NEXT MORNING, Pat admired her new tattoo in the mirror of the bathhouse. Her first. They'd all been given the same one: the Stop & Glow logo, of course. The lines were a crisp black on the pinkened skin of her left forearm. It throbbed, but it was a good pain. A purifying pain. Celeste said she was going to skip breakfast, that she wasn't feeling so great, but Pat knew she just wanted to sleep in. The smoothies were back, and this time there was a beauty about the uniformity of the women drinking the bright blue drinks, Stop & Glow logos over where their pain had been summoned. Pat felt something like community among them all, a sisterhood, a bond she hadn't felt in a long while. The vibe of the gathering was no longer middle-school cafeteria but instead felt like that of a neighborhood bar, or a party where she knew and liked everyone. A group of women at a picnic table made space for her and she sat down. They were talking about the Pyre, tomorrow's ritual.

"You bring an object that symbolizes an obstacle and throw it into the fire," said Priya, a gaunt Indian woman in an army-green boilersuit sitting across from Pat, gesturing with her hand to the distance beyond the dining tent. "My friend did it last year and said it changed her life."

"Brooke is so daring," said the sunburned girl with a nose ring (Jess? Jessie? Jessa?), who looked far too young to be involved in anything entrepreneurial. "Like, no one else would do something like that. It's just so inspiring to be here." The others at the table nodded, and Pat found herself nodding along with them.

Priya turned to Pat. "So, where's your roommate?"

"I'm not her keeper," Pat said with a shrug.

Priya nodded, a smirk on her face. "Did she end up getting the tattoo?"

Last night, Celeste had refused to receive the tattoo—totally silly, in Pat's opinion, since she had so many already. What was one more? Brooke had sat her down on the stool and firmly asked her *Why?* Why wasn't she ready to let her pain go? And then, when Celeste had angrily stood, nearly knocking the stool into the fire, and run off into the dusk, Brooke had used the experience as a "teachable moment" about the importance of knowing what your boundaries were in order to push through them.

"No," sighed Pat. "I suppose she's just figuring out her boundaries." The table nodded approvingly.

"I really don't understand why someone would invest in an opportunity like this if they weren't completely ready for the challenge," said Jess-Jessie-Jessa. "She's acting like a BOB."

A "BOB," Pat had learned, was what Brookies called a person outside Brooke's fold who was critical of her teachings. An acronym for "beast of burden." Someone who was too loaded down with their own baggage to fully participate in life. Who kept their mind closed when it should be open. ("Like horses. *Neigh*-sayers, get it?" Brooke had quipped on an episode.)

"We're all on our own paths," said Priya. "Some of us just have more brush to clear."

"Season 3, episode 5!" exclaimed JJJ, referring to the podcast episode that Priya had borrowed the idiom from.

"Did she give you guys samples of her fragrances?" the stout, olive-skinned woman wearing a Stop & Glow T-shirt whispered to the group. Her tattoo peeked out from underneath her right sleeve.

Priya nodded and held her nose as the rest of the table descended into giggling fits.

That was when Pat saw Celeste entering the tent in a pair of Cookie Monster–blue combat boots, sunglasses on, hair tousled with sleep. She saw Pat too and came and sat down at the table. She smelled of a strange perfume, something sharp and almost rotten.

"So," Celeste sneered, a fake smile on her face, "what have we all learned about leadership so far?"

Priya snorted. JJJ raised her eyebrows.

"Why are you here?" Priya spoke defensively, as if Celeste were an infiltrator, a BOB.

Celeste was unfazed. "I'm here for the same reason we all are," she said, and sullenly sipped her smoothie.

"It's okay if you're not ready," said JJJ. "It's an intense program."

"I know Brooke is kind of eccentric in her podcasts sometimes," said Celeste, "but this all feels a little cult-y."

Priya shook her head. "No offense, but you have no idea what you're talking about."

The table was silent, until JJJ chimed in: "What Priya means is that you should trust the process," she said.

"Pat, can we go for a walk?" said Celeste.

Pat didn't want to go for a walk. She wanted to stay in the dining tent, talking about Brooke. Celeste was a dramatic person, and lately she'd been trying not to associate with dramatic people. Roman was always saying she cared too much about other people's problems, that she should pay attention to her own life. Boundaries, he said. She needed better boundaries. She stood anyway and followed Celeste out.

"I'm so embarrassed," said Celeste. "Brooke has her own way of doing things, but I thought this would be team building and networking. Tell me I'm not overreacting."

"You're probably still adjusting," said Pat. "Give it time."

"So none of this is weird to you?" The woman reeked of desperation.

"Well, yes, but not in a bad way," said Pat. "I think I needed to be shaken up a little bit."

"I don't know," Celeste said, staring down at her hideous boots. "I'm starting to not feel like myself anymore here. It's strange."

"That's a good thing, right?" said Pat. What was the point of self-improvement if you left feeling the same?

"I'm not so sure," said Celeste. "And you seem different too."

"You don't know me," said Pat. It came out harsher than she'd meant it to, but it silenced Celeste for the rest of the walk to the morning Inspo Session.

* * *

DURING SUNSET, THE FIREPIT had been majestic, but now, in the daylight, it was scorched and sad. Pat wondered if maybe Celeste had a point. But then Brooke appeared, resplendent in her earth tones and a floppy straw hat, and everything seemed to fall into place once again.

"Today we begin with an exercise called the Reclamation. This is a guided meditation, so get comfortable. Start by closing your eyes."

Pat had tried meditation at the urging of Roman, who'd sworn by it ever since he quit smoking. He had a little pillow and everything. But she could never get past her own body, could never focus on her breath. Her brain always went elsewhere, to her to-do lists, to memories, to all the other useless detritus that builds up in a mind over the years. But today she followed Brooke's instructions with ease.

I want you to imagine a body of water.

Pat pictured a generic tropical ocean. She was fairly certain it had been the default desktop wallpaper on an old computer of hers. The ocean swished in and out. The air was balmy.

Now that you've spent some time in this place, I want you to begin to wander through your own memories. Flip through all the moments of guilt in your life the way you'd flip through an old photo album. You are seeking your Root Guilt, the earliest and strongest memory of guilt.

There was a brief text flirtation with Jeff, Roman's work buddy, that had led to nothing, but she'd thought about it for weeks. There was the fact that she hadn't spoken with her elderly parents since the store closed, had ignored their calls and emails. There was the lot of Lilly Pulitzer dresses she'd bought off a grieving daughter at an estate sale for a fraction of what they were worth; there was the film studies paper she'd written in college after only reading synopses of the films. The general guilt that she felt for being a straight, white, nondisabled, upper-middle-class woman when there were so many others who didn't have the opportunities that she had, and what did she have to be glum about anyway? Further and further back.

And then the tropical air of the beach chilled; the ocean at her feet became a frothy suck. Pat was back on one of the annual camping trips to Big Sur with her family—that one trip, the one that Celeste's perfume had brought back to her. They'd always driven through fogbanks on their way up the coast, which made it feel as if Big Sur were in some alternate dimension, far from the heat and dust of Tujunga, where she lived with her family.

On those trips, her parents and their friends would pitch tents and let the children run wild through beaches and redwoods while the adults got high, threw back beers, and became teenagers again, shirking any responsibility foisted upon them by parenthood, society, et cetera.

The beaches were wild too—water frigid and choppy, with the constant threat of riptide sweeping you away. Despite this, the children shivered and shrieked in the waves, built sandcastles, scaled rocks, pelted one another with slimy kelp fronds, and collected shells from along the shore.

Pat would spend these beach days roaming with the girl closest in age to her: Judith, who lived in Oakland and whom she only ever saw on these summer trips. The two wreaked havoc on the ecosystem of the ocean: smashing open mussels to feed to eager sea anemones in tide pools, building seagull traps out of buckets and driftwood, and creating hermit crab obstacle courses, a cruel game that involved yanking an unlucky crustacean out of its chosen home and setting up a maze of small rocks between it and the shell.

Then, the summer when they were both twelve, a new girl appeared: Frankie, the daughter of some friend of Pat's mother's who'd joined the trip that year. Frankie was just a year younger than Judith and Pat but acted as if she were in kindergarten. She was timid and frail, always shivering in her swimsuit, and had a host of allergies that she liked to remind them of at random intervals. She believed in things like fairies and ghosts and Santa Claus. Pat and Judith resented her immediately but let her hang out with them to appease Pat's mother, who was blind to the injustice of saddling the girls with someone so uncool and immature.

So they made an unspoken pact to make her time in Big Sur as miserable as possible, in the hopes that Frankie would never come on one of these trips again. They stole her diary from her tent and performed dramatic readings of the parts about her crush on her classmate Vince Mahoney. They pretended to speak a secret language that only they knew, while Frankie looked on, helpless. They told her fibs of all sorts: that Judith was dating a high school boy, that Pat's cousin was Scott Baio, that they'd seen Bigfoot stalking the campground at night. But Frankie stayed easygoing, never complained. Just laughed, as if she hadn't the faintest idea that these pranks and fibs were happening at her expense.

One day, while digging a moat system around a sandcastle they'd built, Judith began spinning one of her tales to Frankie, this one about how if you dug in the sand deep enough, you'd come out in China.

"Liar!" Frankie accused, but Pat and Judith insisted, holding back their giggles as Frankie's eyes widened at their details of all the many species of giant snakes, monster worms, and crabs the size of VW Bugs you'd find on your way down there.

Finally it was decided that to prove it, they would dig. They armed themselves with the best of the plastic shovels and buckets, sweating and grunting as they worked, bailing out the water that filled the hole so that it wouldn't cave in. Below the sun-warmed surface, the sand was damp and cold and full of wriggling gray sand fleas whose bites stung Pat's feet and legs as she flung water out from the hole.

"Hey Pat," shouted Judith from above, "ever wanted to know what it's like to be buried *alive*?" Before Pat could stop her, she dumped a bucketful of sand on her head. Frankie followed suit, kicking sand into Pat's face, shrieking and giggling.

"Quit it!" Pat shouted back, and spryly vaulted out of the hole. "You guys are bitches," she said, shaking the sand from her damp hair.

"*I* want to be buried," squealed Frankie. "It's my turn now."

"It's gross down there," said Judith, clearly tired of the hole. "Plus there are giant crabs that will bite off your toes."

But Pat, irritated that Frankie had so gleefully gone along with Judith's sand games, saw an opportunity for revenge. "Sure," she said. "Get in."

Judith shot Pat an annoyed look as Frankie climbed into the hole. They shoveled in silence until Frankie was nothing but a tiny, wet-haired disembodied head on the beach.

Pat couldn't remember what excuse she'd come up with, but for whatever cruel reason they'd left Frankie there, screaming in protest, to go explore the tide pools.

When the shadows began to change, Judith asked Pat if maybe they'd better check on Frankie. Pat sighed and consented, and they left the pools and the anemones behind. The beach looked different when they rounded the cliff's edge. The tide had come in.

Judith splashed across the shallow water, screaming Frankie's name. Pat stood there, suddenly chilled, realizing what they'd done. She imagined jail doors slamming, her parents refusing to speak to her ever again, the look of horror on Frankie's mom's face. She ran into the water after Judith, who was crying now, and dove under, feeling around for any evidence but only grabbing fistfuls of sand and broken shells.

Eventually they made the solemn decision to tell parents, and the campsite descended into panic. At some point the coast guard was called. To Pat this was all a swirl of horror and guilt, as she sat clutching a sobbing Judith's hand.

Then who should saunter up to the campsite but Frankie, who, as it turned out, had wrested herself free from the hole moments after the two of them had abandoned her and gone to search for fairies in the nearby forest.

For four hours, Pat had lived with the knowledge that she was a killer. It weighed on her. It still weighed on her, in fact, after all these years. That, and the cruelty of the prank. The beach trips were never the same after that. Pat cocooned herself in the tent with her paperbacks while Judith roamed the campground with the older girls, looking for boys. Of course, Frankie and her mother never returned.

Now I want you to see this Root Guilt from another angle. See it in a positive light. See it in an empowering light. How can you turn it into something useful?

Pat reviewed the scene she'd recalled. The moment she'd realized the tide had rolled in, that dark feeling that she'd done something irreversible. She stuck with the dark feeling for a moment, turning it over in her head. The power that came with doing something permanent to someone else. In her life, she'd had so little power, so little control, it seemed. Nothing like the power she'd had that day at the beach.

Open your eyes.

All the women wore complacent smiles except for Celeste, who glared at Brooke.

"Beautiful," said Brooke. "I could really sense everyone's energy. I want you to take that energy and carry it with you into all aspects of your existence. Guilt is a natural feeling, but once we learn to overcome it, anything is possible. This power is what I want you to keep in your Soul Well for the rest of the week. I want you to think about all you've learned so far about sacrifice and reclamation. There will be more challenges, but I know that you are up to them, phoenixes. The goal is self-actualization. My mind knows, my heart shows, my self glows. Say it with me."

The group did as they were told.

As the women were leaving the firepit, Tanya put a hand on Pat's shoulder and told her that Brooke wanted to see her. Pat followed her, casting a glance back at Celeste, who stood, hand on hip, the same pissed-off expression still on her face.

"Pat," said Brooke, taking Pat's hands in her own and clasping them. Pat felt a stir, something deep within her awakened. "Will you join me for a quick check-in?"

They walked away from the firepit, into the desert, Pat matching Brooke's relaxed gait. Tanya followed several yards behind. "I want you to know that I've really valued our time together here, and I think you're a very special person," Brooke finally said. Pat's feet tingled with nerves. Her palms clammed up. Had she done something wrong? Was she being kicked out?

"Thanks," she said, carefully.

Brooke stopped and turned to face her. Her beatific glow seemed to darken; her expression fell and hardened into something cold. "What I'm about to tell you is very serious. This is a small group, and one person's negative energy is contagious. Your bunkmate, Celeste, how well do you know her?"

"I don't," said Pat. "Not really." The relief!

"The incident at the Letting Go, which you witnessed, alerted me that something was not right about this individual. Then Tanya caught her following me back to my camper van. This happens sometimes, at these intense sessions. People lose their path. Sometimes they even become BOBs, talk to journalists, spin lies meant to discredit Stop & Glow's mission." At the mention of journalists, her face twisted into a look of disgust. Then she looked into Pat's eyes, and her radiance returned. "But I'm hoping you, Pat, can guide her back. We're halfway through this time together, and the last thing I'd want is for Celeste to come away with a negative retreat experience. Can you do that for me?"

"Of course," said Pat, returning Brooke's warm smile.

"Thank you," Brooke said, and clutched Pat's hands again. "I can see your Soul Well is deep and full. I'm so grateful the universe brought the two of us together. I can tell I have much to learn from you."

Then Tanya stepped between them and signaled that it was time to go.

* * *

AFTER MINDFUL SILENT SERVICE that night, Celeste was morose, curled on her cot like a petulant teen. The Santa Anas were blowing through, and the canvas yurt bucked and creaked in the wind.

"My mother called the Santa Anas the devil winds," Pat said, hoping to break the toxic silence.

Celeste only sighed in reply.

"What is it?" said Pat.

Celeste sat up on her bed and turned to face Pat. "I can't anymore. The tattoos? The smoothies? Let's ditch and get some real food. Maybe these kids can handle them, but they're doing a number on my stomach."

Pat wrinkled her nose at the mention of stomach issues, which she preferred not to talk or think about. Celeste was still looking at her with that pleading desperation in her eyes. It grossed her out, in complete honesty. The codependence of it all. Glow Time was not a place for codependent women. It was the same disgust she'd felt for clingy, sniveling Frankie all those years ago. She summoned up the power she'd felt at the Reclamation and seized the opportunity to direct Celeste back to the path.

"You really should just trust the process," Pat said. "I mean, we all ended up here for a reason, right?"

"You *would* say that," said Celeste, chilly now. "She's chosen you, God knows why, but she has."

"You shouldn't have followed her," said Pat. "It's creepy."

"I don't think she lives in her van," said Celeste, ignoring Pat's accusation. "How does she shower?"

Pat rolled her eyes. "Probably in the bathhouse, same as us."

"But have you *seen* the van? I mean besides in pictures on her Instagram? If you were in a camper van, wouldn't you park walking distance from the bathrooms?" Celeste went on like this, as if Pat weren't even there. There was, Pat realized, no persuading this woman, and as she let her prattle on with her half-baked conspiracy theories, her annoyance turned to anger. Celeste needed to shut up.

Outside, the wind howled, snapping the canvas. Something clanged in the distance. Pat imagined the yurt collapsing on them both, a rod impaling Celeste. That would solve this problem.

"Maybe we'll all just blow away," Celeste finally said and was quiet.

DAY FOUR

CELESTE WAS NOT IN HER BED when Pat woke to the gentle toll of the wake-up bell. She'd probably gotten an early start and was trying to avoid Pat after their talk last night. Pat checked the showers—no Celeste. She showered and amped herself up, wiping the condensation off the bathroom mirror to look at her reflection. She was tan and svelte: a rugged heroine. She'd been using the Set Your Intention Facial Serum, and her skin glowed with health. Her body was powerful now, elevated to more than just the slab of meat she punished at the gym five days a week. It vibrated with excitement, as if it anticipated the coming self-actualization.

There was still no Celeste at breakfast. Or at meditation. When she didn't show up to Flow Intention Yoga, Pat became worried. Had she defected? Followed Brooke again? She arched into a downward dog, sank down into plank position, and sprang into an upward-facing dog. Her gaze drifted across the desert. Celeste was out there somewhere. It was up to Pat to find her, wasn't it? To lead her back on the path. That much Brooke had made clear. Brooke depended on it. Stop & Glow depended on it.

When lunchtime came, Pat dropped two of the glass-bottled smoothies into her pack when Tanya wasn't looking. As the group scattered to perform their Mindful Silent Service assignments,

Pat went back to her yurt and outfitted herself in her sunglasses, a windbreaker, a silk Chanel neckerchief, and the ugly moisture-wicking sun hat that Roman had insisted she bring with her on the retreat. Then she slipped off across the desert.

It didn't take long for the retreat center to shrink to a dollhouse on the horizon. Pat felt small out there, a speck against the land. The wind had picked up again, and bits of sand stung her face, so she took shelter under an outcropping of rock. She sat there for what seemed like hours, listening to it howl around her. Had Celeste hitched a ride? Stolen her cell phone back from Tanya and called an Uber? And what had she meant, saying that Brooke had chosen Pat? Surely the woman was jealous of the connection that she, a new Brookie, had made.

When the wind died down, Pat set out again. Before long, Touchstone Retreat Center had disappeared completely. She looked at her compass and out at the mountains, trying to orient herself. Celeste had likely gone toward the road, which was east of them. She could do this: growing up she'd often been the one to route her parents back to the trail when they wandered off. She was scaling a small hill of boulders when she heard it—that dreaded percussion. There, staring right at her, was a rattlesnake. Pat backed away from the serpent, in her panic dropping the compass, which skittered down a small crack in the rock.

She froze against a boulder, wishing she could sink into its cool mass. She squeezed her eyes shut. When she opened them, the snake was nowhere to be seen. Though she was still trembling with panic, Pat managed to hoist herself up to the flat top of the rock, hoping to get a better view of her surroundings. But it was as if the road had never existed.

Perhaps all of this—the wind, the snake, the compass mishap—was some sort of test orchestrated by Brooke. Pat was starring in one of Brooke's Inspo Sessions, that's what was happening. She stared at the sun, half expecting to see the letter *S* inside. She laughed to herself, giddily, as she climbed down from the rock and walked in the direction she was sure the road must be. The group would love this story. She'd find Celeste soon. She had to.

DAY FIVE

THE SUN WAS SO, SO HOT. Pat couldn't remember it ever having been this hot before. She'd spent last night lying at the foot of a boulder, using her windbreaker as a pillow. Her entire body hurt, and with only a quarter of her water bottle left, the GlowShakes long gone, she wondered if she was a dead woman. She refused to let that happen, though. She had the blazing sun to guide her, and her Soul Well to nourish her. She was sure she could get back to camp on foot.

Her bare arms stung with sunburn, but it was too hot for her windbreaker. Her tattoo was sore, crusted over with something pale and gritty. She was exhausted, a wrung-out washcloth, though Brooke had said that was to be expected, hadn't she? That connecting with one's inner self was a tiring process. A soul workout. The Reclamation had been quite the soul workout. She felt stronger, lighter, leaner without that guilt inside her. She was powerful. There was no room for guilt anymore. Just the present.

The bushes all looked the same: dried out and unwelcoming. She felt like she was walking on a treadmill through the landscape, like time had stopped. A treadmill. She fantasized about the climate-controlled utopia that was her gym, with its AC blasting, enabling her to run endlessly, to turn on Brooke's voice in her headphones and let it flow through her as she exerted herself. *My mind knows. My heart shows. My self glows.* She recited Brooke's affirmations as she trudged on, their cadence punctuated by the rhythm of her boots on the sand. *My mind knows. My heart shows. My self glows. Mymindknowsmyheartshowsmyselfglows.*

Had they noticed she was gone? Were they looking for her? Would she perish out here? Was she even still living? The only proof she had was the soreness of her joints, her dried sweat hardened to a shell of salt on her scarf. Her parched throat. She took another tiny sip of water. How would she know when she was actualized? She smelled a campfire somewhere; perhaps she'd find some helpful campers who could guide her back or, better yet, give her a ride.

Dust coated her army surplus store canvas boots, and she wondered if this was how soldiers in Iraq felt. She was a warrior too. Roman had told her that there was a marine corps base around here. That they'd constructed mock Iraqi villages, and even hired actors to play villagers for simulated attacks. Did soldiers also feel the power of taking lives? The clean pop of a gunshot, the thud as an enemy fell in the dust. Again she felt the surge of energy she'd accessed during the Reclamation. That moment from her past, once dripping in shame, would become her Soul Well, her energy source. It propelled her forward so that she almost stumbled over a ledge. At the bottom of the ledge was a field of Joshua trees. Could she use one for shelter from the sun, at least until it grew a little cooler? And then she saw it: sitting against one of the Joshua trees was a figure.

She scrambled down, slipping on the loose sandstone, creating rivulets of rocks and dirt with her boots. Though she considered herself to be in good shape, her ankles were not used to this kind of exertion. The trees were black, except for places where their bark had peeled off, which were bone white. The air was still and funereal. Whatever fire had come through had left the desert greenery standing but dead, a forest of dark corpse-trees on the pale dirt. The entire valley was silent, devoid of life, except for the seated figure in the distance.

When she came nearer, Pat was both surprised and not surprised at all. "You left," she said to Celeste.

Celeste looked up at her through those glasses, reflecting Pat's own haggard silhouette. Her face was scuffed with dust, reddened from the sun. She smiled, grimaced really. "I took your advice," she croaked. "I trusted the process."

"Here," said Pat, and reluctantly held her water bottle out to Celeste. Celeste held her hand up, refusing the offering.

"I trusted the process," she repeated, "and the process is bullshit." She spat on the ground, leaving a dark spot on the sand. It looked like blood. "I think my ankle is broken."

Pat's ears rang with rage. No, alertness. Her anger made her more alert, more present.

Celeste looked past Pat at the sky. "Those dragons need to fuck off," said Celeste, speech slurred.

"You're hallucinating," said Pat.

"See for yourself," she said, gesturing upward with her chin.

And that was when Pat saw them. The vultures, circling, waiting. They seemed to know something that she didn't.

"Celeste," she said. "Come on. I think I know the way back to camp." This was a lie.

"No way. I'm not going back there. I'd rather live in the sand now. Be one with the rocks. You know, I found her house." She leaned her head back on the spiny tree. Somewhere, an animal screamed.

"Brooke's house?"

Celeste gave a sober nod. "I was right. The van thing is bullshit. She lives in this giant mansion with a pool and everything. I'll bet you can see parts of it if you go through her videos."

"So?" said Pat. "Who cares? We all tell stories from time to time."

"Don't you get it? If she's lying about this, who knows what else she's lying about? That serum? Vaseline with cooking herbs sprinkled into it. The face spray is tap water with a few drops of witch hazel. She's full of shit is what she is, Pat! I know it hurts to lose something, but wouldn't you rather know the truth?"

"I haven't lost anything," said Pat, rage simmering to a boil.

"Help me up. We've got to tell everyone. We'll find a road. I'll post it on all the Brookie forums. They deserve to know." Celeste leaned back on the Joshua tree, exhausted.

Pat was about to deliver a piece of her mind, but she restrained herself. Instead, she readjusted her pack and began to walk across the scorched field, away from the hysteria. She couldn't handle this drama right now. But what if Celeste was right? She pushed that thought away and refocused. Pat was no BOB. She would return, she would tell Brooke that Celeste was a lost cause. Brooke would praise her for making the effort.

Breathe in, breathe out, step in the dirt, imagine yourself actualizing, how free it will feel. Her breath and footfalls filled her ears, until she became a machine, all parts working in sync. And what was the body after all but a machine? Or was a machine like a body? It boggled the mind: the processes inside us that all just happened whether we wanted them to or not. We didn't even know what they looked like. Mind-boggling that the whole red mess of ourselves didn't just exit through our orifices—which had been what she'd thought was happening when she got her first period, thanks to her mother's failure to talk to her about her body's inner workings.

The shadows were changing now, the distant mountains becoming more grandiose in the contrast of the afternoon light. How many steps had she walked? How would they ever find her? Speaking of shadows: there was another one, another slouching figure in oversized sunglasses. Another Celeste. Pat's first thought was that she'd walked in a circle, but this was impossible. She'd been walking toward one mountain peak the entire time—westward, the sun was heading that way.

She knew what heatstroke could do, so she decided to ignore the fake Celeste. But as she walked past, a hand gripped her ankle, sending her toppling downward. She rolled over and surveyed the damage: the sting of gravel on her lower palms and a bloody knee where she'd caught herself. Her Pradas had somehow managed to skitter from her face and she'd fallen on them, crushing the frames.

"What the *hell*?" she spat.

"Sorry," said Celeste. "Take mine." She held her sunglasses out to Pat, who took them, warily, and slid them on. The lenses were smeared with dust, the frames light and cheap.

"I know what you want," said Celeste in a low voice. Her face had grown gaunt and skeletal, the skin under the eyes droopy and quivering, as if a single tug would rip the whole epidermis from the flesh. Her white tank top was filthy and drenched in sweat. She stank of something feral.

"What?" said Pat. "What do I want?"

"Control."

Pat eyed a jagged rock near Celeste, small enough to pick up with one hand.

"I don't know. . ." Pat began. But she did. She did know.

"Help me," pleaded Celeste. "We can help each other. We can tell the truth. People are grifted all the time. It's the American way. We'll be forgiven for believing."

But Pat's mind was radio static. All she could see was the stone in front of her, the black trees looming above. She wrestled the rock out from the ground, its underbelly cool against the palm of her hand. She raised it up over Celeste's head with some effort, her wounds stinging in the dry wind. A bestial cry erupted from somewhere. The vultures? Or some other animal? The screaming dominated her ears until she could hear nothing else. *My mind knows, my heart shows, my self glows.* She brought the rock down on Celeste's head, again and again and again and again. The screaming stopped.

She began to dig, using the rock to help her loosen the gravelly dirt. As she dug deeper, the dirt became finer and finer until it turned to sand and she could clear it with her hands. The hole kept filling with water, which Pat bailed out with cupped palms as best she could. Strange, she thought, this much water in a desert. Then she rolled Celeste's body into the shallow hole and covered her up.

She couldn't be sure how long she sat there. She must have slept at some point, because when she woke, the sun was setting and she could hear the trills of shorebirds somewhere. The vultures were gone, and up above her, looping in the fading blue sky, was a seagull. In the distance came the unmistakable hush of waves crashing. She stood, running toward the noise.

Her knee ached, her wrists stung, she was sure she looked like a complete maniac. That didn't matter anymore. Where was this energy coming from? A salty wind licked her face as her feet pounded the damp sand. The ocean was so close. She would throw herself into the frigid sea, wash the filth off, and emerge renewed, actualized.

Then everything seemed to flatten, and she was back in the desert. What had sounded like an ocean was a highway. The sea breeze vanished, and the hot, dry gusts picked up again. She collapsed on the shoulder, panting. Her hands and arms were covered in Celeste's blood, brown and thick. She wiped them with her scarf as best she could, finally letting the wind carry it away.

A car engine sounded in the distance. With the last bit of her energy, Pat stood, holding her hat aloft. As the car came closer, she saw the lights on top, the mirrors. She'd hailed a highway patrol car. The officer was a white woman, about her age. She pulled her aviators down to get a better look at Pat. "You part of that group that was out at Touchstone Retreat Center?" she said.

Pat nodded, mute, dizzy with nerves. The officer continued to stare for a few fraught moments. Celeste's blood was smeared all over Pat's shirt. She zipped up her windbreaker, knowing she was done for.

But instead of cuffing her, the officer told her to get in the back seat and help herself to some bottled water. "I'm headed that way," she said. "There was a fire. Wiped out nearly the whole place. Luckily they contained it before it could spread, but I guess there are some people that aren't accounted for. There's a burn ban for a reason. It's a tinderbox out here."

Dozing in the AC, sipping from the tiniest of plastic water bottles, Pat listened to the officer chatter on about fires, invasive species of grass, her own heroics. She caught a glimpse of herself in the rearview, Celeste's glasses obscuring her dusty, sunburned face. She was untouchable, all-powerful, a phoenix. She was actualized.

CLEAN HUNTERS

Emily was ten years old when she saw her first ghost. It was 3:00 AM and she was in the kitchen of Michelle Beach's house, rooting through Tupperware and yogurt containers in the fridge, searching for the foil-wrapped plate of the sleepover party pizza that she'd watched Mrs. Beach put away earlier in the evening. She'd woken up with a roaring hunger. (Later, she'd learn to recognize these hunger pangs as a reaction to an otherworldly presence.) The house was silent save for the humming refrigerator and the gentle crinkles of the plastic tarp that hung over an unfinished wall—the Beaches were remodeling their kitchen.

She found the pizza plate behind a Pyrex casserole container and stealthily lifted it out over bottles and jars, Jenga-style. If any of the girls woke up, they would tattle in two seconds, she knew it. She set the plate down on the counter and gingerly pulled open the foil, her breath quickening with the thrill of the transgression and the anticipation of the congealed cheese's salty tang in her mouth. She held a slice in her hand and was about to take a bite when she saw her, standing at the kitchen table: about her mother's age, hair pulled back in a scarf, frowning. Her gray skin reflected moonlight, though the room was almost completely dark. Her pupils were the silvery phosphorescent sheen of a cat's eyes.

The slice of pizza she'd been holding hit the floor with a gentle thud as Emily ran back to her sleeping bag in the living room, leaving faint footprints of drywall plaster on the parquet floors behind her.

Time passed. It wouldn't be till she was a lonely teenager that she would share this experience, in a chat room devoted to paranormal encounters. She would click on a link that someone posted in response to her story, which would take her to the CleanSpirit listserv. CleanSpirit for clean hunters: practitioners of holistic ghost hunting, a response to the proliferation of EVP recorders and other electronic paranormal investigation devices that clean hunters believed muddled the experience of being in a space with a ghost. If you could turn your mind into a reader, make yourself the medium, like in the old days, then the spirits would reveal themselves. Clean hunting required a daily meditation practice and abstaining from caffeine and alcohol. Emily was drawn to it for its simplicity, its honesty.

The screen would become a glowing beacon of inclusion as she fought through the isolation of high school and college. It would be the place where she learned how to do what she did best, and where she'd meet Gabe, whom she'd eventually marry, who was in the passenger seat of their rented Prius now, scrolling through his phone and reading the National Weather Service's report about the storm that was projected to dump a foot of snow on the little Connecticut town they were currently driving toward, where they'd be spending their honeymoon.

She wondered aloud if they should turn back.

"Are you joking?" he said, looking up from his phone.

"I just don't want to get stuck up here."

"We won't get stuck. These projections are usually wrong anyway."

"If you say so," she said.

Gabe went back to his phone. Emily pushed her foot down on the accelerator and watched the LCD numbers tick up to seventy, eighty. The brown trees on either side of the highway became a muddy blur. This was what they'd left Los Angeles for. The landscape was hostile, she thought, ugly. Dead and cold and brown. The Dixon Inn had been Gabe's idea. The boards, both clean and traditional, had raved about the paranormal experiences at the old inn. Emily had wanted to go to Venice, or Paris, or Cancún. But Gabe had convinced her that this place would be special, would be different, and so she'd conceded. The moment the plane took off from sunny Burbank, she'd felt the dread gathering in the pit of her stomach.

Gabe had stopped looking at his phone and was shoving handfuls of the overpriced kettle corn they'd gotten at a rest stop into his mouth, chewing loudly.

"Want some?" he said.

The idea of the treacly puffed kernels turned her stomach. "No."

"Are you PMSing or something?" Gabe said. "Because that's cool. I can handle that."

Emily sighed. She wished she could be an easy wife, the same bubbly creature she'd been when they met two years ago. But lately, it felt like something in her had been shaken loose and couldn't be put back.

"I just want to get there, is all."

"It's okay." He patted her leg, leaving a streak of sticky popcorn residue. "We'll be there soon."

* * *

LIKE ALL HAUNTED PLACES, the Dixon had its share of lore. The inn was located on the historical grounds of a seventeenth-century Puritan meeting house, where the charismatic reverend Floyd Godwin had led the congregation in outlandish rituals that were said to involve animal sacrifice and bloodletting. Convinced that 1666 would mean the end of the world, Godwin led his flock in shackling themselves to their pews and setting the church on fire in the hopes of fast-tracking themselves to heaven. The site had a particularly sordid history in the 1800s as a brothel, playing host to three different serial killers at various times, each of whom took the life of at least one unfortunate lady of the night during his stay. In 1918, it was where M. D. Rathbone, heir to a railroad fortune, murdered his wife and killed himself after losing the last of his fortune playing cards in the pub, the very same spot where the taproom stood today.

All of these ghosts stalked the halls, rattled the glasses, appeared in mirrors and at bedsides, pinched and pulled and tugged and bumped and otherwise made themselves known. But the most striking apparition was the teenage girl in ripped jeans and a plaid flannel shirt—this was said to be Beth Kentridge, the daughter of a former bartender. Beth had gone missing in the eighties, her mutilated corpse discovered by some hunters in the woods behind the inn a week or two after the disappearance was reported. Some linked the crime to her father, who moved away soon afterward, but those accusations didn't stick. In the years since, restaurant patrons claimed to have seen her in the dim, dingy bathrooms, applying makeup in a reflectionless mirror.

* * *

THE BROWN TREES TURNED into houses, the houses into boutiques and novelty shops. The Dixon, a three-story French colonial structure with a wraparound porch, stood at the end of the shops. Emily parked the car on the street, and the two of them got out and stared at the building. Canary yellow with peeling white trim, it was out of place amid the more subdued architecture of the buildings that stood around it, more New Orleans than New England. From where she was standing, it seemed to list to one side.

"Does that look level to you?" said Emily, pulling her coat tighter around her.

"It's an old house with quirks," said Gabe. "Ghosts love that shit."

She squeezed Gabe's warm hand with her cold one, and they proceeded up the steps that way. Inside the bar on the first floor, the bartender and several rosy-faced patrons were staring at the television, watching a basketball game.

"Hi there. We're the Montezes. Checking in," Gabe said.

"Hang on," said the bartender, and turned back to the television. He and the patrons cheered as a player landed a three-point shot.

Gabe nudged Emily. "Authentic."

"Very," she said.

While they waited, Emily assessed the bartender, wondering if he knew Beth Kentridge's father. He wore a faded black polo shirt tucked into jeans, and a hat with a team logo on it that she couldn't place. He took a sip from his beer.

At the commercial break he disappeared through a door behind the bar and returned holding a key.

"Room 11. Third floor. Two hundred bucks for both nights," he said. Gabe held out a credit card. "Wi-Fi's out for the weekend, so don't bother."

"I hate how they always assume we need Wi-Fi," Emily said, as Gabe dragged her suitcase up the narrow, creaking staircase.

"I'm sure they get loads of city-slicker asshole tourists here asking about it," said Gabe.

"Isn't that us?"

"No," said Gabe. "We have a reason to be here." He unlocked the door.

As far as Emily could tell, their room was identical to most of the rooms in the rural roadside inns that ghosts seemed to favor. It was small and square and painted an institutional beige, a queen-sized bed with a patinaed brass headboard taking up most of the space. A single window overlooked the town's main road where a truck clattered by, shaking the room and sending a pen rolling off the nightstand and down the slanted floor. Emily tested out the mattress while Gabe opened and closed dresser drawers, jittery with pleasure. He'd done this a thousand times, opened and closed drawers in rooms just like this one, but it still thrilled him. He smoothed his hands over the top of the dresser and ran them over the wall, turned the faucets on and off in the bathroom.

"Come here," Emily said, sitting up on the bed and wriggling out of her coat. Gabe stepped out of the bathroom and held up a finger, indicating for her to be quiet. His eyes fluttered shut and his breathing quickened.

"Oh my God," he said. "Em. They're everywhere." He opened his eyes.

"Can we do this later?" said Emily.

"You can't feel it?" he said, putting his hand to the wall.

Emily closed her eyes and let her thoughts fall away, one at a time. All she felt was a rumble from another passing truck. "Maybe?" she said. "This room is just really loud. Do you think they'd let us switch?"

"No way," he said. "This is the hub, I know it. I'm not taking my chances."

"I guess I just need a little more time to settle," she said.

He sat down next to her and took her hand as the mattress groaned beneath their weight.

"Of course, babe," he said, and kissed her lightly on the lips. "This place is the real deal, I can tell. Trust me, you'll feel it soon if you don't feel it now."

Emily felt sick. "Why don't we go walk around town before the snow starts?" she said.

"You go," he said. He'd closed his eyes, and he had a serene smile on his face—he'd started hunting already. "We'll meet back here for dinner."

Emily tried to stifle the frustration she felt welling up inside her. It was their damn honeymoon. Couldn't he lay off the ghosts for two seconds? But she knew that if she'd felt anything, she would have gladly sat beside him with closed eyes and let the icy tingles of the spirits wash over her.

On the staircase, she gazed through the window that faced the woods where the Kentridge girl's body was found. A shudder went through her, but she couldn't tell if it was spectral or just her own reaction to the idea of slowly bleeding to death in the woods.

* * *

THE AIR HAD a heavy, damp feeling to it, and already Emily knew she'd dressed inadequately from the way the cold penetrated her neck and fingers—a coat, yes, but no scarf, hat, or gloves. She crossed over to Main Street, hoping to find a boutique that sold knitwear. She passed a discount liquor store, a nail salon, and an antique shop with a jumble of furniture and knickknacks hastily stacked against its dusty windows.

She stepped inside, hoping to detect ghosts lingering around an old photograph or some ancient toy. Wind chimes tinkled as she pushed the door open, and an older woman with wild white curls poked her head up from behind the boxes of junk that surrounded the register. She gave Emily a brief smile before plunging back down into whatever it was she was doing.

Emily wandered through rows of bureaus, desks, and hope chests. There was an entire section devoted to kitchenware of yesteryear: glass mixing bowls, china teacups, hand whisks, two dozen sets of decorative porcelain salt- and pepper-shaker figurines in the forms of various animals. She thought of the West Elm dinnerware set from her registry in her kitchen back home and wondered if it would end up somewhere like this, decades from now.

There were books piled in the back—moldy old tomes with brown spots on the pages and covers falling off. Maybe there was some spirit here, among them. She'd heard of it happening before, on the listserv. It was more common with diaries, but occasionally an inscribed copy of a novel or collection of poetry was revealed to have a spirit clinging to it. Emily felt nothing but the soft, decaying spines beneath her fingertips.

She let her mind drift back to the party at her coworker Mara's, the last time she'd made contact. A Valentine's Day party, nearly a year ago now. She was finishing up in the bathroom when it had hit her. That unmistakable hum, that faint vibration, that intense hunger. No water came out of the sink's faucet when she turned it on to wash her hands. Pulling aside the shower curtain to try the one on the tub, she saw an old man, seated with his bony gray knees drawn to his chest. He stared at her with those empty, silver eyes. She stared back, holding his gaze, feeling the tingling that came with being in the presence of his kind. A knock startled her and she broke eye contact for a brief instant. When she looked back at the tub, he was gone. The water began running from both the sink and the bath.

In the Uber back home she told Gabe what she saw, and he told her, holding her hand, that he had sensed something, too.

"But I didn't see him," he confessed. "You always see them."

She'd felt a glow of pride then, akin to the feeling she'd gotten as a girl after beating a boy in a footrace at recess.

"It just takes practice," she told Gabe.

"I don't know," he said. "I think you're a natural. I'm jealous."

"Stop it," Emily said, nestling closer to him as he played with her hair.

"It's true. I just hope it rubs off on me."

* * *

HAD SHE KNOWN it would be her last sighting, she would have stayed in that bathroom longer. Even in places where people with the tiniest bit of Sense could feel it—Suicide Bridge, Union Station—Emily drew a blank. They became backdrops that she whisked by on her way to wherever. She hated the injured way Gabe looked at her when she said no, she didn't feel it. She knew these denials made him lonely, led to the funks of self-doubt that plagued him from time to time. So Emily had started doing what she thought was the right thing to do as a wife, as a partner: she pretended.

She pretended at the open house in Atwater—the former home of Shelley Martin, who'd put rat poison in the coffee of her abusive husband and hid his body in the garage deep freeze for three years until some curious neighbor kids hoping to steal ice cream discovered it. Gabe and Emily had posed as prospective buyers and spent ten minutes in the garage, doing their breathing exercises, until the realtor chased them out.

"His rage was so potent," said Gabe, giddy with the thrill of contact.

"Such an angry man," she agreed. "I've never felt an energy quite like that." But really, Emily had felt nothing, just the vague chill of the cool concrete.

She pretended at the ruins of picnic table #29 in Griffith Park, where they sat on a blanket in the dark, waiting for the ghosts of the lovers who'd been crushed by a tree mid-coitus to make themselves known. ("They want us to leave," she'd finally told Gabe, when she'd had enough of the mosquitos draining her blood.)

She pretended at the Culver City restaurant turned laundromat where a mob boss had been assassinated; she pretended in the courtyard of the Los Feliz apartment complex where the actress had fallen and broken her neck after a night of drunken revelry; she pretended on the staircase through the Echo Park hills that was said to be haunted by an eight-year-old who'd died of smallpox in a nearby orphanage over a century ago.

It was too easy. She'd been through enough hauntings and read all the books. She was careful to always let him feel the spirit first, and then embellish on his sighting—and he never questioned her. What she was doing, Emily knew, was breaking the most revered rule of clean hunting, but her marriage was worth it. The community was worth it. She had seen how the ones who lost their Sense were ostracized, left off certain threads, and eventually forgotten. Surely this was just a phase.

* * *

SHE STOPPED AT A SHELF of nineteenth-century medical books and lingered over a heavy volume full of anatomical drawings, some in color, featuring graceful braids of muscle inked in delicate reds and blues. Whose bodies were those? How did they die? The medical profession was a haunted one. The listserv insisted that you never saw old ghosts in cemeteries—grave robbers had long ago pilfered their bodies and given them over to medical schools at universities and private practices in exchange for reward money. When she turned to a page with a diagram of a teenage girl's body, she shut the book.

Snow was beginning to fall by the time Emily stepped out of the antique shop, and for a moment, she felt the way a regular vacationer must feel—aimless and calm, with a desire to wander and explore. She popped her collar, slid her hands into her pockets, and continued on down the sidewalk, away from the inn. As she walked, the snow came down harder and harder, the flakes cold and wet on her scalp. The houses were spaced farther and farther apart until the sidewalk ended abruptly and there was only the shoulder of the road and the dead-looking forest, but she kept walking, her boots crunching in the thin layer of white that had accumulated.

She should be with Gabe, she knew, drinking hot cider, watching the snow fall, cuddling in the creaky bed. But Gabe had chosen the room, the ghosts. She imagined him there now, scribbling down his sightings in the leather-bound notebook she'd given him as a birthday present. Didn't distance signify trust? And wasn't trust the ultimate expression of love?

* * *

THEY'D BEEN SEEING EACH OTHER for several weeks when Gabe disclosed to Emily what he'd had to sacrifice for clean hunting. He'd discovered the forums his freshman year of college, when he was trying to find an explanation for the disembodied whispers in his room and that deep-seated animal instinct that someone was watching him. He came across the CleanSpirit listserv and knew instantaneously that he'd found his people. As the weeks passed, he became so involved that he stopped going to class, preferring instead to seek out ghosts around campus. By the end of his first semester, his parents had taken notice and the doctor visits had begun; he was prescribed meds that turned his days into a hazy blur.

Gabe continued to lurk on the forums, but the Sense-dulling pills made finding the spirits a challenge. For five years he lived like this, until he received a message from Emily, replying to an old post of his: she had also experienced the cold spot in the Glendale Galleria food court, and did he want to grab lunch sometime? It wasn't long after that that they began hunting together. Once he had Emily to confirm that what he was seeing was real, Gabe's pills became unnecessary. "You saved me," he said after he'd told her everything, as they lay entwined on her mattress in her old Echo Park apartment. "I'm free."

He stopped speaking to his parents after that, a decision Emily supported. Skeptics had toxic energy—better to remove that element from your life. In Emily's case, she'd decided early on to keep things to herself, and had spent her adolescence like most girls she knew: trying to stay off her parents' radar. It was easy to do when her older sister, Clara, angsty and mercurial, was constantly getting nabbed by mall security for shoplifting. Emily never shoplifted, and she kept her grades up. She went to movies with one or two similarly well-behaved girlfriends and was home by curfew. These girls knew about her crush on

Sam Moretti, and they knew about the time she'd stolen a can of her father's beer and gotten tipsy, but they knew nothing about the apparition of the young boy that materialized at the foot of her bed at 11:24 PM every night, knocking a one-armed GI Joe doll against her bed frame. This she saved for the boards, detailing the rhythmic thuds of the plastic against the wood. *His way of trying to talk to you*, said the listserv in response. And with her parents focused on disciplining Clara, Emily had no trouble peeling out to explore the neighborhood in search of new hauntings to bring back to the boards. They'd tell her she should lead ghost tours or become a medium. They heaped praise on her, even came to her for advice. *Your abilities are exceptional*, they'd say. *Brava. Tell us more!*

* * *

SINCE THE NIGHT Gabe had revealed his past to her, Emily had felt love, but also an intense responsibility. Pre-Gabe, her intimate desires were just another need to fulfill, a drink of water on a hot day. To satisfy this need she would occasionally fool around with Noah from HR, or wiggle her way into a pair of control-top tights and sit alone at the bar sipping bitters and soda until someone—anyone—took interest. But once she and Gabe were together, all that was over. Guys like him, Emily felt, didn't come around very often, and when Gabe had proposed on the pedal boats at Echo Park Lake one autumn weekend afternoon, she'd thought: *What else can I say?* The two of them had only been dating a year, had only just signed a lease on their tiny one-bedroom apartment in Eagle Rock. And they were young: twenty-four and twenty-five. But her parents loved him; her friends loved him. And most importantly, she finally had someone she could share her sightings with—not just a handle on a message board but a living, breathing person. "When you know, you know," everyone said.

Now she wasn't so sure what she knew.

The daylight was fading fast, and soon Emily would have to make her way back to the inn in darkness. The trees thinned out again, giving way to snowy fields. Checking her phone, she realized she'd been gone for well over an hour. She approached a diner, the light from its blue and pink neon sign turning the snow to rainbow sherbet, and felt an intense craving for a hot drink and some french fries. Cravings were good signs—could her Sense be coming back? She pulled open the door and was greeted by a middle-aged woman with tightly gelled curls and pink lipstick.

"Sit anywhere you'd like," she said, showing off her clear braces when she smiled. The place was empty except for a withered old man in sunglasses at the counter, hands wrapped around a coffee mug. Emily sat a few seats away from him and ordered fries and a hot cocoa.

The cocoa was a travesty—dehydrated marshmallows bobbing in a slurry of tepid water and half-dissolved powdered chocolate mix, but the fries were hot and crispy and scalded her fingers and tongue. Losing herself in her hunger, she dunked them, three at a time, into a blood-red pool of ketchup. She pulled her phone out of her pocket. One text from him and she would turn back, get a car to take her through the weather to the inn. There was nothing. Her fingers left greasy smears on the touch screen as she scrolled through her work email, looking for a distraction. By now Gabe was probably holding court with Beth Kentridge's spirit, asking her what it was like to die. It really was a sick habit, their ghost hunting. You became attuned to tragic places, a divining rod for the violence of the past. Would it be so horrible to leave it all behind and take up knitting?

But she knew she never could. What would it do to Gabe?

She finished the fries and ordered a slice of apple pie à la mode, despite the growing ache in her stomach telling her she'd had too much. The waitress took the empty basket away and replaced it with the steaming pie and vanilla ice cream, which Emily began to devour methodically, one forkful at a time. The old man at the counter, she could sense, was staring at her through his sunglasses, waiting for her to do something that could lead to a conversation. That was one sense she still had, at least—but she ignored him and continued shoving the dessert into her mouth. When she caught his eye again, he picked up a fork from the counter and softly tapped it against his mug. Clink, clink, clink.

She stopped eating and stared at him, remembering, with a little chill, the way the ghost boy had tapped his doll against her bed. *His way of trying to talk to you.* Could this finally be another sighting? Had he been here all along, this spirit, waiting for her to find him? His skin was a map of delicate lines and folds mottled with liver spots. She searched for the telltale phosphorescent eyes, but his sunglasses revealed only her own anxious reflection, hair disheveled from melting snow.

The waitress was folding napkins around the silverware that had just come from the dishwasher. She paid no attention to the clinking, which was growing progressively louder, just kept wrapping forks, spoons, and knives, humming along with the song on the radio. Almost as if she couldn't hear him.

What was it he was trying to communicate?

Just when his clinks grew so strong it seemed he'd chip the ceramic, the waitress spun around and laid her hand on top of his. "Dad, will you give it a rest?" she said. He dropped the fork, frowning.

She turned to Emily, rolling her eyes: "Dementia. My sister was supposed to take him but she bailed, so I had to bring him to work with me again—didn't I, Dad? Because Stacy cares more about her poker game than her family."

The old man shook his head slowly.

He was no ghost. Not yet, at least.

"You need anything else?" asked the waitress.

"No, just the check," Emily said, tossing her napkin on her plate.

* * *

SHE'D HAD NO IDEA how dark the woods got in this part of the country. She trudged down the shoulder of the road toward the inn, guided only by the wan yellow circle of her phone's flashlight. Cars honked as they drove by. Snow was getting in her boots, and she leaned over to scoop it out.

If she were to fall into a snowdrift and never come out, would she haunt Gabe? Would Gabe even try to find her ghost? Or would he meet someone else on the listserv—a taller, blonder, thinner version of Emily who would take him in her arms and comfort him and not need to pretend to see ghosts? The two of them would sit together with serene smiles on their faces, as she and Gabe had so many times before, meditating, attempting to reach entities beyond death, to prove that there was something larger than their sad, simple lives.

She could see the lights of Main Street in the distance. She'd make it after all.

* * *

EMILY SQUEEZED HER WAY through the Dixon Inn taproom, roiling with noisy patrons, and up to the third floor. She paused outside their room. It was dark under the door, which meant that Gabe was mid-séance. She pushed it open and slid into the room, silent as a phantom.

In the dim glow of the streetlamp that shone through their window, she could see Gabe's silhouette. He was in lotus position, perfect posture, measured breathing, so lost in concentration that he didn't flinch when she came in. He looked like the Buddha statue in her mother's garden.

She slipped out of her coat and boots and sat down next to him on the bed, its creaking springs disturbing the silence of the room. She closed her eyes and let her breathing slow, listening to the sounds of the bar through the crooked floor, the hiss of the cars driving through snow on the street outside. Gabe placed a hand on her thigh.

"Do you see her?" he whispered. "She's here. She's looking straight at you."

Emily opened her eyes. The glass of the TV screen glinted in the darkness, but that was all.

"Yes," she said. "I see her. She's beautiful."

REAPER RANCH

APRIL 23

TODAY IN GRIEF GROUP, Nurse Gale gave us all notebooks and told us to write journal entries to our dead. Well, Lee, here goes: James and Rebecca, our James and Rebecca, the children we fed and bathed and loved for so many years, have finally done it. Sent me to live at Roeper Ranch. Reaper Ranch, as you call it. "I hope I die," you always say—you always said, I mean—"before I end up there." Ha.

It's only temporary. If it doesn't work out, I can go home, so they say. Like they are doing me some grand favor. I suppose I should be grateful.

I am here in my prison cell, listening to the sink drip. I told maintenance about it when they helped to move me in, and they came by to fix it, but it started dripping again right after the man left. You'd think that in Arizona they'd do a better job repairing a wasteful leaky faucet. I have the radio cranked up to the classical station, but I can still hear the little drips.

Thankfully they allow cats. Zinnia is here with me. She was sulking for the first week or so but has now made herself at home. Would that I were so adaptable. She sleeps on your side of the bed.

The ranch is named after Faye Roeper, a philanthropist whose husband made his millions in silver mining. He left it all to her when he died, and she opened this place, Roeper Ranch: A Community for Independent Senior Living. It's not a ranch at all, but there are plenty of ornamental iron horseshoes and other equine embellishments throughout the property. Her daughter Erin—a real headmistress type, you would hate her—runs the place now.

My hip aches. That's why I'm here. They say I'm lucky I didn't break it when I fell. They say I'm lucky that Lucia was coming in to clean that morning. She found me there on the kitchen floor thirty excruciating minutes after the chair I was standing on gave out from under me and I went down clutching the mason jar of loose tea, which shattered all over the linoleum on impact. I lay there, paralyzed with pain, inhaling the earthy scent of Earl Grey. The phone was on the wall less than two yards away. I would give myself five minutes, I decided, and then I would attempt to move. Every five minutes, I slid a little closer. I began to wonder why I was even bothering. At the moment that I was praying for something to happen—fatal heart attack, a plane to crash into the house—Lucia came in, screamed, and called the ambulance. And that was that.

They'd already taken the car from me after a minor fender bender involving a stop sign, and now they've taken the house as well. All in the name of my well-being, they claim!

The ranch makes a big production for the families here. Move-in day is always Sunday, when they have the best meals—brunch complete with an omelet station and lasagna for dinner, so the kids can feel less guilty about ditching their folks at this place. The rest of the week is supremely mediocre. Remember that cruise we took to Baja? On the cheap (as was our way, Lee, always thrifty)? That's kind of what it's like around here. Except instead of booze to pacify us, we're given weekly ice cream socials.

My Sunday night Grief Group is one of the many weekly activities that one can participate in here at Reaper Ranch. There's been a spate of deaths recently, more than usual, according to the folks in the group. So Nurse Gale, a newer staff member with what you'd call pep, volunteered to host this Grief Group. It's something to do. Hazel from the first floor goes with me. She's one of the few real friends I've made here. A little granola for my tastes—a result of spending the seventies living with hippies in Los Angeles.

In addition to Grief Group, I have my water aerobics on Tuesdays and Thursdays. Mondays I have my Lifelong Learners class on Great Books. There's a van to church on Sunday mornings, if I feel like going (which, if I'm being honest, I often don't), and Friday is movie night but the movies they show look dreadful so I haven't been to one yet. I'd much rather sit with Zinnia in my lap and watch the comet. Oh yes. That's new. Showed up a couple of days after I got here. Comet Jansen-Ito. I have the kids' telescope and can see it from my balcony. It looks like God smudged a star. You would have loved it—you always got excited about beauty in the sky, dragging me out of the house to look at sunsets, meteor showers, cloud formations, even the hawks that would glide over our backyard.

What else? I've been here three weeks now. Friends came to see me. Blake and Maybelle, Pete and his new wife, whose name I can never remember. They acted strange, like they felt sorry for me. They smile and they laugh, but I can read their thoughts on their faces: Poor Grace. I can't stand it when people feel sorry for me. So I've been spending most of my time alone, with this drippy sink and the popcorn ceiling that I stare up at and think about how it will probably be the last ceiling I stare up at. Why did you have to be the one to leave first? You got off so easy. But they say I'm the lucky one.

APRIL 30

BOB FROM GRIEF GROUP HAS DIED. Nurse Gale said it was fast, in his sleep, the way we'd all like to go. He was like me: he'd lost his wife of fifty-three years a few months back. He didn't talk much, but no one blamed him. He mostly just sat in the group's circle of chairs, nodding as the women broke down in tears talking about their deceased husbands.

Nurse Gale was chipper about it, taking sips from a leopard-print travel tumbler that I'd watched her fill with Mountain Dew from the soda fountain at dinner, explaining to us that death was something we should see as an opportunity to learn a little more about ourselves. Ever since Nurse Gale mentioned it, I've been asking myself: What is it that I've learned? I'm not sure. But Nurse Gale has some interesting notions.

Outside of the group, we say nothing about the deaths. I can't say anything to James or Rebecca. That's just what happens to old people, Mom, they'd say, and talk behind my back about how worried they are about me, but never actually do anything.

Kids are supposed to be helpful. Well, not ours. I don't know what we did wrong. It was your brother Bert who helped me after you left. Came all the way out from Massachusetts. He helped me sign the paperwork, divide up the clothes, all the mundane tasks that had transformed into Sisyphean boulders. I was disoriented, and Bert helped right me. But of course he couldn't stay forever. He made me promise to call him and check in, but I can't bring myself to do it.

Also, there's forced socialization here. It's a little fascistic. For your first month, at every meal, you are supposed to try to sit with someone different. And so I met Hazel, and Robin. Tova, one of the few residents who has a car and can still legally drive. Rick and Jean, who came here together, voluntarily. Imagine!

Everyone has stories about their old lives. Jean was a schoolteacher, taught kindergarten in Reno for four decades. Robin owned a jewelry boutique in Taos. Hazel was a hairdresser to the stars in LA. Tova immigrated here from Tel Aviv and was a legal secretary.

"What did you do, Grace?" they all ask, in that sad past tense.

I tell them that I worked for the public library.

"Oh," they say, "a librarian!"

"No," I correct them, "I was in development."

"Ah . . ." They trail off, and the conversation ends, because no one really knows what that means.

It's good that they force socialization, because otherwise I'd spend meals making sculptures with the food on my plate. I mean, that's what I do anyway, but at least I have company. I guess it's healthier to pick at food while watching a table of geriatrics shove lukewarm hush puppies down their gullets than to spend meals staring at the sparrows outside the window, mashed potatoes turning to cold spackle.

I can't get too close, though. Bob's death is number six in as many months. Poor Bob.

MAY 1

I SEE YOU EVERYWHERE. You are shuffling into the dining hall, your back turned to me, wearing the newsboy cap James got you. You're dozing in an armchair in the library, the Daily Star on your lap. But I get closer and it's not you, it's just another resident, a stranger with the same broad shoulders, the same leisurely stride, like they have all the time in the world. And the sunsets. My God, the sunsets remind me of you, who used to make me stop cooking to come out to the backyard to watch that big orange ball sink into the Tucson Mountains. My windows face those same mountains, except I'm close enough that they're crisper. I watch as the jagged rock formations on their faces turn orange, then pink, and finally purple black.

Our things are all gone. There was some convoluted system in place: I was supposed to label what I wanted to keep in storage, what I wanted to get rid of, and what I wanted to bring to Reaper Ranch. "All you need is a Sharpie and some sticky notes!" they barked at me over the phone. "It's not that hard." I walked around the house holding the Sharpie and the damn sticky notes for an hour, looking at the life we'd built. I couldn't bring myself to peel a single sheet from the pack. I put some clothes and photo albums in an old suitcase, some of the houseplants in a box, and told the movers that the junk haulers would deal with the rest. Better to get rid of it all, I thought at the time, than to live with your ghost hanging around all the souvenirs.

Of course, the kids found out. Of course, the kids were mad. Through what I'm sure amounted to at least a dozen frantic phone calls, Rebecca was able to rescue some essential pieces of furniture: a shelf, the dining room set, the bed. She also managed to save the heirloom steamer trunk—your grandfather's—that we used for storage. Among other odds and ends, it held the telescope I now use to stargaze. The rest went to the dump.

After the move, Rebecca booked a flight out here. "I'm concerned about you," she told me over tea. "What's with all the self-sabotage?" How is one supposed to reply to that? I told her I didn't know what she was talking about. She disappeared for an hour, and returned with bags from Target. Silently, she unpacked them. Beige and taupe throw pillows. A hideous goldenrod-and-navy-striped rug purchased, she said, to dress up the dull gray carpet. A framed black-and-white poster-sized print of a saguaro. Dozens of other cheap, generic tchotchkes, which now live on various surfaces in my cell. She did manage to put a few photos in frames, though. One is of us at our wedding. You're wearing your tan fedora that the wind later swept off your head on the ferry during our honeymoon in Vancouver. The photograph hangs on the wall near my front door, where I can look at it before following the slow trail of geezers leaning on walkers to dinner.

It's spring and it's been four months and eleven days since you left this world. If you were here, we'd be grilling salmon on the patio, watching the jackrabbits and roadrunners scamper through our yard.

MAY 6

HAZEL WAS WALKING ME BACK to my room today when Nurse Gale stopped us in the hall. To my shock and horror, she hugged me, reeking of patchouli and rubbing alcohol. She and Hazel traded small talk about their gardens, the weather, the Diamondbacks. I had nothing to add on any of these topics, so I just watched until Nurse Gale said she had to finish her rounds and told me to remember to let her know if I needed anything because she had Erin's ear. She gave her unadorned earlobe a tug and winked at me before she ambled on down the hall.

"Anything you want," said Hazel, after Nurse Gale was out of earshot, "she can get it for you. Anything."

I am still not sure what that means.

Hazel told me that Nurse Gale is a fascinating woman, that she used to work as an international humanitarian aid nurse before she started working in senior living facilities.

When I came into my room, there was a gecko on our wedding portrait. I don't know how on earth it came in, seeing as I'm on the third floor. It's still there. Zinnia is sitting on the carpet, tail flicking, staring at it. I've called maintenance. Hopefully they come before she decides to take care of it herself.

MAY 11

IT'S HALF PAST THREE in the morning. Zinnia woke me up howling at the sliding glass door to the balcony. I pulled the blinds aside, thinking that perhaps some animal had climbed up to the third floor, but there was nothing there. I stepped outside, Zinnia on my heels. The nocturnal chatter of the nightjars and tree frogs seemed louder than usual at this hour. Jansen-Ito was bright in the sky, pulsing almost.

Hazel got in trouble with the management here. Absolutely ridiculous. They found her cannabis gummies, and since she doesn't have the proper paperwork, they took them away. She said they asked her where she'd gotten them and she refused to tell them. Now there's a flyer on the bulletin board outside the dining hall about the dangers of unprescribed meds.

MAY 13

IT'S NIGHTTIME THAT'S THE LONELIEST. After dinner, when I can hear my neighbors on either side of me watching TV. And that damn dripping sink. I refuse to become one of those dotards who are addicted to that glowing screen. Instead I try to read for my Great Books class. We're reading Shirley Jackson's The Haunting of Hill House, which I read long ago, though now it is not nearly as unsettling as I remembered it. Perhaps now that I've borne witness to so much death, ghosts are less intimidating. The reader is supposed to question whether the spirits are real or just figments of the character's imagination. Such a dull question. What's the difference, in the end?

I write in this when I am too tired to read. Talking to you helps me sleep, and I only hope that it will bring you to me in my dreams, darling Lee. But it seems I've stopped dreaming. I guess I'm stuck in the real world for now. How dull.

MAY 14

THIS MORNING, AS I WAS LEAVING for breakfast, I noticed that our wedding photo had gone missing from the wall! I have not been able to find it and am quite concerned. Did someone take it? Why would they want a photo? How would they have gotten in without keys? Could it have been maintenance? So very strange.

(The drip, by the way, has quickened to a dribble. I put my watering can under it and use the drippings to water the plants.)

MAY 15

LET ME TELL YOU ABOUT HAZEL. Hazel is the girl at boarding school most likely to have cigarettes. Hazel is the one you call when you want to get blotto and forget about your life. Hazel is the friend your other friends worry about and fuss over but are secretly jealous of. Hazel is the voice that says yes, kiss him, yes, take that, yes, one more drink, yes, I'll go. Hazel is pure id.

She has maybe two pictures of her family in her room: one of her parents, and one of her kids. The rest are photos of her when she was younger, usually with celebrities. She ran with the Factory crowd in New York City and later, in Los Angeles, opened a high-end salon.

She offered to do my hair. "This place is like college," she said as she massaged conditioner into my scalp. "A bunch of strangers living together, sleeping with each other. Except instead of dreaming about what we'll become, we dream about what we became."

Then she started asking questions about you. How long were we married? How long were you sick? How was I holding up?

I told her about us, about your decline, about how empty I feel without you. I told her about the missing wedding photo. At this she was quiet. I was afraid I'd said too much, that perhaps I'd crossed a line with her, that she no longer respected me as a sane person.

"Did you ever consider that he may be trying to reach you?" she said. Then it was my turn to go silent. Finally, I said that no, I hadn't considered that. She asked me if I ever wished I could talk to you. I said yes, all the time.

She said she knew how to make that happen, and that I should come by her room again on May 30—the next full moon.

My hair is hard and sticky, but it looks good. Hazel does makeup, too. "Next time you've got a big date," she said, "come to me." I laughed pretty hard at that one. I haven't worn anything besides lipstick since your funeral. As I was leaving, she gave me a hug and told me how glad she was that I'd come to the ranch. It surprised me, her kindness.

Now I am alone, missing you, missing our home, staring at the sun setting over the Tucsons. At least I have them. Zinnia is running around the room, pouncing on invisible mice, forever a kitten. I am listening, again, to the televisions' murmur on either side of me: the musical stings, the laugh tracks, the muffled voices. Why is a sunset making me cry? Why aren't you here? I miss you, Lee. I need you. Are you trying to show me that you're watching?

I tied a string around the faucet today, and that has stopped the noisy drops.

MAY 21

GRIEF GROUP TONIGHT WAS ODD. Nurse Gale got angry, which is unusual. During share session, Norah mentioned that she was considering leaving Roeper Ranch on account of all the deaths here. Nurse Gale cut her off and told us that removing ourselves from the community we'd formed was a terrible idea. That we'd all come so far and needed to stick together, and that Norah was being melodramatic. Norah flushed and looked as if she were about to cry, and then, because it's Grief Group, two other women started bawling. Nurse Gale softened and apologized. Sometimes, she said, she lets her emotions get the best of her. We were all taken aback, since we'd never heard her raise her voice.

Despite her behavior tonight, Nurse Gale seems to be the only one who really, truly cares about the residents—no one talks to us the way she does: like we're human beings.

MAY 23

TODAY IT RAINED. Water aerobics was canceled because of lightning. I could see the cracks of light split open the sky from my window. Remember when we taught the grandkids how to tell how far away the strikes were? Watch for the lightning and then count seconds—one, two, three, four, five—until you hear the thunder. That's how many miles away it is.

I worry about them sometimes, the grandkids. They didn't come to the funeral—stayed home with Marlon. Rebecca was between jobs and couldn't spring for the tickets. Plus, she said, they had school. It's been nearly a year since I've seen them. I miss them; sometimes I fear they've forgotten me.

Rebecca called for the first time in forever to tell me that she and Marlon are separated now. They'd been fighting about everything, was how she described it. It was the usual. He felt stuck, wanted to have some time alone. I told her to suck it up, that it was easier to raise kids living with a partner than without, and she (of course) got emotional. Told me that I should be more supportive of her decisions. She didn't ask at all how I was doing.

I almost told her about how you left, once. Just for a night, when Rebecca was a toddler, before we had James. What was it we were fighting about? I don't even remember. Where did you go? I was too afraid to ask. That that knowledge would make it real. (I guess now I'll never know.) But I remember sitting up that night in Rebecca's room, watching her sleep, trying to convince myself that I could do this—raise her alone—if I needed to. I fell asleep like that. When I woke up, you were in the kitchen making coffee. I'm not sure why I just let that go.

MAY 31

WELL, HAZEL HAS DONE her ritual on me. She charged me five dollars and a bottle of Vitaminwater from the vending machines. I know. I know. It's ridiculous. So unlike your practical Grace, right? But, darling, I guess you could say I've grown soft in my old age. Sentimental in my grief. My reasoning: If someone were to hand you a phone and say dial this number, there's a 0.5 percent chance you'll reach your deceased loved one, you'd do it, right? What's the harm?

I helped her switch on about three dozen little electric votive candles (we aren't allowed to have real candles here) and place them around the bedroom. We draped her bed in towels. She shut the blinds and instructed me to lie down on top of the towels and close my eyes, which I did. The room filled with the scent of lavender, and I felt warm oil dribbling onto my forehead. I started, but she shushed me and told me to be still and focus on my breath. She kept pouring the oil, and soon the dribble became soothing and I dozed off. What did I dream? I don't remember. The next thing I knew, Hazel was wiping my forehead with a damp cloth and telling me that my third eye was open. So that's that. I took the elevator down to my room, feeling refreshed from the nap but otherwise pretty much the same.

JUNE 7

IT IS 4:00 AM and I can't sleep. Zinnia woke me up again with her mewling. I am out on my balcony, writing these words in the light of an old camping lantern. The comet is just barely visible on the horizon. I had this urge to be outside. To breathe something besides the recirculated air of my room. For the first time since you passed, I've been having very vivid dreams. (The power of suggestion, or is it actually my third eye?) A couple of nights ago I woke up to the faucet running in the bathroom. Idiot, I thought. You left it on. Wasting water. Dumb old lady. But I felt something—a presence. And because it was late, because I miss you so much, Lee—I called out your name. When I spoke, the presence disappeared, and I went back to bed and did my best to sleep.

The following day I was too exhausted to go to water aerobics. I stayed in my room and tried to read but could not focus. I'm ashamed to admit it, but after dinner I turned on the television and found a nature documentary about undersea creatures. I became engrossed, hypnotized by the gently waving kelp forests and the erratic darting fish of many colors.

I must have fallen asleep. When I woke up, there was a man standing in the kitchenette. I tried to scream but I was frozen. He was an older man. He looked familiar—I'd seen him around. My fear softened to compassion—he'd just walked into the wrong room. But there was something strange about him. His eyes didn't seem to register mine.

"Are you lost?" I managed to say, but it echoed, as if I were talking into a drain.

He looked at me then, his eyes boring into my own. His pupils were huge, leaking out to the rims of his irises. It was Bob. He opened his mouth and blood dribbled out the side, running down his teeth and chin and finally onto the floor. When I got my wits about me, I pulled the emergency cord near the toilet because it was all I could think to do. I returned from the bathroom and he was gone, a puddle of water on the linoleum in his place. The eternally patient man who works the night shift at the front desk came, and I told him it was nothing, nothing. So sorry. He mopped up the floor for me, said he didn't want me slipping and falling.

I told Hazel about the dream and she got excited and said yes, that means her ritual's working. But I'm not so sure. This whole experience has me thinking about my mother when her illness started to take hold. First she thought angels were sending her messages through radio waves. Then she became a bubbly, brainless child. But happy. So happy. Maybe I'll get there soon. Would like to fast-track—perhaps I can request a lobotomy?

I suppose it's good that I'm writing all this down, Lee. They say writing things down helps with memory, and if my mind is truly leaving me, then at least I will have a record. The kids can read it and remember their poor old mother for the prickly bitch she was. Ha ha ha.

I can't help but wish . . . If only it were you that I'd seen!

JUNE 12

TODAY IS JAMES'S BIRTHDAY, so I called him. He's doing fine, as usual. He and Carlos are going abroad for the next few weeks, to Iceland and then Amsterdam. He seems happy. Calm. More together than his sister, but he's not going through a divorce while raising two boys. Poor Rebecca. But then again, she was the one who made the major push to get me to Reaper Ranch after my fall. Perhaps it's karma. If there's anything I'm learning from all that's been happening lately, it's that there are many different kinds of prisons, and I guess I prefer mine over Rebecca's.

Tova is going to drive us to the movies on Saturday. It's been a while since I've been to the movies, actually. Not since before . . . well, that math is getting so tiresome. The before and after. The days since. Sometimes I find myself wishing I could remove that part of my brain that remembers you and just live my life as if we'd never met. I said as much in Grief Group, and we all talked about the idea for a bit. Nurse Gale said that even though we'd each experienced great loss, we wouldn't be the people we were without the people in our lives who'd died. That the purpose of this counseling was not to make us forget but to help us live with that loss, because that's what our loved ones would have wanted. Easier said than done, of course. I'm trying.

I must get ready for water aerobics now.

JUNE 20

IT HAS BEEN A WHILE since I've written. The truth is I haven't been feeling so great. Tired. All I have the energy to do is doze off to nature documentaries on TV. Blood work looks normal. Dr. R. ran some more tests and should know what's wrong by next week.

Perhaps I have what Hazel has. She's been pretty much bedridden with some sort of nasty flu. I've gone down to visit her a few times, but she's mostly sleeping. Nurse Gale is constantly by her side, flipping through a New Yorker or some other magazine as she drinks from her leopard-print tumbler. (Nurse Gale reads! She actually reads!)

I'm hoping to get better soon so that I can go back to my classes. The cell gets so dreary.

Did you know that whales mourn their dead? It was on one of the nature shows I've been watching. Marine biologists have documented ritualistic behavior where adult pilot whales will carry their dead calves in their mouths for days on end. It's quite beautiful, really, the way the water animates the dead calf, makes it seem alive again.

JUNE 25

I HAD ANOTHER ONE of those dreams last night. Again I heard the faucet running. Again I rose from bed. It was Bob. He lifted an arm and stuck out his index finger, his eyes gazing somewhere behind me. Just then, a bird fluttered onto his finger and perched there. It began chirping in high-pitched whistles. I knew, in the way one knows in dreams, that it was a nightingale. I was enchanted, watching its little beak open and close in the strange blue light that seemed to emanate from Bob. Then it flew into his face and attacked him, pecking at his eyes. He put up his hands to block it but it kept flying into him, making tiny bloody beads on his cheeks and forehead. Zinnia woke up and hissed. I tried to move, but I was unable to. All I could do was shout at it to stop. The minute I opened my mouth, both Bob and the bird disappeared. Again all that was left on the floor was a puddle of water, which I diligently mopped up.

The next morning after breakfast, I went to Hazel's room. Nurse Gale sat in the chair next to the bed, giving Hazel a manicure.

"What do you think of this color?" said Hazel. Her nails were lacquered with crimson polish.

"Very classy," I said.

She looked better—her cheeks had a flush to them—but then I realized it was the makeup she was wearing.

"Sit," she said. "It's been forever."

I sat down in one of the chairs next to her bed.

"I had one of those dreams again last night," I said.

"Oh?" Hazel said, raising her eyebrows.

I told her about the dream. Her amused expression sank to something like worry. She told me that perhaps these dreams were omens, that she needed some time to reflect on what the bird meant, but that in the meantime, I should be careful. "With these kinds of things," she said, "symbolism is everything." I watched Nurse Gale as Hazel spoke. She cursed silently to herself as the brush slipped and she painted a dab of red on Hazel's cuticle.

"What do you think, Nurse Gale?" I said.

Her eyes met my own. "I think Hazel needs to rest," she replied, dipping a cotton swab in a bottle of nail polish remover. The sharp chemical smell filled the room.

"You heard the woman," Hazel said.

I left the two of them there like that.

JUNE 31

THINGS ARE LOW. I've been sleeping a lot. Nurse Gale has been by to see me, which is kind of her. We talked about Hazel, who is now very ill, too ill to see visitors other than family. Nurse Gale is the only one I can talk to, it feels like. There's an easy way about her, similar to Hazel's. She's generous. She asks questions. You can tell she's listening. She laughs at my stories. It's nice to have Nurse Gale around.

But Lee, I don't want to go through this again. Hazel must recover. I am fresh off one loss and can't handle another.

JULY 4

I AM QUITE UNWELL. Spoke to both kids on the phone for the holiday. Rebecca said I need to start thinking positive, that she would send me a self-help book she'd been reading, on how to get over the death of your loved one. That's the phrase she used. "Get over." Do you remember when death was something you faced head-on? When my grandfather was killed in an accident in the factory, my grandmother dyed her white summer dress black—I remember helping her scrub the dye rings from her tub. She wore black for six months. Now, we're expected to hold it all in.

But not here. Not at Reaper Ranch, where death stalks the halls. Ha.

Nurse Gale stopped by earlier tonight, a wide smile on her face. She asked me how I was feeling, called me "doll." I told her I wanted to go out and watch fireworks, and she helped me up in her gentle way, wrapped me in a blanket and brought me out to the balcony. I could just make out some tiny sparkles in the distance, and above those, the comet. She told me that a comet's appearance in the sky is called an "apparition."

"Like a ghost in the stars," she said. "Spooky, right?"

I agreed. (Could it be your ghost? No, that's silly, childish thinking. I mustn't go down that road. But . . . ?)

When Nurse Gale was on her way out, I told her about Rebecca, how she seems to have just moved on, forgotten, and expects everyone around her to do the same. Nurse Gale said that our culture has a discomfort with death, that it no longer happens out in the open like it once did. Now it's in hospitals rather than bedrooms. She saw many deaths while on assignment as a nurse in Yemen. Cholera is not pretty. She went on to describe the sickly blue-gray color that cholera victims' skin turns before they die from dehydration. "You have it easy," she said.

Then she whispered to me conspiratorially. "When the time comes," she said, "let me know, and I'll take care of it. No need to turn blue." She hugged me goodbye.

There was something eager, something hungry, about her descriptions of death. I'm not so sure what to make of it.

JULY 6

IT'S BEEN JUST OVER six months. I still miss you, more than ever, but I think I am starting to see that there is a path for me without you. It's not a steady one. There's some boulder hopping. There are rivers to ford. But it's there.

JULY 8

I FINALLY DREAMED about you last night. You were in the bed next to me, and I pressed my body into yours and you weren't in pain. I felt your warmth and your damp breath on my back and you held me tightly, in a way you hadn't done since before the cancer.

I am very weak. Nurse Gale has tasked herself with making sure I take my pills even though I told her I could take care of it. She is a stubborn one. I asked about Hazel, and she seemed to stiffen. Apparently she's now staying with her family in Prescott. Nurse Gale seemed to think this was a bad idea, that Hazel won't get the care she needs there. She got quite worked up about it, actually, so much so that she started cursing. I felt a twinge of fear, then, that this person—this volatile person—is the one responsible for my well-being. She says I must sleep now.

JULY 9

ANOTHER DREAM: THIS TIME, a figure entered my room covered in nightingales, their dun feathers obscuring the face and torso. The birds clung to its clothing and fluttered about, making their shrill whistles. With enormous effort, I opened my mouth to speak. "WHAT DO YOU WANT?" It was like I was screaming underwater. The nightingales fluttered away, fanning me with tiny gusts of air from their wings as they disappeared into the shadows of my dark room. The figure I stared at was my own. My eyes were frantic and bloodshot. I let out a call that was identical to that of the birds. Their whistling grew louder as more of them joined in. When I awoke, Nurse Gale was at my bedside, reading one of my issues of the Atlantic. I was too tired to move. She is still here. I have trouble even writing this now—my eyes keep closing mid-sentence—but writing in this journal has become a compulsion. I fear that I'll lose track of things if I stop. Nurse Gale is watching me, though she is trying to make it look like she's reading. She takes noisy sips through the straw of her tumbler. I wish she would leave.

JULY 14

I AM OUT ON MY CHAIR, writing by lantern light again.

Three point two billion miles away. That's how far away Jansen-Ito is. There's no way to fathom a distance like that. It's a blurring of science and poetry, the way the mind stretches to conceive it.

Perhaps it is my paranoia, but the more I observe Nurse Gale, the more I suspect she has a connection to the deaths here. The sickness that she carries with her; the time I saw her filling my pillbox when I hadn't asked her to and she brushed it off, said that she was happy to help. There's a part of me that wants to keep getting those visits. Because her final one will bring me to you.

But there's another part of me that knows I must persist, which is why I have stopped taking my pills. They can't be trusted. I requested a different nurse. My joints hurt but I am sharper and less fatigued. I will tell the kids tomorrow, tell them to get me out of here.

JULY 15

SPOKE WITH REBECCA. It did not go well. She became livid, said she'd spoken to Nurse Gale herself, earlier. That Nurse Gale had only my best interests in mind, and I absolutely must start taking my pills again. That really, she was doing everything she could with everything going on in her personal life and her brother out gallivanting around Europe like a twenty-year-old. "For once in your life," she told me, "can you think of someone else before yourself?" She said I should think of what an imposition my stubbornness was on her.

The gall, to speak to your mother that way. I don't even remember ever taking a tone with her. James, maybe, he was always getting into trouble. But Rebecca was the good one, a total breeze. Straight As, Princeton, et cetera. She was the one I bragged about. What terror did we raise, Lee?

The sunset was magnificent tonight. Tangerine and deep red, followed by a bruise-purple sky. You must have been putting on a show. I'm too weak to get out of bed.

I never thought I'd be one of those women who pined. In fact, I never imagined it, not vividly, anyway: me without you. I think often of your body those final days. How fragile you were. How you could stand only the lightest of embraces. Your face became gaunt and your eyes took on a crazed look of ecstasy, your teeth clenched in a skeletal grin. "I'm ready," you kept insisting, but I could sense the hesitation in your voice. Your boldness was always a front, some affectation of masculinity passed down to you from your father and his father before him. And I could see right through it. You were terrified, but you didn't say so. You just stared into the middle distance from your throne of pillows, holding my hand in your bony one, all edges and angles.

JULY 16

I WOKE UP THIS MORNING and I was in the passenger seat of a car. Someone was driving me through the desert. Saguaros and ocotillo went blurring by outside. I turned to face the driver and you smiled at me, Lee. You were wearing your floppy fisherman's cap, the one you wore whenever we went on our adventures. You raised your eyebrows and said, "Soon." When I next woke, I was back in bed, Nurse Gale's shiny pink face hovering above me.

"Reaper Ranch," she said. "Funny."

"Reaper Ranch," I repeated.

"Lee was a clever man, wasn't he?" she said.

So she's been reading my journal. I didn't hide it—didn't even think to, in fact. But now, now I know I'm done for.

"I'll be back for you." The way she said it, it felt like a threat.

Soon, Lee, soon.

JULY 20

I WOKE TO A TAPPING on my balcony door. I stood, shaky, leaning on my walker, and rolled over to draw back the blinds. There in the moonlight was Hazel. I flipped on the balcony light and slid open the glass door. She looked healthy, healthier than she'd been in a long time. Her cheeks were no longer sunken, and her eyes had their sparkle back. Even her hair was full and silky. She stepped into the room and pressed a vial of white powder into my hands. "Put this in Gale's water if you want to live to see another day," she said. Before I could ask her anything else, she had walked through my apartment and out my front door. She disappeared down the dark hallway. The vial was icy in my palm. I slid it under my pillow for safekeeping.

The next morning, I woke and searched for the vial, but it was nowhere to be found.

Nurse Gale came by to do her sordid rounds. I thought I was done for until I watched her pick the vial up from the floor by my bed and inspect it before placing it on my nightstand. She seemed relieved, chirping about how she'd been looking for it everywhere. She sat there, babbling on, and I thought she'd never turn her back. But she did, finally, when she got up to use the bathroom. Into her leopard-print tumbler went the powder. Then she came back and took a long drink. It was almost like she knew what was going on.

Not long after, she began coughing and collapsed onto the carpet.

I pulled the emergency cord by my bed. In they all came.

They've put me in a new cell. A bigger one, though there's not the same mountain view. The police have been here for days now. I can hear the static of their walkie-talkies as they march down the hall.

Suicide, they said. The toxicology report said that she'd ingested cyanide. No note, but law enforcement hot on her trail after unexplained deaths in the Phoenix nursing home she'd been at before Reaper Ranch. I didn't correct them. There are times when being a little old lady works to one's advantage.

Yesterday, I asked Erin if I could see Hazel. Her face fell. "Hazel passed away a week ago," she said. She took my cold hand in her warm one and gave her condolences. Lee, I nearly died right there.

Who was that there that night on the balcony? Was Nurse Gale's death a suicide? I suppose, much like the Jackson novel, it doesn't matter so much. Bob is dead. Hazel is dead. Nurse Gale is dead. You are dead. And soon I, too, will be dead. But not that soon!

Oh! The nice fellow from maintenance found our wedding photo. It had fallen behind the shelf.

JULY 31

I WRITE THIS IN the cramped seat of an airplane, flying across the country. Zinnia is in a carrier at my feet, indignant. Bert will pick me up in Boston and from there we'll drive to his farmhouse in Western Mass, the one you and I never did get around to visiting. He has offered to take me in, so long as I help with some of the chores around the house. Worked it out with James and Rebecca. Said he could use the company.

Rebecca has turned her wrath on Erin for employing Nurse Gale. Of course, she never apologized for not believing me when I told her what had happened, but I suppose siccing her lawyers on Reaper Ranch is her way of doing so.

It's funny: you spend your life trying to build a home, a soft, warm place to retreat to. Something permanent. But it turns out there's no such thing. Or perhaps there are many: one in our little house with the view of the mountains, one in that Reaper Ranch cell, and more before that: the dusty craftsman in Pasadena where I grew up, my tidy little dorm room in college, the vermin-infested boardinghouse I lived in when I met you, Lee. Many homes for many different lives. All only temporary.

AUGUST 25

THE LANDSCAPE IS SO very green here, the opposite of the desert. Zinnia is a little pent up—she spends her day staring at the birds out the window. She's not allowed to leave the room, given that Bert's foxhound seems to have a taste for smaller animals. Other than that, things are fine. A quiet that seems even more pronounced since Rebecca and the grandkids paid us a visit last week and, for a short while, the house was full of the noise of family. Now, Bert spends most days in his woodshop while I spend my time reading, or going on walks through the woods. We eat simple meals together in the evenings and he goes to bed early.

I stay up, though. On clear nights, I'll walk out to the front yard and gaze up at the stars. The night sky here has nowhere near as many as Tucson's, but it's better than nothing. Jansen-Ito is long gone now, barreling through space where we can't see it from Earth. I look for it anyway out of habit, scanning the sky for the apparition, searching for your ghost.

VERMILION

The plume was headed straight toward them. Nancy had been monitoring these conditions for days now, had even raised the issue with Tom a week before they left Brooklyn and asked if they should cancel the trip, but he'd waved her off, told her she worried too much. He'd been looking forward to the Potash trip for months and wasn't going to let any wildfire smoke change his plans. As she sat in the kitchen of the unfamiliar house, clicking through the map of southern Utah on her laptop and following the translucent gray blob that had engulfed the entire region north of them, she heard his phone alarm let out a gentle chime in the bedroom. He'd wanted a dawn start to beat any rush at the slot canyon trail they had planned for today. Fine with Nancy. She rarely slept past 4:30 AM as it was. She took a sip of her tea, hot and bitter, and stared at her bleary reflection in the dark window.

"Ready for adventure?" Tom said, stumbling in from the bedroom in his flannel pajama pants and an ancient, faded Mets

T-shirt. What was left of his thinning white hair stood up in chunks. He peered into the fridge.

"I suppose I am," said Nancy. "I'll put the kettle on for some coffee."

* * *

LATER, IN THE RENTAL CAR on their way to the slot canyon hike, the podcast that Tom had been listening to on his phone came on the car stereo. Some authority figure—a cop, no, a park ranger—was being interviewed about a disappearance. Tom loved his true crime podcasts, though he made every effort not to listen to them in front of Nancy. He knew the missing girl ones especially made her uneasy, brought back memories of losing Esme all those years ago. "You didn't lose her," one well-meaning shrink had corrected. "She went missing." This was supposed to take the blame off Nancy and give agency to Esme. What did it matter, though? She was gone. Semantics wouldn't bring her back.

"Sorry," he said, and fumbled to switch over to some music.

"It's fine," said Nancy, her voice firm. "Leave it on." She'd told him, time and time again, that it was fine, his listening to these stories. Even today, on what would have been Esme's thirty-fourth birthday, something Tom may or may not have been aware of. It had to be fine. She was done letting the grief control her world. She would listen to the podcast, and she would be fine.

"Are you sure?" he said, still holding the phone.

"I'm sure," she said. "Just drive."

The host of the moronically titled *Cave Girl Gone* podcast narrated the backstory in her even keel. Her account was interspersed with interviews of the parents and sister of Maxine

Davies, who'd gotten lost in a cave on vacation only to disappear for good a second time, just days after her dramatic rescue.

A picture of the missing was painted: Max was rambunctious. Max was vivacious. She loved the color green and vanilla soft serve. More than once, she was described as "bright-eyed."

"The ugly ones never go missing," Nancy muttered.

Tom said nothing, but she could sense his discomfort.

On their third date, five years ago, she'd told him about Esme and Rafael and the whole disaster, over the coq au vin Tom had cooked for her. Patiently, Tom had listened, his face slowly draining of color. Surely Stephanie, their mutual friend at whose barbecue they'd met, had briefed him on her tragic past. But if he knew, he made no indication. When she was finished, which was the point at which other men would pepper her with questions or, worse, posit theories, Tom took her hand in his own, rough and warm. "We don't need to talk about this if you don't want to." That was when she'd known he was the one.

Thankfully, they pulled into the trailhead, the first car to arrive.

The air was crisp and the spring wildflowers bobbed and dipped in the light breeze, their colors bright against the ochre sand. The crunch of pebbles beneath Tom's and Nancy's boots and the birdsong were the only sounds at this hour.

She walked a couple of yards behind her husband, who had downloaded an app to navigate the trails, though this one was very clearly marked by the footprints of yesterday's hiking masses. Until she met Tom, Nancy had never thought of herself as a hiker. She was a city girl through and through, though now in her midsixties she could hardly be considered a girl. It was Tom who had changed all that, who had changed so much.

Tom was happiest on the trail. He'd disappear for weekends, throw his pack into his RAV4 and drive out of the city, returning with a mud-spattered car and a musky bag of laundry. She'd joined him on one of these excursions before deciding that she was more of a day hiker, that despite her regular attendance at Zumba and yoga classes throughout the week, she didn't have what it took to lug a pack of her belongings over a mountain, to spend nights on a foam pad.

This trip was a compromise. An old college friend of Tom's had a house in the tiny town of Potash in southeast Utah and would be away for a week visiting his son in Los Angeles. Tom and Nancy would use it as a base camp from which to explore the trails in the surrounding desert wilderness.

Tom walked with a slight limp from a knee injury years ago that he compensated for with a set of trekking poles, but otherwise kept a steady pace. At first, Nancy had been annoyed by his insistence on leading the way; they almost never walked side by side, but after a time she'd come to understand that it was just his nature, going first, protecting her. Having been single for so many years, she wasn't used to chivalry.

Before long, the rock walls rose around her, red and smooth, and they were in the slots. The crunch of their footsteps echoed as if they were traversing a castle corridor. They passed under broken branches that had been jammed between the narrow walls, debris hanging from them. Tom told her these came from flash flooding. She knew this fact already, had read about the foolish hikers who hadn't heeded the warnings of the Bureau of Land Management and had been swept away to their deaths by raging rapids. Nancy tried not to dwell on it. There was so much to worry about all the time. It was exhausting. (She'd checked, of course. No rain. They were in the clear.) It occurred to her there wasn't a single other person on the trail—if something were to happen, they'd be goners.

After about a half mile of undulating sedimentary rock, slants of sunlight and cool, deep shadows, mud puddles and air plants and small birds that made their nests in holes in the canyon walls, they arrived at a clearing of sorts.

Tom pointed out the petroglyphs on the canyon wall—mere scrapes suggesting figures, barely noticeable if you missed the sign chastising hikers for leaving marks of their own—and together they marveled. A reminder that the rocks had been around long before and would be around long after them. That suffering, like life, was temporary. Nancy was sure of this and then she wasn't, as with everything in this landscape. The cliffs changed color with the hour of the day. There was no reference point for anything; rocks could be the size of a house or a small dog, depending on how the light hit them and where you were standing. As awed as she was, it made her uneasy, this contextlessness.

She took out her phone and told Tom to pose for a picture. He stuck his poles in the sand and held his arms out, as if trying to envelop the landscape in an embrace. She examined the photo and showed it to him. "Call AARP and tell them you've found their next cover model," he said, and they both had to laugh.

They listened to *Cave Girl Gone* on the ride back to the house. Nancy realized, reluctantly, that she was invested in the tale. The mother spoke about how losing Max helped her find her faith. She and her husband had become evangelical Christians after Max disappeared for a second time, though the host cast this conversation in a skeptical light, as if Christianity were a disease they'd caught. The sister spoke about the strangeness of being lobbed into the spotlight as a young teenager, but also how quickly the spotlight moved away.

There had been no spotlight for Esme. She'd left of her own volition, if you could call it that. Still, Nancy felt, the cops could have done *something.* Perhaps there would have been more attention on her if she'd been younger and bright-eyed, if upon her birth they'd decided to give her Nancy's Anglo last name, Parker, instead of the Spanish Gomez from her father, Rafael. Perhaps if she'd lost the weight Nancy was always going on about her needing to lose. Perhaps if all the recent photographs they'd had didn't feature her in that hideous eye makeup, shooting a wrathful glare at the camera. She was no Elizabeth Smart, no Madeleine McCann, no Max Davies. She was unapologetically Esme; a hot ball of furious teen angst. Still, Nancy knew her daughter wasn't special. Girls went missing all the time and no one did anything about it.

That evening, on her laptop, after checking the smoke forecasts, Nancy looked at the pictures she'd taken that day. She smiled when she came to the shot of Tom and his hiking poles. It was a good shot. But then, a shadowy figure, dark against the tawny canyon wall behind him. It was blurry, but Nancy vaguely made out a woman's shape. She gasped.

Tom, sitting on the other side of the sectional, looked up. "What is it?"

"Do you see that?" Nancy handed him the laptop and pointed to the shape.

"The person?"

"Do you remember seeing anyone out there? There were no cars in the lot."

"She could have come from another entrance," said Tom. "What is it you're suggesting?"

"Nothing," she said.

"Let's go to bed, darling," he said, shutting the laptop and pulling her up from the sofa. "We've had a big day."

As she fell asleep, the blurred image of the young woman danced through her mind. In truth it made her skin prickle just a little bit.

* * *

IT WAS HARD TO PINPOINT when Esme had left, since she'd been in and out of their lives for some time since meeting Jacob during her senior year of high school. At first, Nancy and Rafael thought it was youthful infatuation. Jacob was a decade older than Esme, earnest and slender, with long blond hair that he wore free-flowing over his shoulders and a broad smile that promised the impossible. He was a bike mechanic; the two had met when Esme had gone to the shop where he worked in Gowanus, Brooklyn, to fix a flat tire. They were always hearing things about Jacob—how he'd been on his own since he was sixteen after his parents disowned him (for what, Nancy never learned). How he was thinking of developing a groundbreaking meal delivery website that Silicon Valley investors had taken interest in. His libertarian politics, much to the chagrin of Nancy and Rafael, staunch liberals. He looked like a boy from Nancy's own adolescence, the kind she'd bring home to her mother just to get under her skin. But Rafael and Nancy weren't those kinds of parents. They were the cool parents, the ones who would rather their daughter and her friends smoke a joint on the roof deck of their brownstone apartment—where they were under supervision—than find some darkened corner where they were vulnerable to the cops and deviants.

What Nancy was not cool with was Esme dating Jacob, so much older. Sure, in the brief interactions they'd had, he'd been nice enough, calling her Mrs. Parker, opening doors for

Esme. But to Nancy, something about these antiquated gestures of politeness made him even more suspicious, like he was trying to cover for something.

Soon Esme was spending entire weekends with him, coming home only for brief stints to pick up clothing or take a shower and graze on leftovers from the fridge before rushing out the door, barely uttering a word to either parent.

"Should we say something?" Nancy would ask Rafael as they watched a DVD on the sofa, listening to their daughter move around her room in that frenetic way of hers.

"They're in love," said Rafael. "Let them have their time together." The thought was that this would all be over when Esme went off to Marlboro College in the fall.

All hell broke loose when Esme told her father that she'd deferred her admission and was instead taking a gap year. This was not the plan Nancy had for her daughter. She'd imagined her at peace with the crunchy but perfectly nice trustafarians of the tiny liberal arts school in southern Vermont. Known that nature would do her good, temper her wildness a little bit. Chill her out.

If she was going to defer, Nancy told Esme, she'd have to find her own place or start paying rent. A perfectly reasonable request, or so she thought at the time. But Esme became vicious in the days that followed, refusing to back down. Every night it was another fight between the two of them over silly things: loading the dishwasher; an errant comment Nancy made about Esme's outfit. And then, one July morning, before her parents woke, Esme left. The note said she and Jacob had decamped to the Pacific Northwest. *I'll call when I'm ready. Please don't worry.* That was fifteen years ago. There had been no word from Esme since. Jacob, too, had disappeared. The last transaction on his credit card was conducted on July 22, 2008, at a Comfort

Inn in Arcata, California. Then the trail went cold. Rafael and Nancy had searched, spent fortunes on private investigators, had been to nearly every small town and major city along the West Coast and down into Mexico.

Five years they searched, until Nancy, after much goading from her sister, who was concerned for Nancy's mental health, gave up. Esme, their only daughter, was gone. That was it. She was there, and now she wasn't. But Rafael refused to accept this thinking—her attempt to let go only made him plunge deeper in. This was their child, he insisted, a proclamation that made Nancy furious with its implications: that she didn't care, that she was a bad mother.

He would never let go. He started paying regular visits to a psychic, keeping little totems and talismans around the apartment—Saint Anthony medals, bundles of herbs bound together with an old hair tie of Esme's, clear quartz crystals on every windowsill. When Nancy realized he had not one but three private investigators on retainer, that their joint savings account had been emptied, she knew she had to get out.

Since then, she'd sought comfort in concrete experiences: A well-prepared meal. A warm bath. A feel-good romantic comedy. Solid ground and steady footing. What little religion she'd had was gone—the requirements demanded of faith, of belief, felt too close to the state of uncertainty she'd lived in all those years, waiting for Esme.

Still, there was always that strand of hope that remained, a loose thread that, when pulled, threatened to unravel everything.

* * *

THE NEXT MORNING, neither of them mentioned the woman in the photograph. They sat in front of the picture window in silence, watching the sun play on the red cliffs. Today was the day they'd climb them. Tom insisted the trail was moderate, with plenty of switchbacks to lessen the climb. Nancy was uncertain. She wanted to do what she'd seen other women her age doing in town—shopping for turquoise, looking at landscape photography and paintings by local artists in the galleries on Kolob Street. But that wasn't why they'd come. They'd come to explore. They'd come to commune with nature. And Nancy, personally, had come to exert herself so much that she wouldn't have the energy to dwell on her tragedy. She tied her bootlaces tighter.

The day couldn't have been more perfect. No smoke, just puffs of cloud in the blue sky, a cool breeze. On the trail, Nancy let herself get lost in the beauty of it all, the simplicity. One foot in front of the other. As they climbed higher into the cliffs, the light breeze turned to wind. Nancy cried out when it picked her sun hat up from her head and blew it off the ledge, somewhere she couldn't see it.

"We'll get you another one," said Tom.

They took more and more breaks as the trail became steeper and the footing more uncertain. Though the view was truly majestic, something out of *National Geographic*, she couldn't bring herself to look for too long before getting sweaty palms and tingling in her feet. When had she become so afraid of heights? There had been a time when she scaled fire escapes, dangled her legs off apartment roofs, dived from high dives. No more. Now there were just the grim calculations of how injured she would be, were she to fall.

In *Cave Girl Gone*, the podcaster had started to cast doubt on the older sister, the last one to have seen Max alive. Bloody sheets had been found jammed in the closet of the family's vacation rental, but it was animal blood, not human. The older sister's insistence that Max had been spirited away by a mysterious cryptid called a mudman made for a good podcast but didn't buy her any credibility. Though Nancy, more than anyone, understood her impulse. With something so impossible, your brain filled those logical gaps. Rafael had fallen into one, believing anything.

But she also knew that in these cases, the simplest explanation was usually the correct one. Max had most likely been kidnapped and murdered. Sad but true.

Esme—she couldn't bring her mind to go there. She refused. *Please don't worry*, Esme had written.

Hours later, they made it to the top, a ridge speckled with conifer shrubs too small to offer any shade and tiny cacti dotting the ground. They found a rock in the sun and ate the sandwiches she'd packed for them that morning. Tom complimented her even though it was nothing special, just the same turkey-swiss combo she used to pack for Esme's school lunches. He squeezed her hand, she put her head on his shoulder. She wanted to stay up there forever, with the howling wind and the trees and the view and nothing else.

"Shall we go?" said Tom, looking at his watch.

"Let's take a picture first," Nancy said. "For Lucas and Anna." She'd promised her stepson and his wife that they would take pictures of the trip.

She held the phone out for a selfie, capturing their faces in the frame with the trees behind. She was sunburned, she noticed, thanks to the wind stealing her hat, but otherwise the two of them looked surprisingly vibrant and youthful. It was rare she was happy with a photograph of herself these days. She sent it to the family group text thread. *Greetings from the top of the vermilion cliffs!* she wrote.

Just as they were getting ready for their return trip, Lucas texted: *Who's that you're with?*

She scrolled back to the photograph. There, where a juniper tree had been, was a woman, face shaded by a blue baseball cap. She was unsmiling, strands of dark hair framing her pale face, which was turned, just slightly, away from the camera.

"How strange," said Nancy, scanning the peak for any sign of human life. She felt dizzy suddenly, as if she were standing at the edge of a precipice, staring straight down.

Tom was also looking at his phone. "I think we should get back to the car," he said.

* * *

THEY WERE QUIET on the hike down, the only noise the howling wind. Nancy stopped twice to slather sunscreen on her face. Tom was hiking fast, faster than she could manage. She let him go on ahead. The grade was taking a toll on her ankles. She wanted to be back at the house, on the sofa, with a book. Enough of the trails and their ghosts.

Walking through the campground at the base of the trailhead, she heard the commotion before she saw it. Tom, trading words with a wiry bottle-blond woman in cutoff shorts, her slender wrists draped with bangles.

"Tom!" Nancy called.

"Stay away from us, you understand?" Tom said to the woman, his voice quivering with anger.

"I don't know what the fuck you're talking about," she said, flapping her arms so her bangles jingled.

"What's going on here?" said a barrel-chested behemoth of a man with beady eyes and neck tattoos as he approached the campsite. He held the hand of a child—a girl no older than five—clutching a lavender plastic pony. With a pang,

Nancy recalled that Esme had nearly the same toy when she was around that age, some candy-colored horse that she carried with her until its mane grew stiff with filth.

"Maggie, honey," the woman said to the little girl, "go play in the tent." The child stared wide-eyed at Nancy for a moment before scampering into the tent behind her mother. "This guy says I've been following him," she said to the man.

Nancy felt herself flush with embarrassment. This woman looked nothing like the one they'd seen on top of the cliffs.

The barrel-chested man put his arm around the woman. "Look, friend, why don't you mind your own business," he said, his tone measured but not without menace. Of course, Tom was no threat to them. Nothing but a crochety old man, likely senile.

"We're so, *so* sorry," said Nancy to the woman, trying to make her voice as sweet as possible. "My husband thought you were someone else." She placed a hand gently on Tom's shoulder. "Time to go, honey," she said to him.

* * *

IN THE SAFETY of the car, Nancy drove while Tom gazed out the window. She knew he was brooding because of how she'd behaved at the campground. Her attempt at de-escalation had bruised his ego. Tom would never say so, though. Not that he needed to.

She was grateful for the quiet, in fact. She needed to organize her thoughts. What was the logical explanation for the clifftop woman? That there had been a hiker there, whom they'd missed? That it was some digital discrepancy in the iPhone's photo rendering? An illusion? She stopped herself from going where her mind seemed to be dragging her—that hole of belief that her ex-husband had fallen into. She wouldn't.

"Maybe I was wrong," she said, finally. "Maybe you were right about that woman. Maybe it was a trick of the light."

"It doesn't matter," said Tom.

"I was afraid that man was going to take a swing at you."

Tom scoffed. "I could have taken him."

"I thought we agreed—no brawls on vacation. I don't want to have to spend our travel savings on bail."

To her relief, Tom chuckled.

* * *

THE WHITE COLUMNS HIKE was what Tom had planned this whole trip around. It was a six-mile loop through otherworldly rock formations and a beauty so singular it couldn't be captured on camera—not for lack of trying, though, since there were photographs of the beige hoodoos in nearly every restaurant and gift shop in town. Because Tom was so determined, and because it was the last hike on the trip, and because it was a once-in-a-lifetime experience, and because he was still sore about her interfering with yesterday's confrontation, Nancy didn't bring up her concern about the plume of wildfire smoke that was currently turning the sun a dystopian orange. Tom was the more experienced hiker of the two. He was perfectly capable of looking out the window.

"Winds are supposed to shift," he said, reading her mind. "It probably won't even be anything to worry about by the time we get there."

The drive to the trailhead was two hours, half of it over a sand and gravel road. Nancy held on to the passenger-side handle for dear life as Tom navigated their rental car around potholes and large rocks. When they'd gone to pick up their hiking permits yesterday, the man at the Potash Visitor Center, a chatty, rotund fellow, had been concerned about the smoke, said they were driving right into it. So early for wildfire season, was what he said, was what everyone said. Tom had waved him off like he waved Nancy off. They'd be fine.

By the time they arrived at the trailhead, indicated by nothing more than a mile marker, the skies had not cleared. They were still a hazy white, and the air smelled like the park on July Fourth.

"Are you sure about this?" said Nancy.

"We don't have to do the whole loop." Tom strapped his pack across his chest, applied another film of sun block. He was ready.

After a short walk through brush and cactus, they were greeted by a forest of sandstone columns ranging from six feet to eight stories high, chalk white, topped with flat brown slabs, phallic and eerie. Stone patterned with what looked like scales was underfoot, as if they stood atop an enormous reptile. They traversed this landscape like children in a fairy tale.

"Isn't this incredible?" said Tom, as they walked past rock formations swirled and ridged like soft-serve ice cream.

"Truly," Nancy responded. The shadows seemed to deepen as the sky darkened.

"What if we wander for a bit and come back and meet here in thirty minutes?"

"Are you sure that's a good idea?"

"I promise you, there's nothing more magical, more transcendent, than being alone out here." He looked at her pleadingly.

Nancy didn't want to transcend anything. She was perfectly fine with her two feet on solid ground. But she also didn't want to be where she wasn't wanted. "Okay," she said. "Thirty minutes it is."

"Holler if you need me," Tom said, disappearing behind a column.

She stepped cautiously into a large basin of white sand and dark brown rock blooming with pale green lichen. The air felt thick and heavy, the smoke smell becoming stronger as she went on. Ahead were more pillars, though they didn't seem to be getting any closer, no matter how long she kept walking. She realized she had no idea where she was or how far she'd gone. Her pack became heavier with each step. The sky had turned from a hazy white to an ominous yellow, and the campfire smell was now everywhere. Her mouth was gritty with who knows what from the air. She dug around in the pocket of her backpack until she found the N95 mask she'd worn for their flight. She fitted it over her face and turned back toward what she thought was the meeting point, but the landscape was covered in such a heavy blanket of haze that she couldn't orient herself. She wished she'd heeded the visitor center employee's warning, wished she and Tom had stayed together rather than going off on their stupid solo walks through these unforgiving structures. She looked at her watch—where had the time gone? Somehow, thirty minutes had passed long ago. Tom would be worried. What, Nancy wondered, did one do when one was lost? Shout? Flash a mirror at the sun? Start a fire? And how would a rescue plane see her in all this smoke? For how long would her trail mix and liter of water sustain her?

Her mind turned, as it often did in times of crisis, to Esme. Their last fight had been about money, or, more specifically, money that had gone missing from the cash envelope Nancy stashed in her desk drawer. For months, Rafael had been telling her to move it somewhere safer, that of course Esme had been borrowing from it because that was what teenagers did. But on that particular night, when she opened it to get cash to pay for their pizza delivery and found it completely empty, Nancy became apoplectic. She should have kept her mouth shut, should have let it go. No amount of cash was worth what she'd then set in motion.

It was a violation, she'd told Esme, quivering with rage, a severe breach of trust that wouldn't soon be repaired. She remembered her daughter's glossy eyes, the flecks of silver eyeshadow among the racoon rings of black. What had Esme spat back in reply? "Go to hell," or "You're a horrible mother," or "You're psycho, I didn't take shit." In truth the fights all seemed to blend together into one horrible crescendo of screams and door slams, of flushed faces and racing hearts. Whatever it was, it ended with that final door slam, the last time she saw her daughter.

She was searching the ridge above her for any familiar landmark when one of the rocks moved. Not a rock. A person. At first she thought it might have been Tom, but this was clearly a woman. Nancy walked closer to the ridge, breathing heavily into her mask, trying to process what it was she was seeing. The figure wore a blue baseball cap and a familiar red JanSport, just like Esme used to carry to and from school.

"Mom!" She heard the voice against her will, sweet and sharp with a tinge of annoyance. The figure still had her back to her, strands of dark hair animated by the smoky breeze. It was the smoke, it was the desert, it was something deceiving her.

"Esme?" she said under her breath. The last thing she wanted was for Tom to hear, if he was even nearby.

The figure turned to face her. What Nancy saw was impossible. Impossible because it had been a decade and a half and Esme would have aged by now, impossible because what were the chances of her being out here, in the middle of this desert, at the exact same time that she, Nancy, was? But there she was, five yards away, backlit by the fiery yellow sky. Nancy ran to her, boots crunching brush and cactus, not looking out for boulders or rattlesnakes or anything. She ran to the base of the ridge, but when she looked up, there was no one there, just the end-times smoke.

With some difficulty, she found footholds and hoisted herself up, her joints screaming with the exertion. The girl was sitting on the ground, her hands caressing the red sand.

"The sand," she said, "it's so smooth, it's like water." Her voice was raspy, her hair matted under her cap.

"Are you okay?"

The girl seemed to notice Nancy for the first time then. Long eyelashes, heavy lids. Her sunburned face was smudged with red mud, lips chapped. She was young, maybe in her twenties, though it was getting harder to gauge these things at Nancy's age.

"Mom?" she said again. Nancy felt her face grow hot, but she knew what was happening. The girl was high. Mushrooms, maybe. Or acid. Nancy would become part of her legendary trip. *I thought my mom was out there, but it was really just this random lady.*

Nancy felt it then, the unraveling. The desire to throw herself to the ground, to pound on the rocks and yell at the sky for every lost milestone, the birthdays, the weddings, the graduations, the triumphs and the disappointments that she'd never be able to witness. For Esme, for Max, for all the missing girls and the broken people they'd left behind.

"Here," said Nancy, handing the girl a water bottle with a shaky hand. "Drink."

The girl did as she was told, then looked around, frowning. "We shouldn't be out here," she said.

"I completely agree," said Nancy. She held out her hands and hoisted the girl up. In the distance, through the smoke, she clocked the sandstone pillars that indicated the meeting point. Tom would be there, worried but still waiting, and would drive this girl back to her boyfriend, girlfriend, friends, parents—whoever was waiting for her. "Follow me," she said, and the two of them walked back toward safety.

CREDITS

I WANT TO EXPRESS MY GRATITUDE to the publications that published these stories in earlier forms: *Epiphany* ("Dogs"), *Joyland* ("You Can Never Be Too Sure," formerly "Wasted State"), *CRAFT* ("Mystery Lights"), *Ninth Letter* ("The White Place"), *Electric Literature* ("Trogloxene"), the *Rejoinder* ("The Reclamation"), the *Masters Review* ("Clean Hunters"), and *BOMB* ("Vermilion"). Small magazines are integral parts of the literary ecosystem. Subscribe and support when possible.

NOTES

THANK YOU to Hannah Marshall at the Chinati Foundation in Marfa, Texas, for providing the translation of the German phrase in "Mystery Lights."

The biographical details of the painter in "The White Place" are loosely inspired by parts of Georgia O'Keeffe's life—though it should be noted that all events are purely fictional. To better understand some of the UFO theories of the 1970s that Sandra espouses in "The White Place," I referred to *The UFO Experience: A Scientific Inquiry* by J. Allen Hynek (1972).

The print hanging in Julia's apartment in "Bright Lights, Big Deal" is a reproduction of the following painting: Georgia O'Keeffe, *Brooklyn Bridge*, 1949, oil on masonite, 47 x 35 ⅞" (121.8 x 91.1 cm), Brooklyn Museum, bequest of Mary Childs Draper. The house in Jamaica, Queens, that this story references is the home of the musician Milford Graves (1941–2021).

While writing "The Reclamation," I relied on the following sources for research: the podcast *Guru: The Dark Side of Enlightenment* by Matt Stroud (Wondery), which chronicles James Arthur Ray's "Spiritual Warrior" retreat; and *Cultish: The Language of Fanaticism* by Amanda Montell (HarperWave, 2021). The Georgia O'Keeffe quote Brooke refers to is quoted in "Georgia O'Keeffe's Vision" by Calvin Tomkins, *The New Yorker*, 1974.

The haunted Los Angeles places in "Clean Hunters" are imagined, with the exception of Suicide Bridge (the Colorado Street Bridge, officially), Union Station, and Griffith Park's picnic table #29. As far as I know, there have been no reports of a cold spot in the Glendale Galleria.

In the wake of my grandfather's death in 1996, my grandmother Robbie kept a diary to help manage her grief. She addressed all entries to him and recorded dreams, thoughts, memories, and daily activities (including sightings of the Comet Hale-Bopp). The narrative voice in "Reaper Ranch," along with the story's form, are inspired by this diary, which she gave to me several years before her death. Grace's dream on p. 206 and her memory of grilling salmon with Lee on p. 193 are paraphrased directly from the diary, as is her speculation that the comet might be a sign from her beloved from beyond the grave. The rest is fictional. The nature show that Grace is watching that features pilot whales mourning their dead is *Planet Earth: Blue Planet II*, episode 4.

ACKNOWLEDGMENTS

THANK YOU to my agent, Michelle Brower, for championing my work, and to Nat Edwards, Elizabeth Pratt, Allison Malecha, and the entire team at Trellis.

Thank you to the team at Tin House, including Masie Cochran, Nanci McCloskey, Becky Kraemer, Jae Nichelle, Jacqui Reiko Teruya, and Nicole Pagliari, for helping to usher this book into the world. Thank you to Beth Steidle, for her bewitching cover design. Thank you especially to my editor, Elizabeth DeMeo, who saw the potential in these stories early on and did so much to help shape them into what they are today.

Thank you to the One Story community, especially Maribeth Batcha, Hannah Tinti, and Patrick Ryan, for the advice, support, and cheerleading throughout the time I was writing these stories. I feel incredibly lucky to work for a literary organization whose mission to nurture authors also extends to those on its staff.

Thank you to the early readers of these stories: Kendra Allenby, Jenny Blackman, Maria Bowler, Sarah Bridgins, Ryan Britt, Megan Cummins, Molly Gandour, Zack Graham, Hal Hlavinka, Nathan Ihara, Jacob Kaplan, Brent Katz, Anjali Khosla, Hannah Labovitch, Ben Lasman, Chris Leslie-Hynan, Matthew Mercier, Wah Mon, Artie Neiderhoffer, Stephanie Saunders, Robert Silva, Leigh Stein, and Anne-E. Wood.

Thank you to the Elizabeth George Foundation for their financial support as I was crafting the collection. Thank you to the following residencies for providing time and space to draft these stories: Vermont Studio Center, Virginia Center for the Creative Arts, and Dorland Mountain Arts. Thank you also to Linnea Nan and Ari Bhöd.

Thank you to Julie Buntin, Clare Beams, Kelly Link, and Rachel Lyon for their generous early support for these stories.

Thank you to Theirry Kehou and May-Zhee Lim, and everyone in my Poets & Writers Get the Word Out cohort—I've learned so much from your publication journeys.

Thank you to the editors who published these stories in their journals: Katelyn Keating, Sadye Teiser, Kyle Lucia Wu, Michael Colbert, Marissa Castrigno, Liz Harms, Rachel Lyon, Halimah Marcus, Benjamin Samuel, and Raluca Albu.

Thank you to all who offered support, advice, mentorship, and wisdom at various stages of the path to publication, especially Ilana Masad, Rachel Cantor, Vanessa Chan, Mila Jaroniec, Talia Lakshmi Kolluri, Ethan Chatagnier, Christopher Hermelin, Susan Bell, David Archer, Nedjelko Spaich, and Ariel Alter.

Thank you to my brilliant family: my parents, Rita and Kirby, and my brother, Joey, for always encouraging my creativity and continuing to inspire me with their own artistic, spiritual, and intellectual pursuits.

Thank you to my husband, Ryan, whose dream of a strange woman appearing in our vacation photos inspired "Vermilion," and who has supported me at every step of this process. Your love is a light in the darkness.

RYAN SPENCER

LENA VALENCIA's fiction has appeared in *Ninth Letter*, *Epiphany*, *Joyland*, the anthology *Tiny Nightmares*, and elsewhere. She is the recipient of a 2019 Elizabeth George Foundation grant and holds an MFA in fiction from The New School. Originally from Los Angeles, she lives in Brooklyn, New York, where she is the managing editor and director of educational programming at *One Story* and the co-host of the reading series Ditmas Lit.